Total

Over the Line
In His Cuffs
For the Sub
In the Den

Bonds
Crave
Claim
Command

The Donovan Dynasty
Bind
Brand
Boss

Master Class
Initiation
Enticement

Impulse
Shockwave

Single Titles
Her Two Doms
Bound and Determined
This Time
Fed Up
Signed, Sealed and Delivered

Anthologies and Collections
Homecoming: Unbound Surrender
Night of the Senses: Voyeur
Subspace: Three-Way Tie
Bound Brits: S&M 101
Bound to the Billionaire: Bared to Him
Halloween Heart Throbs: Walk on the Wild Side

Clandestine Classics
Jane Eyre

MASTER CLASS
Volume One

Initiation

Enticement

SIERRA CARTWRIGHT

Master Class Volume One
ISBN # 978-1-78686-092-7
©Copyright Sierra Cartwright 2016
Cover Art by Posh Gosh ©Copyright 2016
Interior text design by Claire Siemaszkiewicz
Totally Bound Publishing

This is a work of fiction. All characters, places and events are from the author's imagination and should not be confused with fact. Any resemblance to persons, living or dead, events or places is purely coincidental.

All rights reserved. No part of this publication may be reproduced in any material form, whether by printing, photocopying, scanning or otherwise without the written permission of the publisher, Totally Bound Publishing.

Applications should be addressed in the first instance, in writing, to Totally Bound Publishing. Unauthorised or restricted acts in relation to this publication may result in civil proceedings and/or criminal prosecution.

The author and illustrator have asserted their respective rights under the Copyright Designs and Patents Acts 1988 (as amended) to be identified as the author of this book and illustrator of the artwork.

Published in 2016 by Totally Bound Publishing, Newland House, The Point, Weaver Road, Lincoln, LN6 3QN, United Kingdom.

No part of this book may be reproduced, scanned, or distributed in any printed or electronic form without permission. Please do not participate in or encourage piracy of copyrighted materials in violation of the authors' rights. Purchase only authorised copies.

Totally Bound Publishing is a subsidiary of Totally Entwined Group Limited.

If you purchased this book without a cover you should be aware that this book is stolen property. It was reported as "unsold and destroyed" to the publisher and neither the author nor the publisher has received any payment for this "stripped book".

INITIATION

Dedication

For Cassandra, Jessica Newcom, Tara Hutchings. Your friendship makes all the difference in my world. And for everyone who gets out of their comfort zone and takes a risk.

Chapter One

Fuck.

Ever since he'd been unceremoniously dumped on his ass three years ago, Logan Powell had done the world a favor by avoiding the fairer sex. Women had very real needs, emotional as well as physical. They deserved to be involved with someone who was a better person than he was.

So what the hell was he doing at a BDSM play party in the dungeon of his friend's home, staring at the petite blonde on the other side of the room?

It wasn't just her strong, athletic build that attracted him, but also the short spiky hair, fuck-me boots, tight black T-shirt and skimpy leather skirt. What did him in, though, was the way she tugged on the hem of her skirt in a betrayal of nerves.

He propped a foot against the wall behind him and watched her fidget as he considered his next move. It had been months since he'd scened. And on the rare occasions when he did play, he preferred to engage with experienced submissives. If his tingling detective senses were anything to go by, the woman in question had never been dominated.

Double fuck.

He shouldn't ache to be the one to give her the first taste of the exquisite pleasure that came from submitting. *Shouldn't.* But he did.

Joe Montrose, the house's owner and tonight's host, walked over and stood next to Logan. "Jennifer..." Joe said.

"What?" Logan cupped his ear to indicate he was having difficulty hearing over the thundering pulse of a Nine Inch Nails song.

Joe repeated himself. "Her name's Jennifer Berklee. She works with Noelle. It's Jennifer's first time at one of these events."

"I'm not interested." Logan shook his head, wondering when he'd become a liar.

"You don't miss it?"

"Playing with a newbie?" Teaching her about her own responses? Driving her to the edge of distraction, keeping her there, then shoving her over it so he could catch her and care for her? "No."

"Not at all?"

Despite himself, Logan watched as Jennifer squared her shoulders and moved toward Simon, a Dom who regularly attended a number of events in the area. Her hips swayed alluringly and Logan adored the way she all but strutted in those booted heels. For a stupid, but thankfully brief, second he wished she was walking in his direction. "Is Simon still looking for someone to collar?" Simple Simon, as Logan thought of him, though it probably wasn't a fair nickname. But from what Logan had seen, the man had a single approach to women, and a boring one at that. He never seemed to drive a sub to the very edges of endurance and give her amazing completion. The man wasn't a bad Dom, just an uninspired one.

"Yeah," Joe replied. "He's been looking since Lisa ditched him."

Shouldn't matter. Nope. Not a bit.

Joe said something that Logan missed. Even though he clearly knew he was being ignored, Joe kept running his mouth. "So, are you?"

Logan dragged his attention away from Jennifer. "Am I what?"

"Coming to Noelle's surprise birthday party? She's turning thirty."

"When is it?"

"Three weeks."

Logan turned and narrowed his gaze at the man who'd been a friend since basic training. Later, after they'd left the service, they'd returned to the Middle East as civilians. They'd survived two years of skin-searing heat and an explosion in which most of their team had died. Because of what they'd shared and how well they knew each other, Logan knew Joe's vague answer meant he was hedging. "What date?" Logan frowned at his so-called friend. "Specifically."

"Ah. February fourteenth."

Logan scowled. "I fucking hate Valentine's Day. You know that." It wasn't just the cloying expectations but the still-raw memories that he preferred to leave buried. Being among happy, loving couples only made it worse.

"Missing the party will make you a bigger asshole than you already are," Joe replied cheerfully.

"Fuck off."

Joe grinned. Not much bothered the man.

In silence, they watched the interplay between Jennifer and Master Simon.

"If you're interested in playing with her, either Noelle or I can arrange it." Without waiting for a reply, Joe moved off, leaving Logan in blessed, voyeuristic peace.

Dom and sub spoke for a few moments and eventually Master Simon nodded at the St. Andrew's cross.

A blaze of unwelcome and unwanted possession arced through Logan as she closed the distance toward the X-shaped BDSM equipment.

As if sensing his attention, she glanced over at him.

He folded his arms across his chest as their gazes locked.

Even across the distance, he saw her shiver.

Smart girl, recognizing the danger he emanated.

After a few seconds, she shook her head and turned away.

Simple Simon took a step in her direction.

Suddenly, Logan realized he did want to be the man behind her, pressing her against the wood, instructing her to lift her arms high so he could affix her wrists to a pair of cuffs.

Instead, another man had that honor.

The man secured her in place and she immediately pulled her right wrist free. If Logan were in charge, he wouldn't have allowed that to happen. Even if all she wanted was a taste of his dominance, he'd make sure she would never forget the experience.

After putting her wrist back in place, Master Simon rubbed her buttocks through her skirt.

Logan's cock thickened.

Because he needed human contact to maintain his sanity, he showed up at Joe and Noelle's events several times a year. While watching others scene interested him, he'd rarely gotten aroused from it.

Then again, he'd rarely had this kind of visceral reaction to a woman.

Master Simon selected a sturdy leather paddle. It wasn't a bad decision, Logan mused. The toy was intimate, but not overly so. And since her delectable derrière was covered by her skirt, the impact would be minimal. *Good choice for a neophyte.*

Master Simon gave the sub three swats.

The third made her move her body to one side — something she did easily since her ankles weren't secured.

That was a mistake Logan wouldn't have made.

He wanted his subs to feel every damn thing he did to them. He wanted them aware, aroused, interested, committed, and he wanted them to stay in place while it was happening.

Without any change to the rhythm, Master Simon delivered two more swats.

Then the man put down the paddle on a nearby bench, and she freed herself from the restraints.

Logan blinked. Was the scene already over?

Jennifer turned toward Simon, adjusted her skirt, then smiled politely before scurrying up the staircase.

With a curse, Logan pushed away from the wall and followed. If she had scened with him, there would have been no bland, polite smiles afterward. At the very least, he would have talked to her and asked questions instead of allowing her to walk away.

When he found her, she was near the front door, reaching to take her coat from a rack.

"May I?" he asked.

"I..." She dropped her hand and turned toward him before meeting his gaze.

Until they were this close, he hadn't known her eyes were blue, bright and vibrant.

He wanted to see them widen with shock, darken with desire. "Logan Powell," he said by way of introduction as he grabbed her coat and held it for her.

"Thank you." She settled into it, then knotted the belt around her waist as she faced him.

"I watched your scene with Master Simon."

Her shoulders stiffened.

"You didn't seem all that into it."

Her mouth was pressed into a firm line, making him realize he wasn't any more adept than Simon had been. Bulldozing on, Logan took a business card from his wallet and offered it to her.

She hesitated and he wasn't sure she'd accept it.

"Feel free to call me if you want to experience a real scene."

"That felt real to me." She rubbed her behind.

"Perhaps I'm mistaken," he allowed. "But it seemed as if you might have wanted something more. BDSM is not just about impact. There's a mental and emotional component as well. Trust is involved, and so is getting exactly what you're looking for. I think you know that."

She glanced at his contact information before taking his card and stuffing it into her pocket.

After saying good night but not responding to his offer, she left, closing the door behind her with a decisive click.

"Your technique's a little rusty," Joe observed.

"How long have you been lurking?" Logan pivoted to glare at his friend.

"Lurking? I prefer to think of it as making sure my guests find their way out safely."

"He's being nosy," Noelle said, joining them. She pressed her fingertips to her husband's forearm.

Logan didn't miss the sign of deference and affection toward her Dom. Until this moment, he hadn't envied the pair their hard-won relationship. Tonight, though, he felt a twinge of regret for the choices he'd made.

"I was hoping Jennifer would talk to you," Noelle said.

"Maybe if Logan had more tact than your average gorilla, he might have had a chance."

Noelle frowned at Joe.

"She took my card," Logan said in his own defense. And maybe, maybe, she'd call.

* * * *

"You should call him," Noelle said.

"Call who?" Jennifer feigned ignorance.

Noelle snagged a garlic bread stick from a basket and wagged it at Jennifer.

"Who are you talking about?" asked Eden, another member of the infamous Carpe Diem Divas.

To avoid the question, Jennifer reached for the bottle of Chianti. She refilled the wineglasses of the other women gathered around her kitchen table. They'd started meeting two years ago when they'd all been going through relationship challenges. They'd decided to seize life, no matter what it tossed at them. Over a pitcher of margaritas, the Carpe Diem Divas had been formed. Even though Noelle was now happily married to Joe, she still attended. Jennifer couldn't blame her. Everyone brought something delicious to eat, and the drinks were always plentiful.

Tonight, they were meeting in her somewhat renovated Highlands bungalow for the first time. To save money, she was doing most of the remodeling herself, which meant some things were almost finished and others were nowhere close, including the dining room walls that were still a shocking shade of canary yellow.

"We're talking about Logan Powell," Noelle explained to Eden. "He's a hunky Dom." She folded her arms triumphantly. "And he's interested in Jennifer."

"What?" Eden demanded, turning to face Jennifer. "Details. Now. All of them."

Hyperaware that she was the focus of everyone's attention, she took a sip of wine and stalled. "There's nothing to tell. Really."

"Okay," Eden said, apparently undaunted. "Where did you meet him?"

"At a play party at my house," Noelle replied.

Jennifer scowled. "Do you mind? What if I wanted it to be a secret?"

"No secrets among friends," Morgan insisted.

Noelle grinned.

"You went to a party?" Eden prompted. "About time."

About a year ago, she and a few members of the Carpe Diem Divas had gone to see a movie about BDSM. Of course Jennifer had heard about BDSM, but seeing it played out, larger than life, with one of her favorite actors in the leading role as a Dom, she'd been intrigued. She'd watched, unblinkingly, as the man had removed his shirt and flogged his helpless submissive. She'd imagined herself in the heroine's role, helpless beneath a man's sensuous lash.

At a bar afterward, she'd pestered Noelle with dozens of questions. But it had taken Jennifer a number of months to gather the courage to accept an invitation to experience it for herself.

"So," Eden persisted, "did you play with this Logan guy?"

Jennifer shook her head. "No. With someone else."

"And what did he do to you?"

"He, um"—she ran her finger over the base of the wineglass—"gave me a few swats."

"A few swats? Is that all?" Eden demanded.

"What did he use?" Ava asked.

"A paddle," Jennifer replied.

Noelle sat back, sipping her wine, following the conversation as if it were a tennis match.

"Wait a minute." Morgan scowled. "You have a thing for floggers."

Definitely, there were no secrets with this group of friends.

She and Morgan had recently gone shopping for a bachelorette party that Morgan was hosting. They'd ended up at an adult bookstore. And, encouraging each other, they'd slipped through the curtain that hid the shop's dungeon area. Maybe because of the movie, she hadn't been able to get the idea of floggers out of her mind. Fortified by the mojito she'd had at dinner, she'd allowed the sales guy to show her the expensive leather pieces. Morgan had encouraged her to buy one. Before the end of the night, she was the owner of a flogger—still unused—that had cost her half a paycheck.

"Back to the story." Eden leaned forward. "What kind of paddle was it? A wooden one like in the movie?"

"It was leather."

"How did it feel?" Ava asked.

Jennifer wrinkled her nose.

"You didn't like it?" Eden demanded.

"It was a bit disappointing. I was dressed, so…" She shrugged. "I didn't really feel much."

"That's why you should call Logan," Noelle said triumphantly, joining the conversation. "He'd give you a paddling you'll never forget. Better yet, a flogging."

Jennifer squirmed and a flush crept up her cheeks.

"You have been thinking about him." Noelle narrowed her eyes.

All week. Jennifer had remembered the way Logan had held her coat and the way he'd skimmed his strong hands across her shoulders. He'd ignited her nerve endings along with her imagination. But there had been something about him, his implacable tone and the way he'd looked at her. He'd regarded her intently, and his jade-colored eyes had unnerved her. It was as though he'd seen beyond the surface and wanted more. "He's not my type." She hoped to convince herself along with her friend.

"Why not?" Noelle demanded.

"He looks…" She paused then settled for, "Too dangerous." Too masculine. Too broad. Too big. Too handsome. Too focused.

"His scar's sexy," Noelle said.

It was.

"Scar?" Eden looked between the two of them. "What kind of scar?"

"A jagged one. It runs from the corner of his eye up into his hairline," Noelle replied for her. "When I asked him about it one time, he changed the subject. And Joe told me to leave it alone. I know Logan is a detective of some sort, but I don't think it's for a police department. It could be his own company." She shrugged. "All Joe will tell me about Logan's past is that the two of them were in the Middle East a number of years ago. They were there as civilian contractors. I think maybe they'd both served tours of duty in Iraq or Afghanistan when they were in the service, so going back made sense to them." She shrugged. "I don't know if that's where the scar happened, but that's my guess."

Ava shivered dramatically. "Logan sounds yummy."

"He is." Jennifer had noticed him the moment he'd entered the basement, and her core temperature had shot up. And that sexy scar had continually drawn her attention, despite her intention not to stare.

When she'd gone home after the party, she'd masturbated. But instead of remembering the paddling, she'd imagined that Logan had been standing behind her. Rather than swatting her through the skirt, she'd fantasized that he'd bared her skin and given her hard, deliberate smacks.

But now... The image of him wielding a flogger was all but etched in her mind.

"Why don't you call him? You should." Eden asked, "Do you have his number?"

Her blood went sluggish. "Because I'm a coward."

"No, you're not," Ava countered. "You did go to the party after all."

Jennifer appreciated her friend's loyalty.

"Come on. Here's your chance to live a little," Noelle said.

Until recently, Jennifer had always done the right thing. In school, she'd worked hard so she could get into the college her parents had selected for her. She'd graduated near the top of her class, become a CPA, and joined her father's firm, exactly as expected. Even so, she was still figuring out what *she* wanted.

"He's trustworthy," Noelle went on. "Joe considers him a friend. He doesn't say that about many people. Very few, in fact. And..." She reached for her glass and trailed off mysteriously.

Jennifer didn't want to be intrigued. But damn it, she leaned forward with interest.

Noelle glanced around, heightening the tension. "I've spoken to a couple of the subs he's played with..."

"Quit teasing and tell us," Eden begged.

"They say he's an exceptional Dom. Unrelenting, demanding, but patient."

Ava and Morgan fanned themselves. Jennifer was suddenly tempted to do the same.

"As good as the guy in the movie?" Morgan leaned forward.

"Better," Noelle said.

"No way," Ava protested.

"You could do worse," Noelle finished, leveling a look at Jennifer.

"You can't let What's-His-Face fuck up your whole life," Eden added unhelpfully.

"Brett," Jennifer supplied. "His name was—is—Brett." Not that Eden had forgotten.

"I think you should let this Logan guy flog you," Ava said.

"Master Logan," Noelle corrected.

Jennifer met her friend's gaze.

"Well, if he were swinging a flogger at my naked body, I'd call him Master Logan," Noelle clarified.

Jennifer tried to shove that image from her mind. But it wouldn't budge.

After they'd shared a few giggles, the conversation moved on, thankfully away from her and a fictional scene with Logan.

Ava mentioned the new guy who'd been hired at her firm. She said he dressed in suits and seemed aloof. But she'd seen him last weekend while running in Washington Park. Since it had been unseasonably warm, he'd been in shorts and a short-sleeved shirt, and she'd noticed he had a tattoo. It seemed that Mr. Professional had an intriguing side.

"Did you talk to him?" Eden asked. "Maybe trip him?"

Ava shook her head and finished her wine.

"You should go for it," Noelle encouraged. "Ask him to coffee or something. What can it hurt?"

Though she tried to participate in the conversation and nodded at what she hoped were appropriate intervals, Jennifer was otherwise occupied with the tantalizing fantasy that Logan might demand she call him Master…

Even after her guests had left, the thought remained. More than ever, she wished she had been brave enough to take Logan up on his offer at Noelle's party.

She retrieved his business card from her coat pocket where it had rested, undisturbed, for a week.

It didn't reveal much. His name. Office number. An email address from a service that half the country seemed to use.

There was no occupation listed, no company name, no cell phone number.

She traced his name, and a dragon seemed to roar to life in her stomach. It wasn't butterflies, but something fire-breathing, threatening to consume her.

As much as she wanted to have the courage to dial his number, she didn't.

She dropped the card back into the pocket. Then she told herself that she'd run into him again in the future. If he offered to scene again, she'd accept his offer. She wouldn't be a coward twice. After all, Noelle had said he was a good Dom. And that made him a safe choice.

A chill skated up her spine and caused a cold feeling to seep into her head.

There was no way Logan Powell—Master Logan—was safe, no matter what she told herself.

But that realization didn't stop her from walking into her closet and taking her flogger from its hook.

She traced one of the strands. The leather was firm and thick.

For a frightening, dizzying second, she pictured the handle in Logan's hand as he took a purposeful step toward her.

Chapter Two

Where the hell is everyone?

Logan checked his very expensive, very precise watch. Three minutes after seven. Noelle Montrose's surprise birthday party was scheduled to begin in less than fifteen minutes, and he was still the only one here. He was starting to get pissed off.

Only for Joe and Noelle would Logan have left work early, driven up to unlock the house and put a bottle of champagne on ice.

The doorbell shattered the silence.

Finally.

Jarred from his annoyance and glad someone else was here, he answered the summons.

When he saw Jennifer Berklee standing on the stoop, hand raised to press the bell a second time, he had an instant attitude change. If Joe had mentioned that Jennifer had been invited, Logan wouldn't have bitched at all.

"Logan." Her voice was rushed, her eyes wide.

Until this moment, he hadn't allowed himself to realize how disappointed he'd been that she hadn't taken him up on his offer last month, and, more, that she hadn't called him.

So the fact that it bothered him was an irritation.

She remained outside, mouth slightly parted, her breaths coming in quick little bursts.

Perhaps she'd thought about him as much as he'd thought about her.

"Come in." He opened the door a bit farther and she entered the foyer, stamping a few snowflakes from her black ankle boots. *Damn.* They were just as hot, if not hotter, than the ones she'd worn the last time he'd seen her.

He reached above her to close out the howling, unfriendly wind.

For a moment, their gazes collided, but she shook her head.

"Is everyone else hiding?" She dragged a trembling hand through her short hair and restored order to the weather-tossed locks.

"I'm afraid it's just you and me so far."

She scowled. "I thought I was going to be late. Did I get the time wrong?"

"Joe told me to be here by six." He'd probably figured that Logan would be half an hour late, which he had been. Fortunately, no one had been waiting and Logan had found the spare key affixed to the underside of a rain gutter. That had been fun in the dark and cold.

He took her oversize bag and placed it on the floor, wondering if she had any toys hidden in it.

Jennifer unfastened the belt around her waist, then removed her wool peacoat. He couldn't stop thinking of the way her skin had felt when he'd helped her into it a few weeks ago.

She stood before him, ridiculously close since he hadn't taken a polite step backward.

As he might have expected, she was dressed in a short leather skirt that highlighted her feminine curves. It was appropriate for a kink event—which he anticipated this evening's party might become—but it wasn't so scandalous that it would be whispered about at a vanilla gathering.

Her white turtleneck was another matter. It hugged her body, showing off her breasts and trim waist.

She'd completed the outfit with tights and those sexy boots.

His blood pressure spiked. "May I?" he asked, extending his hand.

"Thanks." She gave him the coat and he placed it on a nearby peg.

"Let me just get Noelle's present and my phone so I can take pictures of her when she gets here."

Jennifer bent to unzip the bag, but the way she angled her body ensured he couldn't see everything in there. She extracted a gift and handed it to him, then she grabbed her cell phone from a small purse before straightening.

"Where are we waiting?"

"In the kitchen." He shrugged. "Unless you have a better idea?"

"I'm not good at the whole surprise thing," she said, following him.

Joe had built the house with entertaining in mind. This part of the home featured an open concept with the kitchen seamlessly transitioning to the dining area adjacent to the living room.

The most stunning feature was a bank of picture windows that faced east and overlooked downtown Denver. Generally the view was breathtaking, but this evening a layer of threatening clouds loomed, making it seem as if he and Jennifer were cut off from the rest of the world. Until now, he hadn't appreciated it.

Festive streamers hung from the soaring wooden beams. Red and white balloons were everywhere, tied to chairs, attached to end tables, floating at various heights over every flat surface.

"The place looks great," Jennifer said.

"Joe missed his calling as an interior decorator."

"He did this, really?" She glanced at him. "I figured they hired a company."

Logan made a circular motion near his temple. "He says it's relaxing."

"I wouldn't think so. Cleaning. Cooking. Inviting people. Tracking the RSVPs. Prep work." She shuddered.

Yet Joe did it routinely. At least once a month, he made the trek from his Cherry Creek home to his house in the foothills to organize play parties for his closest friends.

"If there are only going to be a few people, this is a lot of cupcakes." She looked toward the three-tiered structure on the dining room table.

Plates were piled high, sitting next to the napkins and silverware. Glass dishes were filled with mints and nuts. An inviting, expensive bottle of bubbly was chilling in an elegant stainless-steel bucket.

A chime sounded and Jennifer checked her phone.

A moment later, his phone vibrated and he pulled it out of his pocket. Seeing there was a message from Joe, Logan entered his pass code, then read the text.

Surprise!

Logan frowned.

"What the hell?" Jennifer sounded disconcerted. He glanced up from his screen.

"It's from Noelle," she said. "It says *surprise*."

Logan turned his phone so she could read it.

"Now I'm really confused," she confessed.

Both phones signaled new messages.

Happy Valentine's Day! The house is all yours. Don't do anything we wouldn't, and enjoy the evening! We love you both... Joe and Noelle
P.S. The champagne is for the two of you to enjoy.

"I think we've been had," Logan said unnecessarily.

She closed her eyes for a second, and when she opened them, he again noticed how intense they were, but tonight the blue was spiked with gold flecks of anger.

"Noelle knows I hate Valentine's Day. I'll kill her. Kill her. Long. Painful. Slow. Very freaking slow." She focused her gaze on him.

"I had nothing to do with it. I swear." Still holding his phone, he raised his hands. "I hate Valentine's Day too."

"Do you?" She put a hand on her heart and tipped her head to the side, regarding him skeptically.

"Rather have a root canal than deal with it."

"Yet here we are."

The truth was as cold as the Colorado windchill. "Set up by our best friends," he said.

"Some friends."

He lowered his hands.

"All this stuff. We can't just leave it out since we have no idea when they'll be up here again." She dug a hand into her hair, sending a lock spilling in front of her eyes. As she raked it back, she said, "God."

"What?"

"We don't even get to enjoy the party, and we have to clean up the mess."

"Who says we don't get to enjoy it?"

Their phones lit up again.

We're celebrating in town. So feel free to spend the night.

Jennifer replied to the message. He didn't know it was possible for a person's fingers to move so fast. But then she stared at the screen as if expecting Noelle to respond instantly.

After thirty long, painful seconds, it was obvious no reply was coming. Instead, Jennifer touched an icon to call Noelle.

From a few feet away, he heard Noelle's voice mail message.

"She turned off her phone," Jennifer said, shock echoing in her voice. She tried Joe's number and got the same result.

With a deep sigh, she tossed her phone onto the island. "Now what are we going to do?"

"I have an idea." Logan dropped his phone into his pocket then crossed to the bucket that held the bottle of champagne. After pulling it from the ice, he looked at the label. "Expensive stuff. I'd hate for it to go to waste." He removed the protective wire cage, then gave the cork a quick turn before popping it off. "How about a drink?"

Along with survival instincts, common sense urged Jennifer to get back in her car and head back to Denver. As she'd told the Divas the other night, the man spelled *danger*, in capital letters. It wasn't just that compelling scar that zigzagged between his scalp and his right eye. His size intimidated her. He stood over six feet tall, and he was impossibly broad. Then there was his shadowy past. Noelle had said he was some sort of detective, but what kind of detective wore motorcycle boots, a faded-to-gray button-down shirt and a watch that cost half a year's salary?

His raven-colored hair was cut military short. Everything about him warned her to stay away. The man made her feel vulnerable, but she couldn't make herself leave.

After pouring the champagne, he held up both flutes and tipped one in her direction.

She wanted him. And just as desperately, she wanted *not* to want him.

Noelle's words, though, echoed in Jennifer's head. *'They say he's an exceptional Dom. Unrelenting, demanding, but patient.'*

Part of her still wanted to experience exactly that.

Rationalizing that her friend trusted him and that no harm could come from sharing a simple glass of champagne, Jennifer walked into the dining area.

When she accepted one of the flutes, electricity jolted through her.

Jennifer snatched away the glass. Some of the expensive liquor splashed over the rim. She licked it off, then became aware of his gaze on her.

"So you hate Valentine's Day?" he prompted.

"I didn't always." She took a breath to steady her pulse. "I had a bad experience a couple of years ago." At first, Brett had seemed like the ideal boyfriend. He was thirty-four, wore Italian suits, had an impressive portfolio, a stunning mansion off Eighth Avenue in Denver, a ritzy downtown office and he was a successful criminal-defense attorney. Her parents had loved him. But his expectations had started to wear her down. He was looking for the perfect wife, someone to host his events and organize a high-profile social calendar, and he'd made it clear that he expected her to forget her dreams of starting her own CPA firm.

"What happened?" Logan asked.

Dragged back from the unpleasant memory, she asked, "Does it matter?"

He shrugged. "I'm curious."

Time and distance had helped. "Short story? A public humiliation."

Logan kept his gaze steady.

His silence, nonjudgment and the fact that he didn't immediately jump in with sympathy encouraged her to go on. "My boyfriend proposed at dinner on Valentine's Day. When I said I wasn't ready for his demands, giving up my dreams to become Mrs. Someone Else, he dumped my ring in a glass of water. Then he stormed out, leaving me to pay the bill and find my own way home." Adding insult to the mortification, the meal and wine had been considerably more than she'd been able to afford.

"He sounds more like a child than a man."

She nodded. "I tell myself that the unfortunate incident was better than a lifetime of misery. And honestly? I love my career, and now I have the time to invest in making my business a success. At certain times of the year, I work double shifts. I need the freedom to do that."

"What do you do?"

"I'm a CPA."

"So you're not available the first half of April?"

"From mid-March on, actually. But there's always corporate work, extensions. It never really ends. And I'm hoping to go out on my own within a year or so."

Because of Logan's patience and interest, some of her resistance to him faded. Maybe he wasn't as dangerous as she'd originally thought. Feminine intuition shrieked in her ear. The fact that he was easy to talk to made him more dangerous than she'd originally thought. To silence the roar in her head, she asked, "What's your story?"

To his credit, he didn't stall. "I was an idiot. Actually, the world's biggest asshole. I forgot it was Valentine's Day. Worked late. Didn't buy her a card or a gift." His lips were set in a tight line. Although his words were light and easy, the underlying betrayal of pain in his voice was unmistakable.

Like he'd done for her, she waited for him to continue.

"When I got home, all the lights were on, but Helen and her belongings were gone. She left a note with two words on it. You can probably guess what they were." He grinned wryly.

Their confessions had created an intimacy between them and she smiled back. "I bet I can."

He angled his flute and they clinked their glasses.

"We got off to a bad start the first time I met you," he told her. "I was an oaf, came on too strong. I apologize."

"An oaf?" She toyed with her glass. "I'm not sure I've ever heard anyone actually use that word in a sentence."

"I'm one of a kind," he said. "Say you'll forgive me."

How could she refuse?

"I'm disappointed that you didn't call." His soft, sexy, sultry voice sent pinpricks up her spine.

"I'm surprised you gave me a second thought," she confessed, stunned, thrilled.

"Every day. I'm ashamed to admit I asked Joe about you."

She decided not to tell him that he'd been the topic of discussion at the Carpe Diem Divas' dinner meeting.

"Joe said you were worth having."

"Did he?"

"He suggested I try groveling."

Feeling lighter than she had in months, she teased, "Let me guess. That's not one of your finer skills?"

"Finer skills? It's something I've never heard of. I had to look up the word in the dictionary."

She laughed.

Logan took a step closer. He filled her vision, intimately close, making her nerve endings vibrate with awareness.

"You're a newbie to BDSM."

She wasn't sure whether he'd guessed that or whether Joe had told him. "And?"

"If we had scened the other night, you would have given me your phone number and taken my call the next day. And right now... Right now...?"

Nervously, she gulped.

"You'd be remembering how good it was. You'd have confidence, and you'd be on your knees begging me to take you to the basement."

Jennifer drew a shaky breath. "Look, Logan—"

"Be as honest with yourself as I'm demanding you be with me. If you had been totally into that scene with Simon, you wouldn't have turned to look at me. And at the end, you were disappointed with the experience, wondering if it could have been better. In fact, you've talked to Noelle, maybe read some things, watched some videos. You think it can be better."

Though she wasn't sure why, she hesitated. After another a shallow breath, she nodded. "Yes."

"So why didn't you call?" He paused. "The truth."

Heat rocked her. She wasn't sure any man had ever demanded so much from her. "You make me nervous."

"Because?"

Her mouth went slack. "You can't be serious."

He didn't respond.

"You're..." She searched for words. "Intimidating."

He drank the rest of his champagne and put the glass down.

"Am I?" A smile teased the corners of his mouth. The effect was no less threatening.

"I don't know anything about you," she protested.

"Didn't stop you with Simon."

"That's different," she protested.

"How?"

"He reminded me of most of the men I know. Safe." Knowing her behavior might be reckless, she put down her glass then gave in to the stupid temptation of tracing the jagged edges of his scar.

Logan didn't flinch, didn't pull away.

"He let me tell him what I wanted."

"And you don't think I would?"

"No. Yes." She hesitated. "It's not the same thing at all."

"You're right. I'd push you to ensure that you had the experience you wanted." He clamped her wrist, making her regret not moving away while she'd been able to. "Do you know what a safe word is?"

"Noelle's told me a few things about it."

"Explain it to me." His eyes seemed more opaque, the color like molten jade, revealing nothing, yet demanding everything.

"It's a word that will stop a BDSM scene."

He nodded. "Oftentimes, people will have a second word, one that means *slow down* or *pause*."

"Like *yellow*," she said.

"Yeah. Like *yellow*."

She nodded.

"Right now, you're nervous as hell."

As if she'd missed a tax-filing deadline. "Yes."

"Good."

"Good?" she echoed, stunned, hardly able to breathe.

"A little fear, nervousness, increases your reactions, heightens your awareness. Maybe even makes you wet."

God help me.

"Tell me about your fantasies."

He was pushing her into areas she'd never been before. It was thrilling, frightening. Ever since she'd walked out of the front door of this house last month and left him alone in the foyer, she'd regretted the fact that she'd been a coward.

She reminded herself that she'd vowed not to chicken out a second time. But faced with him, breathing his masculine, overwhelmingly clean scent, it was more difficult than she could imagine.

"Tell me," he repeated.

She tried to pull her hand away but she was trapped, helpless.

"Jennifer…" He said her name softly, implacably, a command as much as an entreaty.

She was lost. Mesmerized by the heat in his gaze. "A while ago, I bought myself a flogger at an adult store."

"Have you used it?"

"You might have guessed I haven't had the opportunity."

"What other toys do you have?"

Were they really having this conversation? "I have a pair of nipple clamps, but I've never actually been brave enough to use them."

"So you want to be flogged, maybe with nipple clamps on."

She nodded.

"What gets you off when you're masturbating?"

He saw her, deeper than anyone else had looked. The knowledge made her dizzy. Suddenly, she was unable to find her voice.

"You're doing fine," he said.

His reassurance combined with his matter-of-fact tone made this easier than she might have imagined. "I envision myself tied up," she confessed. "Helpless. Clamped. Blindfolded." *Writhing. Desperate.* In her mind, the more intense the bondage, the harder her orgasm. She wondered if that would be true in real life.

"And then what?"

Her smile died before fully forming. "I was hoping you wouldn't ask that."

"I'm waiting."

Was she really going to admit this? "I'm flogged. Hard. No matter how much I beg, it goes on and on. I'm..." She swallowed then breathed in. "It's just a fantasy. I know it can't really happen. I'm not sure I really want it." But part of her did.

"You'll always have a safe word. What I'm hearing is that you want to be pushed."

She nodded.

"You're hoping, deep inside, that I'm going to take away your choices and tie you to the St. Andrew's cross," he went on. "You want to be vulnerable, to pull against the bonds while knowing you can't get out of them. You want to know the sensation of surrender as the structure supports your entire weight while you're naked, waiting."

Jennifer's legs wobbled. Suddenly she was grateful for his tight, reassuring grip.

"You're picturing it, aren't you?"

"My God…"

"I can make that happen. *We* can make that happen. It's just the two of us. We have all night. We won't be interrupted. No one will be watching you. It's just you and me and your deepest desires." He released her wrist. "But you'll have to ask me for it."

He was offering to fulfill her erotic fantasies. Yes. *Yes.* That was exactly what she wanted. She only wished he wasn't so overwhelming.

"Oh, and, Jennifer? One more thing. You'll do it from your knees."

Her breath strangled her.

He stood so close she inhaled his scent, that of musk and determination. Heavens above, she wanted this.

"What will it be? A night spent in exploration? Or shall we put away the food and head back to the city before it gets any later?"

Chapter Three

With patience learned during long days and nights of wartime waiting—brutal monotony shattered by occasional life-or-death rushes of adrenaline—Logan waited for Jennifer's answer. He liked the way she'd blushed earlier, and now he enjoyed looking at the little furrow between her eyebrows. He guessed she'd be mortified if she had any idea how expressive her face was, the way all her emotions were so clearly readable. He knew her answer, realized she was waging an internal battle with her own desires. Just as surely, he intended to wait until she was honest with herself.

Within ten seconds, less time than he'd expected, she said, "I'd like to explore."

The words pleased him more than he had anticipated. "Tell me your safe word. Do you want to use *red*?"

She shook her head. "Marshmallow."

"Seriously?"

"I don't like them." She wrinkled her nose in a way that showed her extreme displeasure. "It's the texture, especially when they get warm."

He couldn't help but smile. "You'll remember that?"

"I will."

"And a word to let me know you want to slow down?"

"Can we use *yellow* for that?"

"Absolutely. Did you bring your flogger with you?"

She took her time, and he realized she was a woman he couldn't rush. That would make dominating her all the more rewarding.

"I... Yes. It's in my bag," she said.

Obviously she'd made the same guess he had, that any gathering at the Montroses' mountain home would end up kinky.

"Fetch it for me."

After nodding, she walked to the foyer, unzipped her bag, then dug to the bottom of it.

The sight of the red leather flogger in her hand impressed him. It had long, thick strands. Even from across the room, he could tell it wasn't a twenty-dollar novelty. No doubt it had cost ten times that amount, and that told him just how serious she was about this evening. "Did you bring the nipple clamps?"

She didn't look over at him as she answered, "No." When she was walking back toward him, her steps faltered as if she was unsure what to do.

"Hold on to it until we get downstairs," he instructed. "I want you to formally offer it to me when you're on your knees asking me to flog you."

The hint of red staining her cheeks deepened.

He paused to lock the front door before retrieving his bag.

At the top of the stairs, he turned on the lights, then indicated she should precede him. He was man enough to appreciate the sway of her hips as she moved.

He made a mental reminder to send Joe and Noelle a thank-you note. Maybe a case of wine.

"Go and stand near the St. Andrew's cross," he instructed when they were in the well-equipped play area. After Joe had bought the house, he'd had most of the basement walls taken out. That left a large space for the custom-built equipment and allowed him to rearrange things for each event.

Jennifer stopped where Logan had said, then turned to face him. She clenched the flogger so hard her knuckles turned white.

"Take a deep breath," he instructed. "Relax a little."

"Would you, if you knew someone was going to hit you?"

"Put that way, no." He smiled. "But if I knew someone was going to spend the rest of the evening taking me to heights I'd never imagined, I might."

"That might be even more nerve-racking," she admitted.

He continued past her to put his bag on a bench near the wall, intentionally giving her some space.

Even though his back was to her, Logan heard the scrape of her boots on the hardwood floor, making him aware she had turned toward him.

He began to lay out his equipment—cuffs, blindfold and nipple clamps with a chain running between them. Since she had her own flogger, he left his in the bag along with a tawse and paddle. "Nothing will happen that you don't want," he reassured her when he faced her. "I promise you, you will ask for it."

She trembled.

"Would you like to see what I have?" He extended his hand in invitation.

She hesitated but then came up alongside him.

"Does anything here scare you?" he asked.

"Those clamps don't look like the ones I own."

"What kind do you have?"

"Alligators." She frowned. "But these are the kind that don't come off easily, aren't they?"

"Japanese clovers, and yes. They tighten if you pull on them. But it can be interesting to try to beat them off."

She froze, obviously not knowing whether he was serious.

He wasn't. He might try with the tamer alligator clamps, but not these. "Would you like to skip them?"

For a moment she was silent. "Actually, I wasn't planning to get naked."

At the majority of the play parties that he attended, most women kept on at least a bra and panties. Doms who preferred their subs bare-chested often adorned nipples with pasties or covered them with electrical tape. "Tell me what you want to have happen. But I'll remind you that it didn't work for you when Master Simon allowed you to keep your clothes on."

She let out a shaky breath. "I guess I want all the excitement and none of the risk," she acknowledged.

He inclined his head.

"That sounds ridiculous, doesn't it?"

"Not at all." He'd seen that in all areas of life, from his time in the army and his time as a civilian contractor in the Middle East and now as a PI. Lots of people had bravado. Most of it retreated when the threat became real. "Let me tell you what I want." He waited until she nodded before going on. "I want to give you the flogging you want, one that's so damn good you forget your name. And bonus if you scream mine when you come. Yes, you'll have risk. Yes, it will be scary. Yes, it will be worth it."

"I..." She paused, her mouth open. "Logan... I'm not sure what to say."

"Master Logan," he corrected. "Master, if you're only using one word. Sir, at the very least."

"You're serious?"

"It's a boundary during a scene, helps separate the civilized world from mine."

She shuddered. "Are you calling yours uncivilized?"

"No," he hedged. "I call mine real. *Say it.*"

"Ah..." She wrapped her arms across her chest, and the flogger's leather strands dangled in midair. "Master Logan."

Fuck. The sound of her voice, so compliant, made him ache.

With great effort, he concentrated on finishing their conversation. "I will be touching you, kissing you..." Creating an air of intimacy so complete that she'd be engulfed by it, secure forever. "We won't be having sex, at least until the scene is over. I have no expectations, so it will happen only if you want it, and then we'll use condoms."

She nodded.

"I'd prefer it if you'd take your clothes off, but I'll be satisfied if you strip down to your undergarments. So what will it be?" He waited. Even if it hadn't been on a conscious level, they both knew she'd thought about sceneing tonight. The fact that she'd brought a bag proved it. The obvious problem for her was that he wasn't as easy to sway as Master Simon.

"I want to keep on my bra and underwear."

He nodded. "You can put your clothes on this bench."

Fully anticipating her obedience, he went to the sound system and selected a mix that Joe had cued up. The choices ran the gamut from soft rock to inviting jazz, some Nine Inch Nails with occasional Gregorian chants threaded in.

The preset volume was too loud for Logan's tastes. He wanted to hear all her sounds, no matter how quiet they were. And he wanted to hear the strike of leather on skin.

After lowering the volume, he turned to watch her.

She'd placed the flogger next to his equipment. Everything was in a very orderly line, which he liked. She'd removed her boots and tights, and she was struggling with the skirt zipper.

"May I?" he asked.

After she nodded, he brushed aside her fingers and finished the task. Then he stepped back to watch her finish undressing.

Her choice of underwear enchanted him. The panties were red, which was a pleasant surprise. And they were mesh, making them see-through. That was an even better surprise.

Thin black ribbon was threaded through the waistband. The panties were cut high, giving him a nice view of her curves.

Then she faced him.

The front barely covered her pubis.

Logan's pulse accelerated.

As he silently watched, she caught the bottom of her turtleneck and pulled it up and off.

Her bra matched her panties. The material was gauzy, and the cups were defined by the same black ribbon. Tiny bows were set on each strap, an innocent tease to counter the seductive appeal. "You're absolutely gorgeous, Jennifer."

For a moment, their gazes met. Then she seemed to force herself to look away. As she placed her turtleneck on the counter, her hand trembled.

He bent to scoop up her discarded clothing and handed the pieces to her.

"Thank you."

He watched as she folded the garments and put them on the bench as he'd instructed. "Now I'd like you to pick up your flogger, walk to the cross and stand with your back to it."

She took a deep breath before complying.

Logan transferred the clamps, cuffs and a blindfold to one of the metal tower-like structures that Joe had commissioned for the area then wheeled it toward her.

After ascertaining her height, he attached cuffs to the top of the cross. He was very much aware of Jennifer studying his every motion. That done, he took a step back and said, "Now kneel."

"I didn't know you were serious when you said you wanted me on my knees."

Rather than responding, he pointedly looked at the floor.

Her mouth was open and her breaths were audible, rapid.

Logan watched her silent struggle.

Then long, long seconds later, she followed his command.

"Perfect," he approved. "Now offer the flogger to me with your palms cupped in a beautiful, submissive manner."

With astounding grace, she did so.

"Very well done," he told her. "I want you to spread your legs and lean back just a little." Once she'd done that, he continued, "Good. Now lower your head. Cast your gaze down or close your eyes, whichever is more comfortable for you." He spoke in a low, firm tone, ensuring she could hear him over the music while simultaneously informing her she was ceding power to him.

After the slightest hesitation, she closed her eyes.

"You look lovely, Jennifer." There was something completely erotic about the way she knelt, motionless, nervous, yet fighting past it in order to trust him. The image seared his mind.

Logan appreciatively drank her in before taking a step forward to accept the flogger. He hung it from the metal structure. "Open your eyes. Look at me."

She slowly did, glancing up at him.

Already, he saw the softness in her, the responsiveness, the slide into somewhere sexy and potent. There was no bland smile on her face like she'd had when she'd been with Simon. "Ask me to flog you," he encouraged, desperate to claim her.

"I'm—"

"Ask me."

Her hands trembled, but her voice was firm as she said, "Please, Master Logan. Will you flog me?"

"My pleasure." He extended his hand to help her up, and her smaller one was lost in his much larger grip.

He held her for a while as he looked into her blue eyes, savoring the connection. Eventually he said, "Let's get you on the cross." With his hands on her shoulders, he turned her and guided her toward the wooden structure. "Are you doing okay?"

"Truthfully? I'm somewhere between exhilarated and terrorized."

"Let's keep you on the happier end of that, shall we? Wrists first."

She raised her right arm.

He secured her in place and she tugged against the fabric strap, testing it.

"Can you pull out?"

"No."

"Yellow?" When she didn't immediately reply, he went on, "Take a steadying breath and then answer." He stood in front of her so he could study her reactions.

She exhaled deeply. "I'm all right."

"Good." He smoothed a wayward lock of hair back from her forehead. "It's okay to give yourself over to the full experience. And remember you can stop it at any time. Let me know when you're ready to continue."

After a few moments, she nodded. She kept her gaze on him as he secured her left wrist in place. "How's that?"

She tested both bonds and they held her firm. "It's a bit uncomfortable."

When he moved in to loosen them, she clarified, "I think it's more mental than physical."

"Try to stay in the moment. You were right that you'll do better if you quit thinking about it. Right now, you're fine. Don't worry about what's next. One thing at a time."

"That's probably good advice in all areas of life."

"Yeah." Something he needed to learn as well. Totally focused on her, he said, "I want you to spread your legs, but I don't want you stressing any muscles." Once she'd done as he'd asked, he bent to fasten her ankles to the X. As he expected, she tried to draw her thighs together.

He waited, giving her the time to figure out how much she could move. "You're going to be fine."

"I'm nervous," she admitted. "But not scared."

Her eyes were wide as he picked up the flogger and stood in front of her.

He swept his gaze over her, from her spiked hair to the luscious swell of her breasts, to her slim waist, curvy hips and strong legs. In her bondage, Jennifer was breathtaking. In that moment, with her on the cross, the weight of the flogger in hand, he realized he'd lied to Joe at the last party. Logan *had* missed dominating a submissive. Until now, he hadn't realized how badly.

Wordlessly, he trailed the hilt down the column of her neck and paused at the hollow of her throat.

Her mouth parted.

Still using the flogger's handle, he followed the outline of her bra cups. The lingerie was sheer enough that he saw her nipples bead.

He continued on, tracing downward, between her ribs, down her belly, then lower. Her breaths came in an audible staccato, and her eyes were unbelievably wide, unblinking.

Through her panties, he teased her pussy.

"Oh. That's…"

"Tell me, Jennifer."

"Sexy. Hard."

He adjusted his grip and pressed the flogger's hilt lengthwise between her labia. "I want you to hump it."

Deep red stained her cheeks. Logan was willing to bet no one had ever asked her to do something like this, which made him doubly glad he had.

"Logan—"

"Master Logan," he corrected.

Her beautiful blue eyes were still open wide, fringed by impossibly long lashes.

"There's no one here but us. If something's outside your limits, use a safe word. Otherwise, I expect you to hump this flogger immediately."

She gasped but tilted her pelvis forward.

He nudged the handle a little higher, holding it hard against her clit.

Their gazes fused and he willed her not to look away. "*Now*," he snapped to break her out of her thought pattern.

Somewhat awkwardly, she rocked back and forth.

"That's it," he encouraged. "Give me more."

She shuddered.

"Faster. I want your pussy slick. I want your juices on the leather."

"Logan... Sir..."

"Good girl. Ride it."

She gyrated, pulling against her bonds and leaning forward as much as the X would allow.

He repeated approving words, kept her labia spread, continued to keep the handle pressed into her pussy. "Close your eyes," he instructed a few seconds later.

Once she did, her inhibitions seemed to vanish.

Her movements became freer. She no longer just moved awkwardly, she all but caressed the leather with her clit.

The pungent scent of her arousal drifted toward him, intoxicating him.

Since the hilt slid more easily, he moved a hand to her breast. He squeezed a nipple and rolled it between his thumb and forefinger.

She moaned.

"That's it."

The New Age song trailed away and was replaced by a Gregorian chant. He began to stroke her pussy, and she gyrated faster and quicker. He was into this, into her. "Are you going to give me your orgasm, sub?"

"Oh…"

"Jennifer?"

"Yes. Oh God!" Her body stiffened.

"Ride it out. Give it to me."

She opened her eyes, looked at him, into him.

Right then, nothing existed but them…and her pleasure.

"I…"

"Do it."

With a scream and a sigh, she bent her knees. The bonds captured her weight, and he reacted, releasing her nipple and reaching behind her to support her ass even as he increased the pressure of the hilt against her pussy.

She tipped her head back, closed her eyes and screamed as her body jerked.

Finally, endless seconds later, her head rolled forward.

He leaned in and kissed the side of her neck, then slowly moved his hand from beneath her buttocks.

"That…"

"Yeah." He grinned. "That." Logan lowered the flogger, and she gave another involuntary squirm. "Many times a sub thanks her Dom for an orgasm."

She pressed her lips together.

He raised an eyebrow. "Otherwise, in the future he may bring her to the brink, then leave her there."

"What? Seriously? For how long?"

"She might be lucky if she's allowed to come at all during the scene."

"Oh my God. No way."

He didn't respond.

"What I mean is, thank you, Master Logan."

"You're a quick study, Jennifer. It was my pleasure." He stroked a finger down her jawbone.

She turned into his touch. Desire lanced him. He hadn't just missed playing with a sub, he'd missed being with someone like her, innocent, trusting, new. Experiencing this through her eyes was fucking glorious indeed.

He slowly lowered his hand then rehung the flogger before looking at her. "How are you doing? Mentally? And the bonds?"

"Everything is good."

Her tone was strong and she met his gaze without looking away.

"So now are you ready for me to unfasten your bra so I can clamp your nipples before the flogging begins?"

"Ah…"

"You have a safe word," he reminded her.

She didn't reply right away. He studied her. Was it time to push? Or time to let her succumb to doubt? He recalled that she'd bought herself a set of clamps. "It's like the bondage," he went on. "If it's too much, you can always change your mind. And it's not as if this is your only opportunity to scene. We have the rest of the evening. Even tomorrow if we want." For a man who'd avoided relationships for so long, the realization that his words were both invitation and promise stunned him.

"I'm willing to try."

"That's not good enough," he bit out. "Ask me — 'Please, Master Logan. Put the clamps on my nipples?'"

Jennifer drew her eyebrows together. A potent mixture of apprehension and arousal danced in her eyes, making her pupils flare. "You're relentless," she protested.

"Do you really want it any other way?"

From the sounds of her shortened breaths, he knew he was giving her what she wanted.

"Please put the clamps on my nipples, Master Logan."

He wasn't sure he could deny her anything.

Logan walked behind her to unhook her bra and move the cups out of the way. Then he went to stand in front of her again. Her breasts were gorgeous, full, and her nipples were a deep dusky brown. At some point, he'd love to use his crop on them.

He picked up the set of clamps, but instead of affixing them right away, he sucked on each of her nipples for several seconds, very gently, then increasing the pressure until she moaned.

When he could once again smell her arousal, he pinched her right nipple. It swelled, and he tugged on it, elongating it for the clamp.

She hissed in a breath when the teeth bit into her flesh.

He played with her breast, waiting for the first blush of pain to fade.

"Damn," she said.

"Halfway there."

"I was afraid you were going to say that."

After she'd unclenched her hands, he asked, "Ready?"

"I... Yes."

Rather than immediately placing the next clamp, he decided to play with her. Over her panties, he slid his finger slowly back and forth across her pussy.

"Oh, Master Logan..."

He took his time, bringing her to the edge of an orgasm. He moved away to attach the second clamp, but before she could complain, he put his hand back between her legs. "Tell me what you want. What you need."

"An orgasm," she said with no hesitation. "Please. Please let me orgasm, Master Logan."

"Wait," he warned, voice stern.

She rose onto the balls of her feet and squeezed her eyes shut, seeking release, but not daring. The woman was an absolute natural. Selfishly, he was glad she'd had a disappointing scene with Master Simon. Logan wanted her for himself. He leaned closer, mouth against her ear, and slipped his fingers under her panties before entering her. Then he said, "Come *now*, Jennifer."

She screamed as she climaxed.

The cross and the bonds caught her weight, and he wrapped an arm around her waist. Yeah. She was perfect. And his. For tonight, if nothing else.

Chapter Four

Jennifer heard Logan speaking from somewhere distant. *Master Logan.*

"How was it?"

She wasn't sure she could explain her feelings. But she was aware of him looking at her, watching, waiting. "Not what I was expecting." More than she'd hoped. Her nipples felt swollen and they throbbed unbearably. Not from pain, but from something else, maybe longing for more.

All of a sudden, she understood the dreamy expression that came over Noelle's face when she talked about intimate times with her husband.

Jennifer almost always orgasmed when she had sex, but this time had been more powerful than any other. Being out of control, commanded to wait, then being shoved from the precipice had been sublime.

Logan had been there the whole time, never more than a couple of feet away, touching her. And when she'd come, he'd given her the support of his body as well as his confidence.

She felt connected to him in a way she hadn't with anyone else.

It overwhelmed her.

"Are you ready to continue?"

She might come undone without the mastery of his body. "Yes." Then she remembered his earlier prompting. "Please, Sir."

Devilment played in his eyes, and his scar no longer seemed as deeply pronounced. She wondered if the fact that he'd made her feel so safe took away the perception of danger. A flash of feminine intuition warned her the thought was a risky one. Men didn't get scars like that from choosing a safe, secure life. Noelle had told her he'd been in the Middle East. Obviously he hadn't returned unscathed. Jennifer wondered how deep the scars ran.

"How do your nipples feel?"

His question jolted her from her thoughts. Now that the height of the orgasm had faded, she was aware of a dull ache. "They're throbbing a little."

He plumped her breasts.

She sucked in a breath. The sensation was exquisite, wonderful, sharp, delicious, addictive.

"Just a little?"

"Yes, Master Logan."

"Let's see about that." He threaded an index finger though each of the slender metal rings that were attached to the ends and yanked.

The shocking pain made her scream.

"That's better," he said.

"*Fucking hell.*" Her clit throbbed as arousal crashed into her.

Logan grinned.

She realized his action had been calculated. The man knew how to get a reaction, and, more, how to turn her on.

With an achingly gentle motion, he smoothed his thumbs over the tips of her breasts.

She gulped then let out a soft sigh. The juxtaposition of the sensual and the painful caused her synapses to misfire.

"How are you doing?" He released the rings.

"Fine." Jennifer scowled, as if surprised by her own answer.

A lock of hair had fallen onto her forehead, and he feathered it back before again pressing a finger against her clit.

She rocked forward, silently asking for more.

"So needy," he said.

"Yes." She looked at him through the fringe of her eyelashes. "I want you to flog me. Or allow me to come again. Or take off the clamps. Something." All she knew was, she was crawling out of her mind.

When he didn't react, her thoughts tumbled. Then she remembered he wanted to be addressed formally. "Sir," she pleaded.

"My pleasure."

As she watched, he unfastened the buttons at his wrists and turned back his cuffs. She couldn't look away from his strong hands or the sinews in his forearms. This man...

He placed a finger beneath her chin and tipped it back. "Tell me your safe word."

"Marshmallow."

"You wrinkle your nose every time you say that."

The conversation seemed friendly, at odds with her being secured to the St. Andrew's cross, half-naked, nipples clamped and a mad ache between her thighs.

"And if you need to slow down?"

"Yellow. Can we get on with it?"

His eyes flared with desire. This was so much more than she'd anticipated.

Rather than responding, he picked up the flogger.

She squirmed. Logan looked bigger than he had, broader, more intimidating. Heaven help her, it thrilled her. The throbbing in her nipples intensified.

He moved behind her, increasing her feeling of helplessness.

She expected to feel the leather searing her skin. Instead, he traced his fingers across each of her shoulders, then down her spine, stopping at the top of her panties. Suddenly Jennifer wished she had been brave enough to strip entirely. She wanted his touch on her bare skin.

Through the material of her underwear, he rubbed her buttocks before trailing lower to her thighs.

As she relaxed, she spread her fingers wide and pressed against the wood.

"That's right," he said soothingly.

He made smaller and smaller circles, and her body tingled.

She closed her eyes. Eventually there seemed to be nothing but the sounds of monks chanting and her own rapid breaths.

Then...silence reverberated.

In response to the fear that started to sneak in, she tightened her muscles.

"If you relax, it won't hurt as much."

She took a steadying breath before exhaling.

He draped the leather strands over her shoulder then drew them down in a sensual caress.

The first fall against her buttocks felt like a light sting.

"Unclench your ass," he told her.

"I'm trying."

He stroked her back with his hand and the flogger's strands.

"Let go. Surrender. Experience." He stunned her by reaching between her legs to play with her still-damp pussy.

She bent her knees as much as she could, seeking. "More," she begged, wanting him inside her. "Please."

"You'll get everything you want."

He moved away and gave her the first hit that hurt.

She stiffened. Then, remembering his coaching, she forced out a breath.

Another strike fell, followed by several more, one after another.

Her dreams had not come close to the thrill of reality. The leather was wicked and sensuous, all at the same time. It burned, stung, and when the sensations receded, she was left with an unfulfilled need crawling through her. She was turned on, horny, desperate.

Her nipples hardened, throbbing.

He went on and on, the tips of the strands landing on her buttocks and thighs, her back, hitting every place at once, in dull, biting thuds.

"Breathe," he coached her. "Surrender."

She did, giving up the struggle, willing her muscles to soften.

He then flogged her in earnest, back and forth, crisscrossing her body, blazing trails of sensation.

Jennifer's entire being rose to another level of awareness. Her temperature spiked, and she began to perspire. Her muscles and sinews were supple. As he'd suggested, she allowed the restraints to be a saving grace, and she curled her hands around them for extra support.

Then, as if intuitively reading her mind, Logan increased the pressure.

He hit her ass so hard the wind seemed to be knocked out of her. Jennifer's pussy got wetter, stunning her. The clamps bit deeper.

"You're behaving perfectly."

She wasn't sure whether she was or she wasn't. All she knew was she hoped he wouldn't stop.

For long minutes, he flogged her, his motions rhythmic. A light, glancing blow made her sigh. Then he caught her beneath her buttocks with a sharp upward swing, and she screamed.

"That's it, on your toes."

His constant hits made her squirm. Then they became worse. "Oh God." She wasn't sure whether she said it out loud or whether it echoed in her head.

Relentlessly, he continued. His next few dozen hits seared her. *Yellow* raced through her mind, but before she could form it, he changed his pattern, striking her with gentle smacks. This was more of a dance. Then...all of her thoughts ceased.

Her eyes were closed, but she saw twinkling lights, so blue they appeared white.

She stopped struggling, with him, the process, herself. Until that moment, she hadn't realized what he'd meant when he'd told her to do that, but now she did. There was no conflict, just a calm acceptance, then an expectation, a welcoming.

She heard the faint sound of a bell ringing, then the sound of chants, soft, then louder. She seemed to be floating, between somewhere and nowhere at all.

Every part of her body vibrated, and she'd never been needier.

It took her a long while to realize that the flogging had stopped, and that he'd already released her right wrist. He was rubbing it when she opened her eyes.

"Easy. Take it easy."

If I can move at all.

His body was pressed tight against hers, and the denim of his jeans scratched against her skin. And for the first time, she inhaled the scent of him—the crispness of a winter night, the undeniable appeal of masculine strength.

Earlier, his size and shadowed past had unnerved her. Now it gave her a sense of peace, made her feel protected.

With deft motions, he unfastened her left wrist and rubbed the chafed skin. That he was capable of such tenderness astounded her.

"Let me look at you."

She hadn't realized he'd unfastened her ankles.

He put his hands on her shoulders and turned her to face him.

"I'm going to remove the nipple clamps," he said. "Fair warning. It will hurt."

He removed the first one, and a sharp sting pierced her. But he closed his mouth around the abused tip and sucked on it until pleasure replaced pain.

She drew a breath before he took off the second.

After he was done, he helped her over to a bench. She sat while he turned down the volume of the music.

"How do you feel?" he asked.

Incomplete. Somewhat bereft. Unsure how to explain those emotions, she wrapped her arms around herself. "Earlier, you said we might have sex…"

"And...?" He stood in front of her. His eyes, a darker jade than they had been earlier, banked with intensity, devoured her.

She reached inside for the confidence to ask for what she wanted, the courage to be herself. "I'd like you to fuck me, Master Logan."

Logan crouched in front of her and framed her face between his palms. There was a hesitation in her voice that gave him pause. "Do you want to think about it? Wait until you're a little steadier?"

Dead-on, she met his gaze. "No."

"You were pretty far gone."

"I want sex, Sir."

He liked to give his subs what they wanted after a scene, from snuggling to a long conversation, even sharing a hot bath. One submissive had stunned him by wanting to go for a run, but this...? With a woman he barely knew and hadn't been able to stop thinking about?

"I need you inside me. I..."

He waited.

She exhaled shakily. "I want the connection."

"I'll give you anything you desire, Jennifer. It doesn't have to be through sex," he told her.

"Do you have condoms with you?" Her voice showed her exasperation.

The woman was in complete control of her faculties. "Yes. I have condoms."

"Then get one."

A grin pulled at his mouth. "Get one?"

"That wasn't very submissive, was it? What I meant was, get one, Master Logan."

Her playfulness revealed another side of her personality. The more he saw, the more he liked. "You do have a few things to learn."

"Please," she added.

"Much, much better, sub." Since he'd first touched her, he'd wanted to fuck her. Flogging her had only driven up his need. "Upstairs. In one of the bedrooms." Where he could pin her down and drive into her.

"I'd prefer to do it here."

He was astounded by how wide her blue eyes were. "Here?"

"Now."

"You have something in mind?" He was intrigued.

A Muse song filtered through the play area, all but encouraging sex.

"I do."

"In that case..." He released his hold on her face then stood.

She shrugged off the unfastened bra, dropped it on the nearby pile of clothes then rolled her shoulders back. Her invitation was blatant and appreciated.

Logan pulled out his wallet and extracted a condom.

She held out a hand.

Quirking an eyebrow, he tossed it toward her. Without breaking the bond of their gazes, she caught it and closed her hand.

Yeah. It had been a long fucking time since he'd been captivated so powerfully. Though he'd never admit it to her, this woman had the potential to lead him around by the dick.

He bent to remove his boots, but she stopped him.

"May I?"

He quirked an eyebrow. "Certainly, little sub."

She gracefully slid off the bench then knelt, spreading her legs to make room for his foot.

"This would be better if you'd taken off the underwear," he said.

"Spoken like a typical man."

"Ouch," he replied.

Jennifer removed each of his boots in turn. He couldn't remember if his ex-girlfriend, Helen, had ever performed such an intimate act for him. He enjoyed the purity of Jennifer's little act of service.

She knelt up and shuddered as he tugged his belt from its loops. "Do you want to feel this on your ass?" he asked.

"I'd never thought about it before. But suddenly I'm fascinated."

That made two of them. The idea of her being over his knee, scrabbling for purchase while he spanked her, made his cock throb.

He removed his shirt, and she accepted it, maintaining eye contact as she placed it on the bench next to her. Then he unzipped his pants.

"Commando?" she asked.

"Always."

Her eyes widened when he dropped his jeans and she looked at his erect dick. "Is it because you can't find anything to fit over that thing, Sir?"

He grinned at her humor.

As if mesmerized, she continued to stare.

"The fit will be fine. Just fine."

"Can I have your word on that?"

He finished undressing and said, "Put the condom on me."

With deliberation, she ripped open the package. But instead of rolling the latex down his cock, she stood and wiggled out of her panties.

Seeing her there, small, naked, vulnerable, made his protective instincts blaze. He wanted to possess her and never let her go.

He raised a finger, indicating she wait while he swept his gaze over her, from her full breasts to the tormented nipples that still bore marks from his clamps, to the gentle swell of her belly, the curve of her hips, her neatly trimmed pussy. "You're beautiful, Jennifer."

She grinned. "You are too, Master Logan."

"Cheeky wench."

Without being instructed, she slid to her knees and reached for him.

She cupped his testicles in her left hand and stroked his shaft with the other. At first she used long, sweeping motions, then began to use shorter, faster ones.

"The condom." He put his hand on hers, stilling her. "*Now.*"

"Yes, Master Logan." Her tone was proper. The way she glanced up at him was anything but.

Defiant, disobedient, she licked a drop of pre-ejaculate from the tip of his swollen dick, then touched her tongue to her upper lip.

"Jennifer," he warned. "Unless you want to be put back on the cross to experience my wrath…"

She lowered her head so he couldn't see the expression in her eyes, but he could guess that there was devilment in them. "There might be a spanking in your future," he vowed.

"Yes, Sir. Anything you say, Master Logan."

Her grip sure and confident—and fucking arousing—she placed the condom on his cockhead, then rolled the latex down into place.

Meeting his gaze through that impossibly long fringe of lashes, she stroked.

"No." His hand on hers, he stopped her.

"But—"

"Last warning, Jennifer." He sat and pulled her into his lap facing him.

She landed with a whoosh of breath and a sensual laugh.

This woman... Everything about her responsive body appealed to him. "Lift yourself a bit."

"Anything you say, Sir."

This time, there was no hint of a tease, just pure, unhesitant response.

After wrapping her arms around his neck, she rose onto the balls of her feet while he guided his cock toward her damp pussy.

"I want you, Master Logan," she whispered into his ear. She lowered herself, taking the tip before rising again.

He put his hands on her waist, supporting her, letting her set the pace.

With each stroke, she slowly took his shaft deeper, until he was balls-deep in her.

"Damn." She buried her head against his shoulder.

"Okay?"

"Give me a second."

He stroked her spine, her shoulders, then pinched her bottom.

With a yelp, she arched away from him. "Sir!"

Logan dug a hand into her short, spiky, sexy hair and pulled her head back. Her eyes widened, and the flames of arousal caused spikes of gold in her blue eyes. Then, his motions slow and deliberate, he leaned forward and captured her mouth.

She opened for him, and he accepted her silent invitation.

Their tongues met, and he tasted the headiness of champagne — the seductive sweetness of her surrender.

As he claimed her, devoured her, she moaned a little and pressed herself against him.

It ignited his desire.

Logan raised his knees, adjusting her balance, pitching her toward him, allowing him to explore her more and drive his cock deeper into her hot cunt.

She murmured something he couldn't make out. Maybe *yes*. Maybe *more*. But there was no mistaking the way she clung to him, rocking back and forth, in a silent invitation for him to fill her pussy.

Reluctantly, he ended the kiss and traced a series of smaller ones across her shoulder.

"Fill me," she said.

He dug his fingers into her ass, making sure she knew she was his.

Her sigh told him she understood.

Logan pistoned his hips, fucking her with short, fast motions. Everything he gave, she took hungrily, asking for more.

Her breathing changed and her skin heated.

"I need..."

"Wait," he said. Her pussy muscles clenched around him, urging him precariously close to an orgasm.

"I don't want to," she protested, angling forward.

He tightened his grip.

"Master Logan." Her words were desperate, a plea. Something he'd never be able to deny her.

He lifted her, then said, "*Now.*" He thrust his hips, surging up into her, seeking her G-spot.

She cried out. Screaming his name, she gripped him tight as she came.

He held back for another few seconds, the denial uncomfortable and exhilarating as she writhed on his cock.

When her body went slack, he protectively crushed her against him, a hand in the middle of her back as she gulped for air.

"That…" She exhaled. "Mmm…"

He grinned. "Satisfied, little sub?"

In response, she kissed the side of his neck.

"We're not done," he said.

"I was hoping we weren't."

He adjusted their position slightly, and she dug her toes into the floor to lift herself a few inches. She curled her hands around his shoulders while he pounded into her.

Her cunt was wet, tight. All of a sudden, he was questioning the sanity of avoiding a relationship for so long.

He went deep, impaling her.

"Fuck." She groaned. "I like the way you do me, Sir."

It wasn't just any woman he'd missed, he realized. It was a woman like her, one who was willing to ask for what she wanted, willing to take it.

Logan's balls drew up. Waiting was exquisite torture.

"Yes," she said.

He gave a final thrust, pulling her down, making her take all of him. She cried out and leaned back, enough for him to reach one of her nipples and tweak it.

"Sir!" She clenched her ass cheeks, and the motion drove his orgasm.

He ejaculated in spurts that made him shudder and squeeze her tight.

"That, Sir, hit a few of my fantasy buttons," she said when he opened his eyes to see her looking at him with a smile.

"We've got all night," he said. "Let's see if we can push a few more."

Chapter Five

The idea was enough to make her dizzy.
Being with Logan had been everything she could have imagined, and oh, so much more.
Jennifer accepted his help as she stood. She swayed to one side, and he immediately put his hands on her waist.
"Do you need to sit?"
"No." She shook her head. "I just stood too fast." But it wasn't only that. Her mind was swimming from everything she'd just experienced.
When she'd attended the BDSM movie with the Carpe Diem Divas, she'd fantasized about what it would be like to be under the control of a powerful man who would guide and support her.
Brett had been okay in bed, enough to get her off, but there had been no adventure. Often the lights had been off or, at the very least, dim. Most times, they'd even done it beneath the sheets. He had never been as direct as Master Logan, never studied her the way he did, never pushed her beyond her comfort level into new levels of awareness and arousal. This was

everything she imagined sex could be. And damn, she liked it.

"Better?" Logan asked, looking at her through narrowed eyes.

She pushed back the unruly lock of hair from her forehead and nodded.

He quirked an eyebrow.

"I mean, I'm fine. Thank you, Sir." Part of her was thrilled by his insistence on formality. He was right. It kept the outside world separate from what they were sharing. To her, that made this more intimate.

She expected him to release his grip, but he didn't right away. For the moment, it was nice to feel protected.

He studied her face, as if reassuring himself, before saying, "Let's get you upstairs and maybe into a shower."

She nodded.

When he released her, she reached for her underwear.

"You won't be needing any of that until tomorrow."

Freezing, she looked at him. "You want me naked?"

"Unless otherwise instructed. Yes." He stood.

Until now, she hadn't noticed how much he towered over her. Taking off her shoes and facing him made her cognizant of his size, strength and irresistible domination. He stole her breath.

"But you are welcome to take your belongings upstairs. My things as well." He disposed of the condom. Even without an erection, he had an impressive cock.

As if on cue, she became aware of a tingling between her legs that told her she'd be sore tomorrow. She grinned, unable to remember the last time *that* had happened, if it ever had. In her experience, no other man was his equal.

Logan straightened up the play area, removing his cuffs from the cross and dropping them into the bag. Then he returned to the metal tower and picked up the wicked clamps. "How were they?" he asked.

"I'm...glad we used them."

He continued to regard her, clearly waiting for her to go on.

"They were intense. Almost too much. Well, they were extreme when you pulled on them."

He grinned, and she suddenly felt like prey.

"And your pussy got wet," he said, his voice as rich as cognac spilled on black velvet.

She gulped. "True."

"Be brave, Jennifer."

"I already have been, Sir. More than ever before."

"We have a lot of the night left."

Even though his words sent a shiver of threat through her, she didn't want their time together to end.

He dropped the clamps and the blindfold into his bag, then zipped it shut before going to turn off the stereo. The silence echoed.

Receiving a flogging to the sound of Gregorian chant music had allowed her to get out of her head and stop thinking. Then... Having sex to Muse had been incredible. The thrumming beat had given her courage that she'd never experienced before.

But now, with no outside noise, she noticed the thump of her heartbeat and the frantic, desperate sound of her shallow breaths.

"I want to look at your ass. I'll follow you up the stairs," he said.

Was this what it was like to be a submissive? Subject to the Dom's orders and desires? Having boundaries tested, maybe demolished? An illicit thrill tingled down her spine. If this was what it was like, she wanted more.

"And I want to admire my handiwork, see if you need more stripes to remember me by."

She couldn't tell if he was joking, and that created uncertainty that made her stomach pitch.

"After you."

Jennifer gathered her flogger and the pile of their clothing, including his boots, then finally, his leather belt. She held everything against her chest as she climbed the stairs. Every sense seemed to be on hyperalert. She knew he was watching, making a judgment. It was exhilarating.

"Your ass is a little red."

She glanced over her shoulder.

"But you only have a few lingering marks. I'll remedy that."

His words weren't a question, and they were delivered matter-of-factly—almost as casual as observations about the weather.

Once they were upstairs, he put his duffel bag near the door and said, "Let me get you something to drink."

She continued into the living room and placed their boots side-by-side on the floor before piling the rest of their things on the couch. His earlier words about existing in two different worlds filtered through her mind.

In the window's reflection, she watched him.

Even though he moved with athletic grace, he took in the surroundings. Always a warrior. Always on guard.

She stared, mesmerized.

He collected a water bottle then placed it on the end table before moving in to wrap his arms around her. "Cold?"

For a moment, she held herself away from him, but his grip was firm, relentless, and she relaxed, wondering if she could deny him anything.

"That's better."

The evening felt surreal. She'd gone from expecting a festive evening with friends to the most intimate, mind-expanding, fantasy-filled situation possible.

He rubbed his hands up and down her arms, keeping her close until the chill subsided.

"Come with me," he said.

Logan led her to the couch then wrapped a blanket around her shoulders. He left her long enough to flip the switch to ignite the fireplace. When he returned, he sat next to her, then uncapped the bottle of water and offered it to her.

Until she'd taken a drink, she hadn't realized how parched she'd been.

He pulled her closer. This time, she went willingly, snuggling into his chest, breathing in warmth, comfort and security from him.

"Does anything hurt?"

"My nipples are a little tender. Not bad, though."

"And your back, thighs, buttocks?"

"Hardly a twinge," she confessed, unwilling to admit how much that disappointed her. In the movie she'd seen, the leading man had promised the star that she wouldn't be able to sit for a week after he was done with her. And Jennifer wasn't feeling the least bit uncomfortable.

They stared at the flickering flames, and she said, "I'm curious about your scar."

"Are you?"

She wondered if that was a way to dodge the question or an invitation to probe further. Since she was intrigued, she pressed on. "You're a bit of a mystery. Even Noelle doesn't know much."

"You asked about me."

Was that a note of triumph in his tone? "I like to know something about men I might sleep with." In fact, she generally insisted on several dates before becoming intimate. Yet she found Logan trustworthy, perhaps because of his honesty. He hadn't promised anything other than an evening of exploration, and she'd found that somewhat refreshing.

"Yet we just scened."

She wiggled away, putting some distance between them before turning to face him. "I know Joe considers you a friend. Apparently there aren't a lot of people he says that about. I'm guessing the same is true for you."

"Friends? A handful," he conceded.

"But those few?"

"I'd risk my life for them."

She believed it. "And the scar?" she persisted.

"Pushy for a sub, aren't you?"

"You flogged me, fucked me, said something about giving me some more stripes. I think that gives me a right."

"Does it?"

"Doesn't it?" she challenged, pulling her legs up onto the couch.

He was quiet for so long she thought he might not answer. When he did, his voice was low, rough, containing a jagged edge of pain. "It was an explosion."

"When you were in the Middle East?"

"You heard that from Joe or Noelle."

"Sort of. Noelle said you'd been in the Middle East, but she doesn't know how you got the scar. So I'm guessing the explosion happened while you were over there."

"It did. There were four of us, going back to our compound. IED." He traced the scar back and forth with his forefinger.

The motion seemed so unconscious she wondered if he was aware of it.

"Joe, Matt made it back alive. Matt wished he hadn't, couldn't deal with it. We brought Gary's body back, but we left Matt's spirit, his heart...whatever the fuck you want to call it..." He dropped his hand, curled it into a fist. "He killed himself almost two years later. He had a wife. A kid."

She sucked in a breath. But since words seemed inadequate, she remained silent.

He was staring ahead, not paying attention, as if he were lost.

"At Matt's funeral, Joe and I made a pact to live fully, our way, no matter how lame, to honor Matt and Gary." After several tense seconds, he looked at her. "I keep my hair short so the first thing I see every day is this scar. A reminder of that promise."

Jennifer felt slightly breathless. "Thank you for telling me."

"Sorry you asked?"

"Not at all." She shook her head and offered a wan smile. More fully, she understood what he meant about the different worlds. The things that he spoke of, she would never experience. "I wish I were capable of not being nosy."

"Don't apologize for being who you are."

The timbre of his voice rumbled through her, and she snuggled closer to him again.

In the companionable quiet, woven from the sharing of secrets, they watched the fire, saw clouds fill the sky, making it look mysterious outside.

"I promised you a shower," he said much later. "But it can wait. I want to get you hotter, wetter, dirtier first."

His shocking words shot heat into her cunt, leaving her feeling greedy. "When?" she asked, emboldened in a way she had never been before tonight.

He plucked the bottle from her hand and the blanket from her shoulders, then said, "On your knees. Present my belt to me."

In his tone there was nothing but uncompromising authority. She searched his features and found no hint of the person who'd so tenderly held her moments ago. Instead, he was a Dom who expected to be obeyed. Shocked, she realized she liked both sides of him equally as well.

Silently—since words would have lodged in her throat—she dug through the pile of their clothes until she found his belt.

He continued to regard her, his fingers steepled.

Once she held the leather by the buckle, she was uncertain what to do, how to proceed.

"You've got good instincts. Trust them. You won't disappoint me."

She folded the belt in half before kneeling in front of him. Remembering his instructions in the basement, she spread her thighs wide and leaned back slightly. Then she bowed her head, extended her hands palms up and focused her gaze on the floorboards.

For a long time, he remained silent. It took all her concentration to remain where she was, knowing he was looking, thinking, perhaps planning what he intended to do to her.

Finally, just when she was about to shift or say something to break the tension that was clawing through her, he said, "Exactly right."

She exhaled a slow, shuddering breath.

He took the belt from her and said, "Now fetch my bag for me."

Aware of his gaze on her, she stood with as much grace as possible then went to grab his bag. She deposited it next to him.

With a pleased nod, he instructed, "Over my knees."

He offered a hand, and she accepted. Even though her pulse skidded past every other beat, she drank reassurance from his strong grip.

Within seconds, she was upended, off balance, reaching for the floor with her fingertips.

"Legs farther apart."

Before she could get situated, he placed a finger at the entrance to her pussy and eased it inside her.

Her vision swam.

"How are you with anal?"

"Oh my God…"

"I'll take that as a yes." He played with her pussy, sliding his finger in and out until she was wet and slippery.

Then she felt him at her tightest hole, slowly pressing forward. She had a safe word and a word to get him to slow down. Since she was an anal virgin, she should use one of them. But she didn't. Couldn't.

"It'll be easier if you bear down instead of fighting."

She sucked in a breath, realizing he was coaching her, not asking permission.

He removed his hand. At the sound of the zipper rasping, she froze. She cocked her head to the side to see him pull a small packet of lube from his bag.

He tore off a corner. Then she felt the cool, viscous liquid on her skin.

With his finger, he worked it in deeper and deeper.

"Relax," he suggested, his voice soothing.

She wasn't sure that was even possible.

He swatted her right ass cheek hard, and she yelped, scooting away from him. But the distraction was enough to allow him to wrap one arm around her waist and drag her back into position while he forced his finger all the way in up to the knuckle.

"Ow! Damn it. That's uncomfortable."

"Enough complaining," he snapped. "Unless you want two fingers up there."

"You wouldn't!"

He placed a second finger at her entrance.

"Wait! One is fine. Thank you, Sir."

"Much better. Now ask me to finger-fuck your ass."

In response, she unintentionally clenched her buttocks.

"Jennifer," he warned.

Defiance warred with desire.

"Jennifer..."

"Will you finger-fuck my ass, Sir?"

"Since you asked so nice, of course, little sub."

But as he eased out, then back in, she was astounded by how turned on she was becoming.

"Keep trusting me," he encouraged.

"Do I have a choice?"

"You know you do."

She decided not to safe word out.

After half a dozen more leisurely strokes, he began to move faster and faster. Rationally she knew he only had one finger up there. It felt like so much more, igniting her nerve endings. "This—"

He reached beneath her and squeezed an already tender nipple.

She bucked, and he took advantage of that, shortening his strokes, relentlessly doing her.

"Logan..." She didn't know what she was asking for. "Master."

Before she could orgasm or even really sort out her physical responses, he stopped.

Her breaths were ragged, and her mind felt the same.

He grabbed an individually packaged alcohol swab from his bag and wiped his hand before saying, "Where was I?"

"What?" she demanded, incredulous, trying to turn over so she could glare at him.

Uncompromisingly, with a palm pressed against the middle of her back, he held her in place.

"Are you serious?" Her empty cunt throbbed. And her ass burned slightly, not from the fingering, but from the sudden lack of attention. She felt ready to crawl out of her mind.

"Oh, yes. Leaving you something to remember me by. How many stripes from my belt, Jennifer?"

"How many?" she repeated. "What?"

He rubbed her buttocks vigorously and squeezed her upper thighs.

"Give me a number. More than two. Fewer than ten."

His commanding touch was enough to make her forget her protests.

"I'll give you more for stalling." He dug his fingers into her flesh.

"Four." The word was more a gasp than anything.

"Four it is."

Knowing what was coming terrified her and she tightened her muscles.

She was learning that this man rarely did what she expected.

Instead of feeling his belt, she was surprised when he stroked her butt cheeks, then delved between her thighs, compelling her to relax without ever uttering a word.

With a soft sigh, she gave herself over to his ministrations.

"That's it," he said.

She'd never before experienced this kind of attention from a man, and a secret part of her loved it.

The denied orgasm unfurled again, instantly making her wet and hungry.

Her body jerked when the leather connected with her right buttock. She held her breath for a couple of beats, waiting for the pain to radiate, but it didn't. Instead, it was a localized, broad stripe.

She exhaled.

"That was one," he told her.

Jennifer nodded. It hadn't been nearly as bad as she'd expected.

He delivered the second on her left buttock, harder this time, making the pain dig deeper inside her.

"The last two will be a little more challenging."

Could he have possibly known that those words were enough to make her determined to endure it without complaint?

The next stripe caught her across both buttocks, burning into her. She went rigid and her breath caught.

Instantly, he rubbed her with his palm, and the pain receded, leaving behind a hot wave of lust. "Fuck," she whispered.

"Yeah. You understand."

Suddenly she did.

When she'd seen the sexy BDSM movie, she'd been skeptical about a submissive's ability to connect with a Dom through this kind of experience. Even when Noelle had assured her that it was indeed possible, Jennifer had still had doubts. But Logan erased them. It wasn't just the physical act. It was mental, emotional, sexual. In this moment, nothing existed but Master Logan and her. He had hold of her, keeping her secure, comforting her even as he shoved her beyond all of her boundaries.

It was dizzying. Terrifying. Addictive.

"Ask me for the last one," he said.

"Yes, yes, yes. Please, Sir. Yes." *More.*

The final strike seared her. She screamed and dug her toes into the floor, trying to escape. He held her fast, making quick circular motions over her ass, helping to dissipate the pain.

Then he plunged his hand between her legs and inserted two fingers deep into her pussy.

"Come for me," he urged.

A million neurons seemed to fire at the same time, and she couldn't deny him anything.

She rocked back, wordlessly demanding he impale her deeper, and she ground herself against his hand.

"So gorgeous," he said.

A shudder ripped through her, and she cried out as she climaxed. "Damn!"

But he wasn't done with her.

Logan changed the tempo. Rather than the relentless pace, he teased her pussy. In less than a minute, she was ready again.

"That's it."

"I'm…" *Lost. Shattered.*

She was still over his knees, fingers brushing the floor. Helpless. And she didn't want the evening to end.

"There's more I want to give you. Take it?" he asked.

"Always?"

She didn't think she'd be able to, but she whispered, "Yes."

Master Logan was as skilled as he was patient. Then he smacked her ass on a place she was already burning.

The exquisite pain made her insides ripple, and he surged his fingers deeper in her, giving her what she needed to come hard.

This time, her body went limp and sweat dotted the back of her neck.

"Now it's time for that shower I promised you." He stood and offered his hand.

She accepted.

Logan continued to tug until she was in his arms. She rested her head near his heart, hearing the powerful thud beneath her ear.

"If you think this means you're done for the evening, you're wrong."

She tipped back her head and looked at him. "I never expected otherwise."

His eyes became molten jade.

Jennifer wasn't sure how much more she could survive. But, as he held her, she realized she was willing to find out.

Chapter Six

"Down the hall. Second door on the right," Logan told her, although he didn't release his grip. He liked having her in his arms. Since Helen had left him, he'd been so caught up in running his detective business and outrunning his inner demons that he hadn't realized how much he'd missed having a woman around. During the first few days he'd been alone, he'd told himself that a relationship was too much effort, that it interfered with his ability to do his job.

And now he was questioning that.

Until this evening, he hadn't acknowledged how lonely he'd been.

By slow measures, Logan released Jennifer, rationalizing that they still had the rest of the night together.

He led her to the guest room. "Bathroom is through there," he said, pointing.

She froze, obviously realizing he intended to follow her.

He maneuvered around her to turn on the faucet and set the temperature. "After you."

"You're getting in with me?"

"No secrets, no privacy when we're together."

"Are you serious?"

Rather than replying, he placed a hand on her ass and nudged her. Once they were in the oversize stall, he reached above her and took down the showerhead. "Face me and spread your legs."

Without a single argument, she did as he'd instructed. She was a quick study—something he appreciated.

Logan directed the spray toward her pussy. But rather than just rinsing her, he parted her labia to bathe her.

Her eyes widened, and the blue seemed even deeper than before. He moved the nozzle closer so the spray was more powerful. Her lips were parted, and the sound of her breathing increased. Her knees began to tremble. After a few more seconds, he could tell that the pressure had become torment, exactly as he'd planned.

"Master Logan..."

"Hmm?"

Jennifer put a hand on his shoulder. "I..."

He brushed his thumb across her clit.

She jerked.

Then he grazed her with his nail.

She gasped, obviously already on the verge of an orgasm—one he wanted to observe.

He slipped two fingers inside her and sought her G-spot, not with a gentle touch, but a relentless, tormenting press. He directed the spray toward her tightest hole, seeking to drive her mad.

"Sir!"

Oh, yes. She was so freaking responsive to him. "Ask me to let you come."

Her knees buckled.

"*Ask.*"

"Please," she whispered.

"I can't hear you."

"Fuck."

He eased off the pressure slightly, but then he kneaded her clit.

"Please," she begged.

She sagged against him. The change in position made it easier for him to access her G-spot, and he did, all but wrenching an orgasm from her.

"I need…" She closed her eyes.

He knew she couldn't last another ten seconds unless he stopped. He was tempted, so very tempted, but at this point, he wanted it as much as she did.

"Please, Master Logan." She tightened her jaw. "Now?"

"Yes," he said, pushing more forcefully against that sensitive flesh deep inside her.

She cried out his name as she climaxed, her internal muscles contracting around his fingers.

Jennifer's body went slack, telling him she'd lost all sense of time and space.

And he was there for her.

He captured her against him and somehow managed to put the showerhead back before he swept her from her feet and carried her out of the shower stall.

His dick throbbed with a demand he intended to deny. Until much, much later. For now, he wanted to care for the submissive who'd offered so much.

When she began to squirm, he set her down on the floor and reached for a towel from the rack. She held out a hand to take it, but he shook his head. "I'll finish what I started."

"That's not…"

"It is necessary," he countered. He raised an eyebrow and waited.

"Yes, Master Logan," she finished.

Damn. Her use of the honorific pleased him. *She* pleased him.

Jennifer remained still, only a few inches from him, while he dried her neck and shoulders. Then he continued down her front, over her chest. He paid extra attention to her breasts, then abraded her nipples with the nubby cotton.

She sucked in a sharp breath, but she didn't protest.

"I like you being sore for me." It meant she'd think about him even after their time ended.

He rubbed the towel over the soft swell of her belly before crouching to pat her pussy dry.

"Oh, that's…"

He licked her.

Her legs shook. She grabbed his head and held him tight. He circled her clit with his tongue. She moaned. Already craving more, she tilted her hips toward him.

"Insatiable sub," he said. He gave her another few, teasing licks before pulling back.

She moaned in protest.

"Orgasms are mine to give or withhold."

"But…" She'd never had a man who left her so hot yet unfulfilled.

Ignoring her, he continued to dry her thighs and shins. "Turn around."

This time, he started with her calves and moved up, pausing when he reached her buttocks. "I like your marks." Now she had some from his belt as well as the flogging. "Satisfying. Very satisfying." They'd fade by morning, but he appreciated them now.

He finished with her nape, and he pressed his index finger to the pulse speeding in her throat. "Let's get you to bed."

"Uhm..."

He raised his eyebrows.

"Are you sleeping with me?" she asked.

"It's your choice."

She licked her lower lip then glanced at the floor.

"I'd like to," he added.

"Me too."

He wasn't sure how long it had been since he'd protectively curled his body around that of a willing submissive. Or, more, how long it had been since he'd wanted to.

The idea of waking up with her in his arms appealed to him in a dozen different ways.

In the bedroom, he pulled off the extraneous pillows, then tossed the fluffy, overstuffed comforter onto a chair. "Come here." He turned back the sheet.

Jennifer obediently crawled onto the mattress. Then he joined her.

A burst of wind shook the window, and she shivered.

"Come here." He rolled onto his side and tugged her against him.

"Thank you," she murmured.

He grabbed the sheet and wrapped it around them then brushed back that tantalizing stray lock of hair from her forehead. "Get some rest," he told her. "You'll need it."

She splayed a hand on his chest. Seconds later, he suspected she might already have fallen asleep.

He stared straight ahead. With a jolt, he recognized that he wasn't just thinking about the past. He was thinking about the future, something he'd rarely allowed himself the luxury of.

* * * *

The cold woke her.

Instinctively, she reached toward the middle of the bed but realized she was alone.

Disoriented, she sat up.

It took her a moment to remember she was at Joe and Noelle's house. Logan had been holding her when she'd fallen asleep. No, not Logan. *Master* Logan.

Memories flooded her, and her pussy throbbed with need despite how tender she was.

Outside, night was starting to lose its grip, and the sky was a milky, cloudy gray. She wondered what time it was.

She waited a few minutes, and when he didn't return to the bed, she grabbed the sheet, secured it around her upper body, and went to find him.

Logan was sitting on the couch, fully dressed in his jeans, a long-sleeved shirt and his boots. The cupcakes were nowhere in sight, and the entire kitchen had been cleaned up. She wondered how long he'd been awake or if he'd gotten back up after she'd gone to sleep. He had a cup of coffee in hand and was staring into the blazing fireplace.

The fact that she was wearing only a sheet left her vulnerable and uncertain. Even though she had moved silently and stood there motionless, he turned his head in her direction.

His features were set, jaw tight. He looked intense, brooding…and he stole her breath.

"Are you always on guard?" she asked.

"Occupational hazard," he replied.

"Complicated man."

"No. Very simple, actually. Awareness keeps you alive."

She shook her head. "You scare me a little."

"I scare myself." Maybe from the weak morning sun, his eyes were lighter in color than they had seemed last night. "Join me," he invited.

Unable to resist, she walked toward him.

He scooted over, and she sat next to him on the couch. The leather was warm from his body as well as the blazing fire, and she realized it had been a long time since she'd been this content.

"Coffee?" He offered his cup.

She took a sip and wrinkled her nose. "No sugar?"

"You're one of those," he said.

"Those?"

"Amateurs," he teased.

"And no desire to become a pro." But because she was chilled and the cup was steaming, she took a second sip.

She liked sitting this close to him, enjoyed his scent, the reassurance of his masculine warmth.

"Any ill effects?"

"If you're asking whether or not I hurt from the flogging..." She looked at him. "No. Surprisingly."

"Or the sex?"

"I think I managed your monster-sized cock just fine, Mr. Powell."

"That you did." He grinned. "And your ass?"

"From your belt?" She was guessing that wasn't what he was talking about.

"From the reaming I gave it."

Unconsciously, she shifted. "It's fine."

"I'll keep that in mind."

"What?"

"That you can take more. Do you need to get home?"

"I usually run errands on Saturdays, but I have nothing pressing."

"There's a small breakfast place just down the mountain. They specialize in skillet meals." His eyes darkened. "I recommend you keep your strength up."

Jennifer regarded him over the rim of the cup. "Because…?"

"There are toys in my bag. And I'm not done with you yet."

She squirmed, from fear, from anticipation.

"How long do you need to get ready?"

"Depends on whether or not there's more of this high-octane coffee. If there is, I'll be ready in two minutes."

"They have one of those cup brewers."

"There's a God and he's smiling down on us." She returned his cup to him and wiggled off the couch.

She took a step toward the kitchen, and the sheet stayed behind. Jennifer glanced over her shoulder to see a corner of the material bunched in his fist.

"I told you I want you naked. That didn't change because it's a new day."

The reminder of his expectation made heat pour through her. "Yes, Sir."

"Move your ass, little sub."

Conscious of his gaze on her, she pulled back her shoulders and crossed into the kitchen. She opened a cabinet and found box after box of choices. Apple cider, hot chocolate, tea, organic coffee, decaf, French roast and her favorite, mocha. Best of all, there were packages of sugar.

She popped a pod into the coffeemaker. Within seconds, it hissed and popped and she began inhaling the faint, but welcome, scent of chocolate as the beverage brewed.

He watched, eyes wide with horror, as she tore apart five sugar packets and tipped the granules into the cup. Then she added a generous helping of cream before stirring.

She inhaled the steam. It smelled sweet and creamy. She sipped then wrinkled her nose.

Unsatisfied, she dumped in more cream.

"We could have gone out for lattes," he observed with an interested twist to his lips.

"We still can." She snatched up her cup, grabbed some mascara and an eyeliner pencil from her purse and headed back to the bedroom.

He watched every step.

A few minutes later, minimum makeup in place and hair finger-combed, she rejoined him.

"We'll take my car," he said.

Fine with her since he obviously knew where he was going. After donning their coats, they headed for his black SUV.

Wind whipped around them, and the temperature seemed just as cold as it had last night. The sky was gray, as if the sun hadn't been able to part the curtains on the day.

He opened her door first and waited until she was settled in before closing her in and walking around to the driver's side. The moment he started the engine, she pushed the button to turn on the seat warmer. Even though she set it to high, the cold leather bit through her tights. "It looks as though it might snow," she said.

"Couple of inches are possible in town." He shifted into drive and slid her a glance.

"Which means we could get more than that up here in the foothills."

He nodded.

Logan drove them down the mountain then turned onto a road she had never before noticed. A couple of minutes later, they arrived at a quaint shopping center. There was a coffee shop, a breakfast place, a clothing boutique, a liquor store and a restaurant that specialized in tacos. "Heaven, all in one place."

The breakfast place wasn't anything like she'd anticipated. She'd been expecting something a bit more upscale, maybe with waitresses and delicious coffee choices.

Instead, wooden tables were packed into a small place. The tops were scarred from years of use. Even though it was still early, most of the sturdy chairs were occupied, and the dining room was loud. But the way it smelled, of coffee and fresh-baked goods, made her mouth water.

There was a line of people in front of the counter, and the restaurant's meager offerings were scrawled on a black chalkboard hanging from the wall. One special had already been crossed through.

The menu seemed to consist of a limited number of skillet meals and a few sandwiches, but a glass case was stuffed with a dizzying array of scones and pastries.

Her stomach urged her to order something substantial, but her mouth demanded a chocolate croissant.

Obviously noting her dilemma, he suggested, "Get a croissant to go."

"The calories," she protested.

"The exercise," he countered. "I'll take it upon myself to make sure you work them off."

Suddenly warm, she untied her belt and opened the buttons on her coat. "In that case, I want the spinach scramble. With a side of bacon."

"What'll it be?" the woman behind the counter asked when it was their turn. She plucked a pen from behind her ear and poised over a pad all without making eye contact.

Must be the way she managed the large crowd.

"Coffee?" he asked Jennifer.

"Water is fine. I'm holding out for a mocha latte."

"I should have guessed." He placed their orders.

Impressively, the woman still didn't glance up as she grabbed a mug and filled it with coffee before replacing the carafe on the burner. After tucking the pen back into place, she slid a plastic glass across the counter toward Jennifer, pointed to a pitcher, then put two croissants in a bag. "Anything else?" she asked, her fingers already flying over the keys on the cash register.

When she announced the total, Jennifer reached into her purse for a twenty-dollar bill to pay her part of the tab, but froze when Logan said, "Put it away."

"Don't be ridiculous," she said.

His eyebrows drew together formidably.

The woman behind the counter finally looked up. She glanced at Jennifer then Logan before taking his money.

She gave him change, and he dropped it into the tip jar. "Your number is twenty-one. Pick up your order at the end of the counter when it's called." She plucked the pen from behind her ear again. "What'll it be?" she asked, moving on to the people standing behind them.

Effectively, efficiently, they'd been dismissed.

Jennifer grabbed her glass, while he picked up his coffee and the bag containing the pastries.

"Look, Logan, there's no reason I shouldn't pay my fair share. It's not like this is a date or anything," she said after they'd selected napkins and silverware, filled her glass and were seated at a table for two near the window.

"I'd appreciate it if you didn't disagree with me in public again." His tone was clipped, tight, as if it took effort to exercise control.

She squirmed when he leveled a chilly stare on her. "It wasn't really an argument," she protested.

"I wanted to buy you breakfast. I'm happy to discuss that, but not in front of others."

"You're overreacting."

"Am I?"

He scowled, and heat chased up her spine to settle at the base of her neck. He looked ferocious, every bit the Dom.

"Look..."

He waited.

"Just because we..." She picked up her water and took a drink, pretending her hand wasn't trembling.

"Had a D/s scene that had you screaming my name?"

"That's not a reason for you to buy me breakfast."

"Then what is?"

She felt as if she'd been dumped into the ocean without a life raft. Were all Doms like this? Annoying? Frustrating? Rigid? And if so, that might be a good reason to avoid a relationship with one.

"Not everything is worth an argument," he told her. Then his lips twitched. "There are certain times to just say thank you."

"But..."

"It's just breakfast. It's not like I threw you over my shoulder and carried you off to my dungeon, stripped you bare, shackled you to my overhead hook and imprisoned you for life as my sex slave."

Fuck. The image seared itself into her brain. Heat danced across her nape. To distract herself, she shrugged from her coat and draped it over the chair back. Still, the thought remained, gaining energy.

"Choose your battles," he suggested.

Their number was called. After tapping the table twice, as if to punctuate his point, he rose to fetch their food.

She thought over his words. It wasn't so much that she objected to him buying her a meal as the way he'd handled it. But, really, was it worth an argument? Ruining what they'd shared and what might still be ahead?

That idea tantalized.

When he slid the scramble in front of her, she sighed.

He waited, head tipped, regarding her.

"Thank you for breakfast."

His smile made her day brighter. Then he ruined it by opening his mouth again. "Much better. I prefer you compliant."

"Well, I don't." She scowled.

"You might find the tradeoff worthwhile, if you give it a try."

"I'm not sure I want to."

"Stubborn to the end."

Jennifer took a bite of the steaming, delicious scramble. "Good choice on the restaurant."

Logan grinned, a slow, consuming expression that melted her reserves. He looked ten years younger and infinitely more approachable. Instead of relaxing her, it increased her tension. An engaging, charming Logan would be so much more difficult to deny.

"Joe and I ate here a couple of times when I helped him with some remodeling at the house."

"The basement?"

"Gives me some ideas for things I might want to do at my place."

It occurred to her she had no idea where he even lived. "Where is that?"

"A house in the south part of Denver. Got it at a steal when the market was down. But honestly, it needs a lot of work. And I'm always on a case."

"Is that by choice?"

He took a drink of his coffee. "Unconscious, I suppose. How about you?"

"We have something in common. My house is a fixer-upper, but not by choice. I would have preferred something that was move-in ready, but I couldn't afford it."

"What part of town?"

"The Highlands."

He nodded. "Historic home?"

"If by historic you mean old money pit, yes. Furnace. Painting. Refinishing floors. Needs appliances. All my time and savings are going into it. I told myself the tax write-off is worth it." She shrugged. "So far I'm not sure it is."

"You're doing the work yourself?"

"Most of it. I watch a lot of how-to videos online. And I go to classes at the local hardware store."

"You're serious?"

"This week, I plan to learn how to use an air sprayer."

"A power tool?"

She rolled her eyes at him. "Are you being a pervert?"

"I might be. Are you going to wear coveralls?"

"No." Jennifer laughed. "Sorry. I just want to get rid of the canary-yellow walls as quickly as possible. Though I have to admit that when I don't have coffee, the color wakes me up just fine."

He grinned. "I'd like to see the house."

"It's not much more than a construction site at the moment. You'd have to bring your own hard hat, I'm afraid."

"I could teach you about those power tools."

His voice was husky, and his tone was somewhere between a tease and a promise. But the idea of having him at her place, dominating her, maybe tying her wrists to the headboard...

A busboy collected their dishes, and Logan asked if she was ready to go.

"It's getting so loud, it's difficult to hear you," she said.

"What?" he mock shouted, cupping his ear.

Outside, wind had whipped up, blustery and biting. "That snow is definitely on the way," she said. It would be smart to head back to Denver now, but she was reluctant to end the weekend so soon. She wasn't sure when or if she'd have the opportunity to play with him again, and she wanted to experience as much as possible while she could.

"Still want that mocha?"

She looked at him and scowled.

"That's what I thought." He cupped her elbow and led her toward the coffee shop.

A frisson of desire teased her spine at his casual, possessive touch. And she realized she'd never been with a man who was this hands-on.

He held the door for her. This time, she didn't argue when he paid for their drinks.

"Well done," he said into her ear, the words tantalizingly rough. "I'd much rather reward good behavior than punish bad."

"Either one sounds good to me," she replied, hardly able to believe she'd been bold enough to say that aloud. Was she brave or foolish? Maybe both.

"I'm looking forward to getting you back to the dungeon."

Her shiver had nothing to do with someone opening the door and letting in a cold burst of air.

An extra-large cup in hand, they went outside.

A woman inside the boutique flicked on the neon 'open' sign and smiled invitingly.

Since a long black skirt that would look great with boots caught Jennifer's eye, she asked, "Do you mind if I have a look?"

"Not at all. Shopping is one of my favorite things," he replied.

She frowned. "Are you being sarcastic?"

"Me?" He opened the door for her.

She zipped past him, glad to be out of the soul-sapping cold.

After exchanging a few words with the owner, Jennifer meandered to the skirt rack. Logan dutifully held her cup while she selected one and held it in front of her to check the length. "It'd be perfect for work."

"Can I start a fitting room for you?" the owner asked, appearing at the perfect time.

"Thanks." Jennifer handed over the skirt then wandered toward a tabletop stacked with sweaters.

"The red one," Logan said.

"It looks as if it's a size too small."

"Try it."

Skeptically, she picked it up.

But once she had the outfit on, she knew he was right.

"Show me," he said.

She slid back the curtain and exited the fitting room.

"I was wrong." His voice was tight. "You're not wearing that sweater anywhere but on a date with me. It's sensational."

"It's perfect," the proprietress agreed.

Even though Jennifer was reluctant, she changed back into her other clothes.

The shop also had a selection of lingerie.

"I'd like to see you in these," he told her, picking up a pair of purple panties and a matching bra.

She met his gaze then looked at the delicate briefs in his strong hands. Wanting to be dominated by him again, she nodded.

And didn't protest when he purchased the gorgeous, feminine undergarments.

"Thank you for not arguing," he said when he opened the shop door for her. "I told you I prefer to reward good behavior. And I will."

She shivered in a way that had nothing to do with the gusting wind.

They stopped at the taco place and picked up ingredients to make fajitas later. She could get accustomed to spending time with Logan if he was going to treat her this way. That thought was as terrifying as it was thrilling.

As he opened the vehicle door, her phone signaled an incoming message.

"Noelle," she said.

She let her friend know she wasn't in trouble for setting up the evening.

Weather looks bad. You should stay over tonight, too.

Jennifer's heart lurched. She'd been planning to spend part of the day with Logan, but any longer seemed far too intimate.

"Anything important?" he asked when he was seated next to her with the engine running.

"That was from Noelle." She debated how to reply before settling on, "She said the place is available and we don't have to leave."

Another text came in.

Don't worry about cleaning. We have a housekeeper scheduled for Monday.

He looked at her.

Instant response slid through her. She already had it bad for this man.

"What do you want to do?"

"I'm not sure," she hedged.

"I'm a greedy man, Jennifer. I'll take as much of your time as you're willing to give me. An hour, a day, another night, a week, maybe even more."

"More?"

"Yeah. But for tonight, I have a few ideas on how we can pass the time."

"Oh?"

"The first one involves the coffee table."

"The…" She stared at him. "Really?"

He nodded.

"I'd never thought of it as bondage equipment."

"Everything is. Tell Noelle we're staying."

A big fat snowflake plopped on the windshield. Despite that, his comment had warmed her insides.

She was curious. And it turned out that she, too, was greedy. "In that case, Sir...consider it done. Show me what you have in mind."

Chapter Seven

Once they were inside with the door sealed to block out the blustery wind, Logan discarded their empty cups then put away the food before calling out, "Please take off all your clothes and bend over the coffee table."

Though she should have expected the order, the suddenness of it caught her off guard.

She went into the living room. Her pulse stuttered as she toed off her boots then pulled down her tights.

Jennifer looked into the kitchen and noticed he wasn't paying any attention to her.

With a scowl, she finished undressing then got into position, or at least she hoped it was the position he wanted. She bent over and placed her palms on the tabletop.

He went down the hallway, and time stretched.

Outside, the wind whipped against the house and snow started to hit the window.

Her skin chilled, more from the sensual exposure than the temperature. Her shoulder muscles began to ache.

She was tempted to stand or at least stretch. Indecision warred in her. Her Dom expected to have his orders followed. But what would it hurt to move, even a little?

But Logan's earlier words, about rewarding good behavior, teased her subconscious, sending a rush of anticipation through her. The desire to have his positive attention was more powerful than her need to move.

She closed her eyes, took a deep breath, held it for a few seconds then breathed out.

"Bravo."

Jennifer stayed in position, though she curled her toes under. The sound came from a distance, which meant he had been watching her. For how long?

He walked into the living room, stood in front of her and placed his bag on the floor near her.

Then he went behind her and traced his fingertips up the insides of her thighs. It took all her control to remain in position.

"Still no marks."

"No?" Suddenly she wanted one, at least one to remember the weekend by.

He ran a finger across her clit, and she clenched, getting wet, wanting.

Before she could move against him, he removed his hand.

"Sir!"

"Quiet."

He left her to turn on the fireplace before facing her.

She hazarded another glance his direction to see him standing with his back to the flames, arms folded across his chest, jaw set, eyes narrowed, gaze focused on her.

It took all her concentration to remain in place, waiting on his pleasure, sub to Dom.

Mind fuck.

"Spread your legs as far as you can."

Once she had, he returned to her and unzipped the bag.

In her peripheral vision, she saw exactly what he doing. He pulled out cuffs then bent to secure her ankles to the table legs.

Next came the clamps.

He took his time playing with her breasts and teasing her nipples into tight little buds. This time, he didn't ask before letting the Japanese clovers bite into her flesh.

She sucked in a breath but didn't protest.

And when he teased her pussy, the pain faded, becoming pleasure before blooming into the sharpness of need. "Sir…"

He immediately dropped his hand.

She gritted her teeth. And she stared as he removed a tawse.

"Remind me of your safe word."

"Will I need it?"

"Potentially."

She tightened her muscles and tried to press her thighs together. "Marshmallow," she whispered.

"I'm going to push you harder than I have before. Three strikes on each thigh. Keep your hands on the tabletop. Unless you'd like them tied together?"

"No."

He dug his hand into her hair.

"I mean, no, Sir. I'll keep my hands in place."

"Better."

She was aware of him taking a small vibrator from a side pocket. He tucked the tawse beneath his arm before cleaning the toy with an alcohol wipe. Then he turned the vibrator on to a low hum and pressed it against her clit.

"Oh... *Crap.*"

He flicked the metal chain of her clamps, and she jerked to one side, only to be stopped by the ankle restraints.

After moving the vibrator aside, he seared the inside of her right thigh with the double-stranded tawse.

Before she could protest, he put the vibrator back against her clit.

He flattened his palm between her shoulder blades for a moment to reposition her. Before she could orgasm, he once again took away the vibrator and marked the inside of her left thigh.

The area burned, but the pain quickly receded.

She pushed her hips back, silently asking for the stimulation again, hoping he'd relent and get her off.

But the wicked Dom refused.

Instead, he laid the tawse to the outsides of her upper thighs before tugging on her clamps.

She swayed, bucked, screamed.

"So fucking hot," he said.

As if completing a design, he scorched her skin, right beneath her buttocks.

The tawse clattered to the floor.

From behind, he finger-fucked her, circling her clit with the vibrator and going inside her wet cunt, knuckles-deep with each thrust.

She was going out of her mind, from the horrible burning sensation on her skin to the evil grip of the clamps.

Even last night, she hadn't experienced anything near this intense.

He overwhelmed her.

"Logan..." She shook her head and immediately regretted it when the clamps swayed again.

"Master Logan. Use the right term if you want something, otherwise we can stop right here. Now."

"Master Logan," she said. "You're going to make me come."

"Oh yes. I am."

He pushed the vibrator fully against her, spreading her labia, throbbing against her clit a dozen times a second. He continued his relentless sensual thrusting, splitting her apart.

She screamed as the climax rocked her from the inside out.

The world shattered, went bright, then... Nothing. Silent. Still. Empty.

He released her ankles then the clamps before helping her to stand.

"Thank you, Sir."

"I love a fast learner."

He helped her to the couch where he pulled her into his lap and rubbed her arms against the chill.

Outside, a storm now raged. Wind whipped the snow sideways, obliterating the view of Denver. It was as if they were sealed off from the rest of civilization.

She recalled his earlier response when he'd talked about keeping the civilized world separate from his.

"I guess we're staying," he said long minutes later.

She became aware of the scratchy denim on the tawse marks and also the strength of his arms. If this was his world, she liked being part of it.

He fetched a blanket from the bedroom and covered her with it.

They turned on the television to watch classic movies, but he kept the volume low enough that they could talk.

A few hours later, he straightened the area then poured her a glass of white wine while he warmed up the ingredients for lunch.

She scooted around so she could watch him work, and since her body was naked and a little fatigued, she felt no guilt in letting him wait on her. "How does a private eye become so adept in the kitchen?"

"I don't know about that," he said, as he removed lids from the sour cream and guacamole. "I'm great with reheating and putting takeout on plates. I'm more interested in consuming enough calories than the way they taste."

"Seriously? I enjoy cooking."

"Don't misunderstand." He met her gaze. "I like eating excellent home-cooked meals."

"It wasn't an invitation."

"Damn."

She grinned.

"But in the military, I learned to eat when I could. And now, on surveillance, sometimes food is the only thing that keeps me awake and focused."

"Do you do it a lot? Surveillance, I mean."

He turned away to stir the peppers, onions and chicken. "More than I want."

"What are you looking for, cheating spouses?"

Logan looked over his shoulder at her. "Not once."

"So what do you do?"

"I generally don't talk about it."

"I'm curious about the guy who spanked my ass and fucked me until I almost passed out."

"Me?" he asked, turning back to her.

She grabbed a pillow and tossed it at him.

Effortlessly, he captured it and set it on a counter.

Realizing he was almost finished, she stood.

"Going somewhere?"

"Uhm, to put on some clothes."

"Was there a part of *I want you naked* that you didn't understand?"

Heat bloomed in her face. "But—"

"The BDSM thing isn't pretend for me," he said. "Unless you'd like to forgo it for the rest of the weekend?"

It's a boundary during a scene, helps separate the civilized world from mine.

"This isn't a scene." She blinked. "Unless I'm confused? I thought unless…"

"Go on."

"Unless you were flogging me or we were having sex…" Her entire body felt as if it were filled by pinpricks. "Well, that we were just friends."

"I don't have a lot of interest in being just friends, Jennifer."

"Then…what?"

"We're in one big long scene."

"We can't be friends?"

"I want to be more than friends."

She looked at him over the rim of the wineglass. "I'm not sure I understand."

"I like you, Jennifer. We're compatible. At least the way you screamed my name and came all over my hand seems to indicate you enjoy sex with me. And maybe I'm premature, but I'm guessing you may want to do it again."

"Friends with benefits?" Her voice oozed the sarcasm that churned in her.

"Don't be crass."

"Me? Isn't that your suggestion?" she demanded. "That we meet up again later to fuck?"

"With us being exclusive to each other."

"And me being naked."

"Yes. And exposed to me. For me. I want to explore this with you, Jennifer. See where it goes. Don't diminish what we have." His eyes were dark, and lines of annoyance were etched around them. "I told you, I will take whatever you're willing to give."

All of a sudden, she realized she'd offended him without meaning to. How the hell they had gone from chatting to this, she had no idea.

"Let go of the blanket, sub."

His tone was melded from steel. And she knew this was much more than a battle of wills. Did she want to see him again? Agree to his demands? All she knew was that the sex had turned her on. The flogging, his supple, unyielding belt, the dastardly tawse...she'd liked them all. Even though she'd only had a short time with him, she wanted to see him again. The future of missionary-only sex now seemed unacceptable.

She dropped the blanket.

"Glad that's settled." He gave her a curt nod then turned back to the stove.

Damnable, infuriating woman. Sub.

Logan allowed his gaze to linger on her feminine shape. He couldn't get enough of her. The more he scened with her, the more he wanted. He was consumed with ideas of what he wanted to do to her, for her.

He wondered what the hell had happened since he'd first noticed her almost a month ago. Gorgeous, curious, challenging... Jennifer appealed to his base nature. Add in her responsiveness and he was a grinning, happy idiot.

He'd never had this kind of reaction to anyone else. And the idea of letting her go tomorrow and just being friends? Hoping that they bumped into each other at a future play party and that she was alone? Competing for her against other Doms? Not a fucking chance.

He grabbed plates, silverware and placemats.

"Can I help?"

Doing household chores, naked? "Yes."

He admired her crimson bottom when she joined him in the kitchen. At least one of his marks lingered on her thigh, and her abused nipples were taut.

As she worked, he carried in the food.

She'd placed him at the head of the table with her seated to his right. Intentionally? If not, it was further proof of her great instincts. "More wine?"

When she nodded, he topped off her glass. It'd be a few more hours before they scened again, and he'd make sure this was the last she drank if she wanted to play.

"Thank you for this," she said. "I'm feeling spoiled." She picked up a chip and dipped it into the guacamole. "Delicious."

"Made better by the company."

"You say that to all naked women."

"You're the only one I've ever had at my table."

"Even the woman who dumped you on Valentine's Day?"

"So nice of you to remind me." He took a drink of the Mexican beer he'd found in the refrigerator.

"Sorry."

"Said in the *not sorry* tone."

She shrugged, the motion accentuating her breasts. It cost him all his resolve to stay in his seat instead of morphing into a Neanderthal, slinging her over his shoulder and hauling her up the stairs to dump her on the bed before fucking her fast, slow and every speed in between.

"Not even Helen."

"Why me?"

"You had the interest in BDSM. Common ground. Helen came to it through me. And I want to explore it more with you."

"I bring out your inner Dom?"

Yeah. "Or something a bit less civilized."

"But no less polite."

"Shrug like that again and we'll find out."

He expected her to blush. Instead, she folded her arms beneath her breasts, pushing them up and out seductively.

"I will never make you eat naked again," he vowed.

"I may never wear clothes again," she responded. "Sir."

When he was about halfway finished with the meal, she said, "Back to the surveillance."

"I thought I changed the topic earlier."

"You did." She crunched another chip.

"You're persistent."

"If we're going to be fucking—"

"It will be so much more than that."

"Will it?" She sat back.

She said it as if it were his choice, his decision. He knew what he wanted. Her. But could she put up with him? His schedule? His commitment to his work? The ghosts that still shrouded his days? How independent was she? He knew she wanted to pursue her career, and he was fine with that. Maybe, just maybe, they could both get what they needed. "If you're agreeable," he responded finally.

"In that case, I want to know about your business."

"That's something I only discuss with my closest associates."

"I'm the one seated at the table next to you, naked," she countered. "And you told me that you and Helen had issues, some of them because of your job. You kept her out of your private life. If you meant what you said, that you are interested in whatever I'll give you, then I won't be kept out of your private life."

"Fair enough." He considered how much to tell her.

"It's dangerous?"

Logan didn't reply immediately. He didn't want her frightened. On the other hand, there were times he didn't arrive home in time for dinner. He'd been shot at, sucker-punched and kicked in the kidneys so hard that he'd peed blood for a week. He kept his freezer filled with ice packs, and he'd been known to sleep for forty hours at one time. "It can be." Absently he traced the scar then abruptly dropped his hand.

"I didn't know being a PI was risky."

"Depends on the kinds of things being investigated." He took another drink. She was right. If they were going to go forward, if she was eventually going to give him her complete submission, she deserved some information. Maybe more than he'd told anyone but Joe. "At the moment I'm working an illegal arms dealing scheme."

She blinked. "Shouldn't the government be pursuing that?"

"They are."

"And you're…" She blinked, looked away, then back at him as if the last piece of a puzzle had just been tapped into place. "Doing the same sort of thing that you were in the Middle East."

"You could say that."

Jennifer was obviously choosing her words. He'd answered her questions, but he hadn't offered any clarification or further information, and she was smart enough to figure that out.

"So you're working for the government," she surmised.

"Not exclusively. But yes. I do some high-tech business stuff, too."

She closed her eyes. "You do counterterrorism work."

He didn't answer. Didn't need to. "Sorry you asked?"

"I need to know what I'm facing." She leaned toward him and traced the scar that he'd so recently touched.

He was tempted to grab her wrist. Wanted to. Needed to.

Instead, he allowed her to do what she needed to.

"A relationship with you won't be easy."

"Not always," he agreed.

"You told me you forgot Valentine's Day, for example."

"Yes."

"She said you were the world's biggest asshole."

"True." He shrugged. "I'm sure as hell not proud of it."

"Does that go for birthdays? Anniversaries? Christmas?"

"It has. All of the above."

"Is it worth it?"

"Only you can decide."

"What's in it for me?"

"I have more than enough money to take care of us. That will allow you the freedom to start your own business. And I'll encourage you. In fact, I need someone to do my books."

"I'm a CPA not a bookkeeper."

"Meaning you'll do what you need to but it will cost me a pile of money?"

She smiled. "A shitpile."

"That's a lot."

"A lot, a lot," she confirmed. "And it will probably give me insight into your business that you may not be comfortable with."

"I could be talked into taking that chance."

She ran her finger around the rim of her mostly still-full glass. "What else? Spankings?"

"Always."

"Fucking?"

He met her gaze. Her eyes were open wide, those lashes impossibly long. "In your hot little pussy. Your tight ass. And your mouth. Until you cry for mercy."

"I..." She dropped her hand into her lap.

"Heard enough? If so, let's get started on either the mouth or the ass fucking." He gave her a wicked, evil grin. "Since I'm feeling generous, I'll let you decide which."

"You are generous, Sir."

"Your choice?"

"Uhm... Anal scares me a bit. So oral?"

"Nice try. A proper sub would have said whatever I would like best."

The color drained from her face.

"Mercy on a new sub?"

"Oh, Jennifer. Jennifer, Jennifer. Don't you realize yet?" He reached out and put his fingers on hers. "Anything you want."

"So oral?"
"Anything but that."
Her eyes went wide. Her breath caught. Her shoulders were rigid.
"Please stand, turn your chair backward and grab hold of the back."

Chapter Eight

"Are you really going to...?" Breathless, unable to think, let alone form the question, she trailed off.

When he didn't respond, she squeezed her eyes shut momentarily, wondering what the hell she was thinking.

His honesty was a real, raw thing. He'd been open in admitting that he wanted to be more than fuck buddies, and that any relationship would be challenging. Jennifer knew he'd push her physically and mentally.

The scar he bore was a stark, physical reminder of the daily debt he paid to Joe and the friends he'd lost.

He'd never quit. He'd forget holidays and he might be on surveillance, unreachable during key moments.

Yet... Sex with him was spectacular. He didn't expect her to give up who she was to be his hostess. In fact, he seemed to want to push her to explore her own wants and desires, to become more of the person she wanted to be.

He scared her in the most delicious way possible.

"You always have a safe word. I hope you won't need it, want it. But I'm reminding you that it's available in every area, in discussion, in sex, in reality. You're in charge."

Feeling unbelievably sexy and sinful, she stood and did what he'd said, holding on to the top of the chair.

He took another drink of his beer before putting the bottle down. "Your ass is mine tonight."

The storm raged, as intense outside as it was in her.

"And first..." He pulled a small package from his pocket. *Lube.*

"You knew this was going to happen, Sir?"

"Jennifer, I think about you all the time. I'm planning the next scene when we're in this one."

"You think about it ahead of time?"

"There's a script in my head."

She frowned, but he nodded and said, "Always."

"Now put your forehead on the cushion, reach back and spread your ass cheeks for me."

"My pussy isn't sore." She hoped he'd select that option.

"Good to know."

She could safe word, but she was more uncomfortable with the idea than anything else. She knew he wouldn't hurt her, but being here, in the dining room with their reflections stark in the plate glass window, seemed lewd.

He tore open the package, seemingly content that she would comply. Which she did.

Swallowing her trepidation, she bent, rested her head on the cushion then reached back to part her buttocks.

"You can skip the embarrassment," he assured her. "That has no place between us."

"I wish it were that easy."

"It is. Or it can be, if you stop worrying and start experiencing."

She closed her eyes and tried to be as easy with it as he wanted.

"On your tiptoes."

Before she was settled, his finger pressed against her anal whorl.

She gasped and moved her hands. Because he was generally so gentle, she'd expected him to tease her pussy instead of going straight for her ass.

He smacked her right ass five times, hard, in quick succession.

"Damn it!"

"Do as you're told, sub. We can do this easy and nice or I can blindfold, clamp, spank and fuck you now."

She fought her own fear and shyness as she struggled back into position.

"Two fingers," he said.

"I was afraid of that."

"Three if you throw another tantrum."

The sting on her skin and the undeniable heat in her pussy convinced her to press her lips together.

Last night had been easy compared to this.

She could feel that he'd placed his forefinger on top of his middle finger. Inexorably he moved into her tight hole.

"Breathe and bear down."

"I don't like this."

"Would you like a gag better?"

"No, Sir!"

"Stop fighting. Open up."

She felt the unusual, unwelcome pressure against her sphincter.

He reached beneath her to tweak a nipple.

The shock made her gasp, and when she released it, she inadvertently relaxed, allowing his lube-slickened fingers to penetrate deeper.

She tried to pull away, but he cupped the back of her head with his palm, holding her firmly, reassuringly.

"Stay still."

For at least thirty seconds, he didn't move. She became accustomed to the full sensation. It wasn't comfortable, but it wasn't unbearable.

"Good. Good."

She could subsist on his approval alone.

With his fingers, he began to fuck her ass. She squeezed her eyes shut, in a ridiculous, stupid hope that it would help keep the embarrassment away.

"Relax, my little subbie. I've got you."

He was right about that, she thought wryly. With the position she was in and the way he held her, she wasn't going anywhere.

After a few seconds, she took a deep breath. Maybe it wasn't as horrible as she'd imagined it would be.

"Give yourself over to me. There are more nerve endings here than any other place in your body. It can actually be pleasurable."

"Not sure I believe that, Sir."

"No?"

Every word he said was soft, reassuring, not demanding.

"Think about the way it feels," he said. "Not about what's happening. Focus on the fact I want to do this. This is strictly for my pleasure, and it's not about humiliating you. Can you do that? For us?"

She took a shuddering breath. "I'll try."

"I'm going to let go of your head, but I want you to stay exactly where you are, as if I'm still holding you."

As much as possible, she nodded. "I understand."

He moved his free hand to her pussy and slid the pad of his thumb across her swollen—and shockingly damp—clit. "Let go. And stop thinking," he reminded her.

She forced the tension from her muscles.

"Much better." He moved his fingers in and out, spreading her, filling her.

The sensation stunned her. Combined with the pressure between her folds, she was lost. Without conscious thought, she rolled up onto the balls of her feet, changing the angle, giving him greater access.

"Sensational," he approved. "Fantastic."

He continued to thrust, manipulate, tease. Unbelievably, an orgasm began to unfurl deep inside her, the pressure unlike anything she'd ever experienced. "God. Logan... Master... Sir..." She wasn't exactly sure what she was saying, all she knew was that she wanted the climax that loomed just seconds in her future.

"Are you going to come from me fucking your tight ass with my hand?"

"Yes! Yes, yes, *yes!*"

"Tell me what you need."

"Harder."

"Anything."

He gave it to her, relentlessly. She spread her ass cheeks even farther and ground her heated cunt against his hand.

"You couldn't be sexier."

"Sir."

He quickened his motion on her pussy. "Take it."

Screaming, crashing, shaking, she orgasmed. "Damn." Blood rushed between her ears, and every muscle seemed frozen even though her legs felt weak. "*Damn.*"

Slowly he moved his hands. Her knees buckled.

"Stay there," he said.

She heard his footsteps fade then the sound of water running. Within a minute, he was back with a warm, damp washcloth.

As he cared for her, she shook her head. After this, there would definitely be no embarrassment between them.

When he was finished, he helped her to stand and face him.

"Now you're properly prepared for tonight."

"There's more?"

"I promised you that your ass is mine tonight. I always keep my promises. My cock is going up there, balls deep."

She flushed scarlet, even though she no longer thought that was possible.

He wrapped her in the blanket she'd used earlier and told her to have a seat while he put away the leftovers and loaded their plates in the dishwasher.

A fire blazing, a sexy man thoroughly dominating and caring for her. "I really could get used to this." She took a sip of her wine and looked at the raging storm.

"You will," he agreed.

She glanced over her shoulder at him and watched as he walked toward her carrying his unfinished beer.

"You're able to sit," he mused.

"Not comfortably."

"Good. Otherwise I'd be afraid I wasn't doing my job properly."

Involuntarily she tightened her ass cheeks. How did he arouse her so completely and keep her there?

And it was beyond hot that she actually was sore.

He settled in next to her then pulled her against him.

She snuggled into his chest, drank from his warmth and pure masculine strength, enjoyed his company.

He turned the television on, and they laughed over an old James Bond movie villain.

When the credits began to roll, he muted the sound.

She scooted away from him and turned to face him. "I'm curious. Were you serious about needing a CPA?"

"Yeah. Someone I can trust. You interested?"

"I might be. Yes. But I meant it when I said I'm expensive."

"I only ever want the best."

And the rest...? She couldn't believe that this was turning out to be so much more than she'd expected. Amazing sex. A potential client. "What about the trying a relationship part?"

His eyebrows settled into a firm, implacable line, and his jaw was tight. Something dark, just this side of anger, haunted his eyes. "I don't joke, Jennifer."

"I need my space. I have a house to remodel, tax season is approaching, and I want to pursue starting my own firm."

"And at times you'll do it all with a plug up your ass."

She shivered as she looked at him. Logan Powell was so freaking sexy and dominant that he stole her breath.

"And watching you use an air sprayer while you're naked will be hot as hell."

"Now you're joking." She regarded him.

"Am I? You said no coveralls, so nude is the next best thing."

* * * *

After the sky had darkened completely and the snow no longer drove against the windows as relentlessly, they ate a few leftovers, and Jennifer devoured one of the cupcakes.

"You can take a dozen of them home."

"You think they'll last that long?" she asked, using her finger to swipe some remaining frosting from the ruffled paper cup.

He watched as she licked it from her finger.

"What?" She blinked a few times, pretending innocence.

"I think you know."

"I was hoping so."

"Move it," he said.

Logan retrieved his bag then indicated they should head down the stairs to the basement.

This time, Jennifer had left embarrassment behind when she'd shrugged off the blanket and placed it on the back of the couch.

"Confidence looks sexy on you," he told her when she sank to her knees near the bench.

"Thank you, Sir." Remembering the way another sub had behaved at the last play party, she put her hands behind her neck.

"Very nice."

Jennifer was stunned by how far she'd come, how quickly. A few scenes, where he'd demolished her inhibitions, had seemingly freed her.

He pulled out the blindfold, the clamps and a paddle. The sight of the implements in his big hands made her wet.

"The cross," he said. "Facing it."

Without hesitation, but not as much grace as she wished she had, she rose and got into position.

After he'd secured the cuffs, she tested her bonds. She'd managed to pull free of the ones Master Simon had used. If she were honest with herself, she'd admit she took comfort from these. She could move, tug, yank, but she was safe and secure.

"They're mine," he said as if reading her thoughts. "And you are, too."

"Yes, Sir." The words rolled so easily, naturally.

He moved in front of her, and she saw he held the blindfold.

"For this scene, I don't want you to know what's coming."

That took more trust. She gave it.

"You amaze me. Delight me."

"Same for me, Master Logan."

"I love the way it sounds on your lips." His touch was gentle but firm as he covered her eyes and ensured the elastic band was placed properly.

Next he set the clamps. She gasped at the shocking bite of pain. Her nipples were still tender.

"When you're at work on Monday, you'll be thinking of me."

She would have been, whether or not they scened this evening.

He turned on some music. The bass thundered, reverberating through her, drowning the sounds of their breathing and making it impossible for her to know where he was in the room.

Sensory deprivation and overload rolled together, leaving her mindless.

He touched her pussy, and she screamed from the shock. But before she could try to draw her legs together, he moved.

She sagged against her bonds.

"Five."

"Sir?"

He rubbed the backs of her thighs, then vigorously massaged her ass cheeks. She knew he did it so she wouldn't bruise.

Then he stunned her with the paddle on the back of her leg, directly above her right knee. This was nothing like what she'd experienced with Master Simon. Though it was a dull pain compared to the flogger, it went deep, completing her. It was everything she'd fantasized about after she'd seen the BDSM movie.

He landed another on the opposite leg.

She exhaled, forcing away the pain.

Masterfully, he played with her pussy, inserting a finger, driving her to the edge.

Then...nothing.

He pulled away his hand.

All she knew was thunderous music, darkness and the kind of arousal that she'd never before experienced.

With the edge of the paddle, he tapped her nipple hard before squeezing it and releasing one of the clamps. She squealed.

"Nice?" he asked her.

She pursed her lips. *Nice? Awful. Debilitating. Wonderful.*

He landed another.

Was that three? Did him hitting the nipple clamp count as one of the five strokes?

The unclamped breast ached, but the other burned from the metal's grip. The backs of her legs stung, and her pussy throbbed.

She'd never experienced anything so commandingly powerful. She wanted more. "Yes."

He released the other clamp, then as blood surged back in, he put it back in place. She screamed. Then she became aware that the sound of her pain mixed with his diabolical chuckle in an erotic sensation that filled her senses.

The weight of the dangling chain and clamp made her eyes tear.

The next two strokes landed on her buttocks, square, but not as painful because of the amount of flesh he covered.

But did she have one more coming? Or were they done?

She waited, unsure whether to be on guard or to relax completely and wait for him to release her bonds.

Long seconds hung, then passed.

Sure it was over, she exhaled and allowed her head to loll to one side, ready for the nasty clover to be removed.

He caught her then with a shocking stripe, beneath her buttocks, lifting her heels from the floor.

It stunned and thrilled.

He shoved three fingers deep inside her pussy, and she orgasmed.

She was hardly aware of him unfastening the cuffs, and she kept her eyes closed for a while after he removed the blindfold. With his reassuring strength, he guided her toward the bench then pulled her into his lap and held her close.

"I still need to remove the other clamp."

She nodded.

He took it off, then he toyed with her nipple until she sagged against his chest.

"How was it?"

"Unbelievable." She breathed in his scent. It seemed the more experience she gained, the more she blossomed. The hesitant woman who'd walked down into the basement yesterday bore little resemblance to the sub she was becoming.

He cleaned up the area, turned off the music, then gathered the bag and told her to head to the bedroom.

"Are we done?"

"We're only beginning. After you."

She walked up the stairs ahead of him, aware of his heated gaze on her. At one time, it might have made her nervous. Now she pulled back her shoulders and lightly gripped the handrail on the way up.

Once they were in the bedroom, he put a bottle of lube on the nightstand and instructed, "Undress me."

"My pleasure, Sir."

Something hot flared in his eyes.

She started with his shirt, baring his strong, broad chest. After folding his shirt, she unbuckled his belt and pulled the leather from the loops, remembering how sexy it had felt on her backside yesterday. And if he were serious about them having a future together, maybe she'd feel it again.

The thought gave her goosebumps.

She looked up at him to see him staring at her, noting her every movement.

Moving faster, wanting connection, she bent to help him remove his boots and socks then knelt to unzip his jeans. He plucked a condom from his pocket and tossed it on the bed.

Her mouth dried.

Even though she'd known he'd be commando, seeing his cock, so thick and erect just inches from her face turned her on. Wanting him, she leaned toward him and took him in her mouth.

"Jennifer..." He dug his hands into her hair and held her firm as she sucked and licked him. "Yeah," he approved, the word mostly a guttural groan.

She adored having this kind of power to please him. And it seemed fair after everything he'd done for her.

With his grip, he guided her, and she took him deeper. Until now, she'd never enjoyed giving head, but she'd never been with a man this appreciative.

"Enough," he said a few seconds later, and he cupped her jaw to force her to stop.

"But—"

"I'm setting the scene," he reminded her.

She knelt back. After wrinkling her nose, she said, "Yes, Sir."

"At some point, I'll come down the back of your throat," he promised.

The naughty image thrilled her.

"But I want you to put the condom on my dick."

She fumbled more than she would have liked, but he didn't seem to object. Realizing that, she took a little more time than she needed to.

"Well done," he said, as if she'd done it perfectly. "Now bend over the bed."

He offered a hand to help her stand, and she glanced at his cock, unable to look away. No matter that he'd had fingers up her, she doubted she could take his entire length and girth up her tightest hole. "I'm more than a little nervous."

"You'll be okay. You've been stretched out."

"Your fingers are nowhere near the size of your magnificence."

"Magnificence?" he repeated, a smile toying around the corners of his mouth, making him seem more approachable, less formidable.

"I mean penis."

"Magnificence is better."

"I can't believe that came out of my mouth. I may regret it forever." She rolled her eyes.

"Over the bed."

Tension knotted in her shoulders. "What if I'm not okay?" she asked.

"Your safe word works here, too. Promise."

Grateful his grin had faded, showing that he'd recognized her sudden nervousness, she said, "Thank you." She got into position, her torso on the bed. He moved the lube onto the mattress then played with her clit, and he pressed the tip of his cock into her pussy.

She looked back over her shoulder at him. "Sir?"

He pressed his dick all the way into her pussy before leaning over to open the lube. She watched him put a generous dollop on his fingers.

She expelled a jagged little breath, knowing he was going to suggest she relax.

Logan began to fill her pussy with long, slow strokes. Trustingly, she closed her eyes, then concentrated on not tensing her body when she felt a cool, wet finger against her ass.

He eased in, but he didn't stop fucking her, keeping her aroused.

Like earlier, she was able to release enough tension that the anal part became pleasurable, even when he inserted a second finger.

Then, before she was mentally ready, she felt his gigantic cockhead pressing against her sphincter. "It's a lot bigger than your fingers," she protested through gritted teeth.

With his other hand, he toyed with her pussy.

"So good," he said. "Bear down. It's really not more than you took earlier."

Was that true? Tightening her muscles would make this more difficult, so she allowed the mattress to absorb more of her body weight.

"You're a quick study," he said.

She gently closed her eyes and surrendered.

"Yes. Exactly right." Logan stoked in deeper, a little at a time, pulling back, then easing forward. "Almost there."

He gave a short, final thrust, sinking in all the way. She gasped, partly from the shock, partly from the pain, and mostly from the realization that he had her thoroughly claimed. Sensation and emotion overwhelmed her.

"Balls deep," he said, tone both graveled and triumphant. "Told you I keep my promises."

He tucked one arm beneath her to hold her tight, and he caressed and fondled with the other as he began to move deep in her ass.

"So damn tight. Hot."

She balled the bedding in her fists as he fucked her hard. Her whole body felt as if she were on fire, alive. Wanting everything he had to offer.

Stunning her, an orgasm began to unfurl.

She moved, grinding herself against his hand, creating even more friction between them.

"What you do to me," he said, pulling her tighter.

"My God. I can't…" Her thoughts fractured. She couldn't take much more.

"You can."

His cock thickened, grew harder. His breathing was labored, and he held her tighter. She was completely captivated by him…her Dom.

"Now. Come for me now, Jennifer."

"Yes, Sir," she whispered.

He eased two fingers inside her pussy.

Combined with the sensation of having her ass full, she shattered, losing her grip.

Her face buried in the mattress, she screamed from the power of the release.

"Damn." The word was somewhere between a groan and a demand. Logan adjusted his arm, lifting her hips a fraction of an inch higher.

"Mmm." Even though she was satiated, she wanted to feel the force of his orgasm.

His strokes were shorter and faster, and he held her prisoner, nearly splitting her in two as he came, his body hot and pulsing.

He remained inside her for a seemingly impossible amount of time, his body protectively covering hers.

She wasn't sure how long they stayed like that, bound together, hot and sweaty. But when reality returned, she noticed that the fingers of their right hands were entwined. "I'm not sure I'll be able to sit comfortably for a week."

He dropped a kiss on her shoulder blade. "Now we're getting somewhere."

Eventually, he helped her up.

They showered together, and when they were back in bed, he wrapped an arm around her waist, his dick shockingly semi-hard against her butt cheeks.

"You can't possibly…"

"Depends on how still you are."

Brazenly, she flexed her hips.

"You sure you want to do that?"

If she weren't so exhausted and warm, she might explore further. Instead, she heeded the warning, settling against him, enjoying the sensation of being protected, not on guard, maybe for the first time in her life.

Tonight was better than last night. Familiarity was its own form of comfort.

But she came to awareness in the middle of the night, beneath him, her hands pinned above her head. His breath was warm on her face, and even in the darkness of night, she read desire in his eyes and intent in the tilt of his chin.

"You can wake me like this any time," she said sleepily.

Where their earlier couplings had been intense, this was sweet. He gave, she accepted.

He made sure she was taken care of before he came in the condom.

Without ever waking up fully, she drifted back to sleep, hazily aware of the way he snuggled up to her and covered her shoulders with a blanket.

The next thing she knew, daylight had crept into the room, and she was alone in the bed, just like she had been the previous morning.

As was becoming a habit, she wrapped herself in a sheet and went into the living room.

Logan stood in the kitchen, hips propped against the countertop, cup of coffee in hand, looking devastating with the shadow of a beard. "I hope I didn't wake you."

"Not at all."

"Coffee? With five sugars?"

"Please."

"The storm has eased off," he said as the machine brewed her cup. "Snowplows should be out soon."

Outside, only a few gentle flakes drifted down. The sun had burst through, and the sky dazzled in its stark blue color.

"I received a phone call around four," he told her. "Potential break in the case I'm working on."

She shouldn't have been surprised. The whole weekend had been borrowed time. Jennifer told herself she should have been grateful for what they'd had.

"We've been monitoring a house to see if our guy would show up. Someone potentially matching his description arrived in the middle of the night. He's been holed up."

"So you need to leave?"

"Soon." He nodded. "I need to take over for Jeremy."

Her stomach plummeted.

"I'm not letting you get away," he said, promised. "I want your phone number." He dug his cellular out of his pocket.

Jennifer gave him her information, and he programmed it in before saying, "I cleaned the snow off both of our cars and scraped the ice from your windows, but I suggest you wait until the sun is up before leaving. The longer you wait, the safer your drive will be." He pulled out her cup and stirred in five packages of sugar, wincing the whole time.

"Thank you. Not just for the shoveling, the cleaning up and the coffee..." She accepted the cup, added a dollop of cream then took an unsteady drink.

As if he had all the time in the world, he waited for her to continue.

"But also for this weekend experience."

"It's only the beginning."

After she had a second sip, he took the cup from her and slid it onto the countertop. His hands firm on her shoulders, Logan tugged her close. "I'll be in touch."

She tried for a casual, 'I'm unaffected by what happened and don't care whether you do or don't' smile. "That would be nice." *Nice* wasn't the word. *Reality-tilting* was closer.

He fisted one hand into her hair and tugged back her head.

She met his gaze. His eyes were the color of frost. But his lips were heated, his tongue demanding.

He ripped the sheet from her body, leaving her naked, her nipples peaked, her thighs parted, her pussy wanting.

He toyed with her nipples, then slid his hand between her legs. Even with their mouths joined, she moaned and rocked toward him, hungrily seeking release.

Just moments before she came, he pulled his hand away.

"What?" Confused, she blinked when he took a step back.

"I want you to think of me."

"I..." *Is he serious?* He intended to leave her unfulfilled? Goosebumps raced up her arms.

Without another word, he turned and headed toward the home's entryway. He shrugged into his jacket, gave her instructions on locking up then picked up his bag.

After he opened the front door, he looked over his shoulder. "Oh, and, Jennifer?"

She met his gaze.

"I meant that I want you to think of me. So don't masturbate." With that, he left. The door closed behind him with a resounding shudder.

Chapter Nine

On autopilot, she went through the motions of getting ready to leave, applying a little makeup, ensuring her flogger was in her bag. She took one last trip through the guest room and tried not to remember the way Logan had fucked her, then in the middle of the night, had made love to her.

Before leaving, she locked up and hid the key where Logan had instructed.

As he'd said, her car had been scraped, and he'd also cleared the driveway and sidewalk. Not only that but he'd sprinkled salt so it hadn't iced over again.

The drive home was slow, but not treacherous.

Her house, though, was freezing cold, and not just from the temperature.

Midmorning, Logan sent a text, asking if she had made it home okay.

She grinned, feeling suddenly warmer.

Around noon, he sent a second message, letting her know it might be a while before he contacted her again. He'd followed mid-afternoon with a third.

Be patient?

She'd replied that she would.
And then...nothing.
Noelle called around four. "Well?"
"I have no idea where to begin."
"Since you stayed two nights, it can't have been terrible?"
"It was amazing."
"So tell me about it."
"Honestly, I'm still processing."
"Let's have drinks with the Divas on Wednesday."
By then, she might have heard from him. Or realized he wasn't going to call. "Perfect."
For the rest of the afternoon and way too late into the night, she checked her phone before giving in to frustration and turning it off altogether.
Not that it mattered. When she woke up, she saw there had been no notifications.
At work on Monday, she placed her phone on her desk and waited for it to ring or signal a text from him. Although she received half a dozen messages from Noelle, Jennifer didn't hear from Logan.
She finally told her friend that she hadn't heard from him.
Noelle advised her to give him time. After all, he was a busy man.
Which was true. But that didn't help.
By Tuesday, Jennifer's frustration made her irritable at the office. It wasn't just because she hadn't heard from him, but also because she'd been stupid enough to follow his dictate not to masturbate despite being desperate for an orgasm.
She asked herself why she was obeying him. They didn't have a relationship. It wasn't as if she were his

sub. She didn't know whether he actually would call again. How the hell long was she supposed to wait?

'I always keep my promises.'

His words haunted her. But so did his silence. The harder she tried not to think about him or the way he'd secured her to the St. Andrew's cross, the more persistent the memories became, growing bigger in her fantasies and invading her dreams.

She gave a silent prayer of thanks when Wednesday finally arrived and she met the Carpe Diem Divas for happy hour at a local bar in her neighborhood.

"You don't look happy," Ava observed.

Not much got past the Divas.

"So, what's wrong?" Ava persisted.

"You still haven't heard from him?" Noelle guessed.

"From who?" Eden demanded.

For the next few minutes, Noelle confessed her part in helping set up Logan and Jennifer.

Then Eden turned to Jennifer. "And? Did you scene with him?"

"Yeah," Jennifer acknowledged. "I did."

"Did he paddle you like that other Dom did?"

"He did. But it wasn't at all like the time with Master Simon."

She fanned herself.

"And he used my flogger."

"The one we bought when we were shopping for that bachelorette party?" Morgan demanded. Without waiting for an answer, she plowed ahead. "I knew it! How was it?"

"Better than I imagined," Jennifer revealed, rubbing her finger around the outside of her margarita glass.

She knew Eden would press for information, but honestly, she wanted to keep most of the details to herself. They were private—not necessarily because of what she and Logan had shared but because of how she'd reacted to it mentally, emotionally. How could she possibly explain what it felt like to be overcome by endorphins, lost inside her own head, in a place so pleasurable she wasn't sure she'd ever wanted to come back?

"You're understanding it better, aren't you?" Noelle asked, more softly. "How complex the whole BDSM dynamic is."

"It's complicated. Yes."

"And?"

Jennifer shook her head. "I'm not sure I wanted to know."

"Why?" Eden asked. "Did it hurt?"

Noelle and Jennifer both glowered at her.

"What?" Eden held up her hands.

"Of course it hurt," Jennifer said.

"Okay. So you hated it, right?" Eden pressed.

"No." She'd loved it. Wanted it. Craved it.

"Ha!" Ava exclaimed.

"Ha?"

"I think you like this Logan guy," Morgan said.

"Master Logan," Jennifer corrected automatically, hearing his voice in her ear. A light shiver traced through her veins.

"So that's how it is." Morgan reached for a tortilla chip. "Noelle said she'd call him Master Logan if he had a paddle in his hand." She gave a little shiver.

"You've got it bad," Ava said, and there was some sympathy in her tone.

Jennifer knew her friend was right. Problem was, he obviously didn't return the feelings. With a wince, she realized what it was like to be the person on the other side of the 'in love' equation.

Even though she spent the next hour chatting with her friends, Jennifer's heart wasn't in it and she had a difficult time paying attention.

Ava said she'd found out that the guy with the tattoo had a boyfriend.

"Better you found out now," Morgan said, raising her almost empty glass.

As they walked outside, Noelle took her aside and squeezed her arm. "I'll call you tomorrow so we can have a more private conversation," Noelle promised. "That is, if you're ready to talk."

"Thanks, but I've got a busy day." Jennifer smiled, hoping to take any sting from the words.

Noelle pulled back, but she nodded as if understanding. "If you change your mind, call me."

Jennifer wasn't sure she was interested in talking about her experiences with anyone, even the one person who might understand what she was going through.

"I can't stand to see you like this. I feel responsible."

"This is all on me," she said. "I made my choices. I don't regret a single one of them."

"Tell me you're okay."

"I will be," Jennifer replied, hoping Noelle couldn't hear the lie. "I promise."

Because she had no plans for the upcoming weekend and she needed to keep herself busy so she didn't slowly go out of her mind, Jennifer stopped at the hardware store on the way home. She selected a gallon of paint for the guest room, a couple for the kitchen and she found a clerk to help her select an air sprayer. Even that conjured images of Logan. *Master Logan.*

After taping a few walls in preparation for the weekend, she went to bed early, slept badly, then dragged all the way through work for the rest of the week. Then, annoyed that she was feeling sorry for herself, she turned off her phone when she got home on Friday evening.

She rewatched the videos on how to use the power tool and followed the clerk's instructions before painting the guest room. It took her less than half the time that it had taken her to do the bathroom.

On Saturday morning, she got up and began taping off the kitchen cabinets and moving out the table in preparation for the primer. It was going to take a lot to transform canary yellow to soft sage.

By Saturday night, she was exhausted and every muscle ached. She drowned her thoughts by listening to music so loud that knickknacks danced in the curio cabinet.

She was only marginally successful in blocking out thoughts of Master Logan.

But once she drew her bath, her efforts collapsed into failure. As she sank in and the hot water soothed her muscles, she began to relax, and that wasn't good. A restless hunger consumed her.

She couldn't stop thinking about sex.

As usual, the harder she tried to shove thoughts away, the bigger they became.

Her clit throbbed, and she wanted an orgasm.

She told herself it couldn't hurt to masturbate. She didn't owe him anything. They'd shared a weekend, a number of great scenes, hot sex and he'd helped her explore her boundaries. Despite his pretty words, they didn't have a relationship. Other than him taking her phone number, there were no future plans.

Jennifer trailed her fingers down her breastbone, then cupped each breast in turn. She gently tugged on her nipples, but she couldn't get any kind of satisfaction from it. She needed more pressure. Or, better yet, some pain.

Frustrated, she sat up and pulled the plug to drain the water.

After climbing from the claw-foot tub, she wrapped a towel around herself and went to find her toy bag.

She pulled out the nipple clamps she'd never played with, and she grabbed a small vibrator, then climbed onto the bed.

As soon as she closed her eyes, she imagined Master Logan telling her what to do. "Yes," she whispered to the empty room as she rolled her right nipple, teased it, pulled on it, elongating it in preparation for the bite of the tiny, serrated alligator teeth.

She recalled the way he'd placed the clamp last weekend, and she did the same.

The grip scored her tender flesh, and she lifted her hips from the mattress. Since she'd been left wanting last Sunday morning, arousal had lain in her belly, low and hot. Now it flared in fervent demand.

Jennifer repeated the process with her left nipple, and this time she moaned. The pain made her clit throb. She didn't just want an orgasm—she needed it.

With her eyes still closed, her imagination still racing, she reached for the vibrator, then turned it on. She parted her labia and placed the wriggling nubby head of the bullet against her clit.

She dug her heels in beneath her, arching her back as she pressed against the vibrator. "Damn..." Wishing Logan were there, she slipped a finger in her pussy, then pushed the bullet hard against her clit, rapidly moving her wrist to create more motion.

Her breaths came faster and faster, sharper and sharper.

"What in the hell do you think you're doing?"

"Sir…"

"Didn't I tell you not to orgasm?"

"But…" *Goddamn.* Jennifer couldn't get there, couldn't come… *Maybe just a little more pressure…*

"I said stop it immediately, Jennifer."

Fuck. All of a sudden, fantasy vanished. His voice seemed so fucking real. Panting, she opened her eyes, then screamed.

Logan stood in her bedroom only a few feet away, wearing a ferocious scowl, his arms folded formidably across his chest.

Petrified, stunned at being caught, pissed off that he was there, and fucking elated that he was, she remained frozen, her pulse racing. "Logan."

"*Master* Logan," he corrected. "I'll take that." He held out a hand and glanced at the still-buzzing bullet she'd somehow dropped onto the mattress. "And then you can get on your knees and explain what the hell you think you're doing."

Chapter Ten

Logan waited impatiently for her to follow his orders.

Instead, she sat up and demanded, "What are you doing here?" She grabbed a nearby robe and dragged it against her.

The motion knocked off one of the alligator clamps. She winced, but didn't attempt to remove the other one. *Smart girl.*

"How did you find me?"

"I'm a goddamn detective."

"If you think…"

He waited.

"That you can burst in here without calling or texting me—"

"I did. Several dozen times in the last twenty-four hours. I was starting to get worried about you. So was Noelle. Check your phone."

Her gorgeous blue eyes went wide. Her expression changed from challenging to contrite. Since his numerous calls had gone straight to voice mail and she hadn't responded to half a dozen text messages, he figured she had probably turned it off. "Now do as I requested."

"Ordered," she countered.

He lifted a shoulder. "Semantics."

Her chest rose and fell in shallow bursts. In coming here, unexpected, uninvited, he knew he'd scared the shit out of her, yet he couldn't bring himself to be overly concerned.

"It's been almost a week," she said. "You could have called."

He pulled out his phone with the shattered screen and tossed it on the bed next to her.

"Did you drop it?" she asked.

"Look again." When she squinted at it, he said, "Turn it over."

Her face drained of color. "It's got a hole…"

"Yeah. It stopped a bullet."

She put a hand on her throat. "Were you hurt?"

"Bruises. Nothing a couple of aspirin won't take care of. We got the case wrapped up around five yesterday. The first fucking place I went was the cell phone store. Not the shower. Not my bed. Not to get a drink or food. To the phone store." The idea of burying his dick deep in Jennifer's wet pussy had kept him sane. The thought of flogging her had been a lifeline in the chaos. The memory of holding her while they'd talked had soothed the savageness of his emotions.

"That's almost worse than getting shot," she said, with a wry twist to her lips.

"Not by much." He'd spent days working his ass off to get back to her, thought about her when he shouldn't have, used the knowledge that he'd see her again as motivation to press through to the end of the case.

He crouched in front of her, being more real with her than he'd ever been with any woman. Jennifer deserved it. "You were the only thing I thought about. I'm a man of my word. If I say I will call, I will. *I keep my promises.* I'll prove it to you, and I'll make it up to you."

She stared at him as if trying to decide whether to trust him.

"Then you didn't answer my texts or my calls. Around ten last night, I called Joe. He told me to give you time. So I called Noelle. She refused to give me any information. But she tried to call you. I went over there two hours ago, and she was getting as concerned as I was. She finally convinced Joe to give me your address. At that point, it didn't matter. I was going to use all my connections to find you." Logan softened the tone of his voice and took one of her hands. "I knocked on the door. Rang the bell."

"I guess I did have the music a little loud."

Which he'd turned down. "You had a key under a fake rock. Only honest people think they fool anyone. No more keys in easy access," he said. Seeing her there when he'd walked in, naked, back arched, moaning in tiny frustrated sounds as she sought a climax she couldn't reach had affected him in powerful ways. He wanted to be the only one to please her. For a man who'd spent years avoiding relationships, he was intensely attracted to this woman. "Then I saw you, trying to steal an orgasm that you promised me. Me, Jennifer. It's mine to give, not yours to take. *Mine.*"

She shuddered.

"You promised you'd be patient."

"I thought... I remembered the story about Helen."

"That relationship was over," he said. "We both knew it. She had the guts to end it before I did. But you... I asked you to wait."

She exhaled, and the color of her eyes lightened.

"Now. Don't make me repeat my order." He held out his hand again.

Her internal struggle didn't last long. He knew she was as hot for him as he was for her. She could have thrown him out or used a safe word, but she hadn't.

She picked up the vibrator and turned it off before placing it in his palm.

"Thank you," he said as he stood.

Slowly she slipped from the bed, and the robe fell to the floor.

He stepped back to give her room. She looked at him for a few moments. Then she lowered her gaze as she knelt.

The free clamp swung, pulling on the one still attached to her nipple. Her wince prompted him to say, "I could take that off for you, but I'm not going to. I want to see you suffer."

"I have been." She looked up at him. "When I thought you wouldn't call." Her voice was breathless, aching...killing him.

"Trust takes time," he agreed, his voice gruffer than he'd meant it to be. "We can start by having you move into my place."

"What?"

"You can keep this one until you have faith in the relationship. In me. In us. And that's built over time. If that's what you want."

"I agree about the trust. But I like this house. It's close to my work, and I like the neighborhood. If you're going to be gone for long periods, I want to be in a place that I chose. I want to stay here."

"Do you have a basement?"

Her pussy flooded with moisture. "Yes."

"And the canary-yellow walls are going?"

"Tomorrow."

"You'll be naked, unless you bought coveralls. I can't wait to clean the overspray off you."

"I…" On her naked thighs, she turned up her palms in supplication. "I missed you."

"Then let's take that first step."

"Yes. I'd like that, Sir."

He was desperate for this woman and fighting his natural instinct to toss her on her back and fuck her ragged. "There's a penance for trying to steal my orgasm."

"Even though I waited almost a week?"

"Even though."

She licked her upper lip.

"What's your safe word?"

"Marshmallow," she said.

"Unless you want to use it, drape yourself over the footboard."

Jennifer didn't hesitate for a moment.

When she started to stand, he said, "I'd prefer you crawl."

Even though her breath caught, she got on all fours. The chain attached to the alligator clamp swung back and forth as she moved. From her wince, he knew it was shooting sparks of pain through her.

She reached for it, but he snapped, "Leave it."

Wrinkling her nose, Jennifer continued past him and got herself into position.

"Stretch your arms as wide as you can," he instructed.

He went into her closet and found a number of long scarves. After tying them together, he secured each of her wrists to the wrought-iron headboard. "This bed is perfect. I think it's meant as bondage equipment."

"Everything is to you," she said, perhaps remembering the coffee table at Joe and Noelle's house.

"Kiss me," he told her.

She pulled up as much as possible and turned her head toward him.

That was all he needed. He framed her face with his palms and held her firmly. "I'll teach you not to doubt me." Then he kissed her hard, deep, with promise and commitment. "And I'll start by letting you know I'm serious when I give you a command."

"I understand."

"Tell me again how many days have you waited?"

"Five, Sir."

"Five?"

"Six. Six, Sir."

He lowered one hand and squeezed the breast that still had the alligator attached.

She cried out, and he silenced her with a kiss that stole her breath and made her grind the balls of her feet into the floor.

He left her for a second, only long enough to grab the loose clamp and affix it to her neglected nipple.

"Sir!"

"You're going to come six times before I fuck you, Jennifer."

"Can we please get on with it, Sir?"

"Impatient?"

"The clamps are driving me batty."

"Yeah. I can smell your heat." Heady stuff, submissive female arousal.

He slid his hand between her legs and rubbed her cunt. The harder she pulled on the restraints, the tighter they got.

She started to breathe faster, and he reached for the vibrator. He turned it on and smiled when he realized the small bullet had a surprising amount of power.

"Sir..." Her eyes were wide as he moved closer.

Then he touched it to her clit.

She screamed and arched her back. "Stop, stop, stop!"

"*Stop* isn't a safe word," he reminded her, slapping her left ass cheek with hard openhanded swats.

"I'm going to come," she warned, promised.

He pressed the nubs tighter against her and told her, "Yes."

She called his name as she shattered, collapsing over the metal. But the moment her breasts touched the mattress, she pulled up again.

"This is unbearable," she said, her voice containing a pitiful wail.

"We haven't even started," he promised.

Logan removed his belt and gave her six strokes—not as hard as the ones he planned to deliver after she was properly warmed up—all aimed at that tender spot at the tops of her thighs.

She squirmed and cried, and her tears were sexy and real.

"You're gorgeous," he told her. And he reaffirmed, "Mine."

"Fucking prove it," she said.

He knew it was a plea and that she wasn't simply goading him. "I intend to." He finger-fucked her hot cunt until she was dripping. "Ask me to touch your G-spot."

"I might die if you don't," she said.

"You'll only think you will." He found the right place and gently touched it.

She whimpered. "More," she begged when he remained still.

"I told you to ask. Be specific."

"Please touch my G-spot, Master Logan."

God, he liked the way that term sounded. He moved his free hand to her ass and dug in his fingers. Then he pressed her G-spot harder, keeping firm pressure until she clenched around him.

"May I come, Sir?"

"Yes," he whispered, enjoying the sound of her crying out.

"How many was that?" he asked when she was able to drag in a couple breaths of air.

"Two," she whispered. "Feels like a hundred."

"Do you have lube?"

It took her long seconds to answer. "In the bathroom," she said eventually. "Under the sink."

He left her where she was, and when he returned, he placed his feet inside her ankles and forced her legs farther apart. "Stay like that or I'll tie your ankles, as well."

"Yes, Sir."

He poured a liberal dose of lube on her, letting it run down her, over her anus. Then he scooped up some with two fingers and pushed into her.

"That's too much."

"Is it?" he asked, unconcerned. "You've done it before."

Even he hadn't recalled her feeling this tight.

She swayed back and forth, trying to get away.

He worked himself in until he was buried up to his knuckles.

"It's…" She bit her lip. "I'm so full."

Logan parted his fingers slightly, then began to ream her, uttering words of comfort. "Take it for me. Stop thinking about yourself and think about your Dom."

She froze for a moment as the words resonated. Then she totally relaxed. "Yes..."

Even as he tormented her delicious little ass, he picked up the bullet. He flicked off the nubby top, exposing three tiny metal nubs. On his next thrust, he entered her pussy with it, simultaneously filling both of her holes.

He fucked her until she came, hard. "That's three."

"I'll never complain again," she vowed. "Even if you go away for a long, long time without calling or texting. Or writing. Or sending a telegram."

He kissed the side of her neck. "Nice try, sub."

"Couldn't you just beat me or something? Flogger? Paddle? That evil belt?"

"Orgasms," he said. "You owe me three more."

"But..."

"Not done with you yet." When she didn't respond, he said, "I didn't hear you."

"Anything you say, Sir."

He went into the bathroom to wash up. When he returned, Jennifer's body was dotted with perspiration, and she looked so gorgeous, spread, bound, bent over, helpless.

With a damp washcloth that he'd brought back with him, he cleaned off the excess lube. Then he released her wrists before sitting on the floor and resting his back against the footboard near her.

"What are you doing?" Jennifer asked.

"Come here. Put your cunt on my face and fuck it," he ordered.

She sucked in a breath before slowly saying, "That's outside my comfort zone."

"This is about what *I* want, little sub. Do it."

"I..."

He waited. She was so fucking hot, and the scent of her musk made his cock ache.

"You're impossible, Sir."

"And you're going to get the insides of your thighs pinched unless you do as you're told."

After a few seconds, she moved over him and bent her knees slightly.

"More." When she didn't immediately respond, he carried out his threat and pinched her hard.

She yelped, and her body instinctively swayed forward to escape the pain.

Then she was on his face, and his tongue was inside her. Her sounds of protest yielded to moans of pleasure.

With his hands on her, he forced her to move until she was humping his face and he was licking her hot pussy. "That's it."

"Sir, Sir, Sir!"

The metal chain jangled as it swayed, and she drew in desperate, labored breaths.

He pulled her down even harder, unbalancing her. But he was there for her, demanding she give him what he wanted, even if her cunt was getting tender.

With his tongue, Logan traced an infinity knot on her clit.

She gyrated and thrashed.

"Give it to me."

Screaming a protest, she came, her essence all over his face.

He stayed where he was, supporting her weight while she regained control of her body.

"Sir..." she began when he stood.

"Hmm?"

Initiation

"If I promised I've learned my lesson..." She turned her head to the side, seeking his gaze. "Will you please fuck me?"

With her lips parted, her blue eyes glazed with desire, he ached to give her everything she desired.

Logan rubbed her body, starting with her arms. He checked the circulation in her wrists, massaged her shoulders, made certain her legs weren't cramping.

"This time, I'm taking you from behind."

"Just take me. I need your cock."

He pulled out a condom from his wallet then stripped slowly, aware of her watching his every move. He rolled on the condom then stroked his shaft a few times as she silently stared.

"I forgot how big it was," she said, slightly breathless.

"It'll fit. I promise." He brushed that stubborn lock of her hair back from her face. "Tell me what you want. Be specific."

"Your cock filling me, Sir. Master Logan."

Anything she wanted. Anytime.

He moved behind her.

Since she was so much shorter than him, he had to bend his knees while she lifted herself onto her tiptoes.

He guided his cockhead to her pussy, then slowly stroked himself in. "I waited," he told her. "Since I asked you not to come, I chose not to as well."

She tried to angle herself so she could look at him, then gave an annoyed hiss when he and the bondage held her tight. "Are you serious?"

"I am." As her body accommodated him, he made his thrusts longer and slower, pinning her with his hips. "This—*you* are worth any wait."

"Damn."

He had no idea whether she was referring to the sex or the fact he'd denied himself. "Come when you're ready," he told her. He wasn't sure how long he'd be able to hold off. Last night after he'd arrived home, adrenaline had still thrummed inside him, keeping him awake. It wasn't simply the remnants of the case, but the fact he'd been unable to reach her. Jerking off would have helped him unwind and get to sleep, but he'd known that being with her would make every sleepless minute worthwhile. "I'm at least halfway to being in love with you," he said.

"Good. Because I'm not going there alone," she said, her words ringing with conviction despite how breathless they were.

"Then we're agreed." He rode her hard, reaching out to hold her hair. By the time he was done with her, Jennifer would know she was his.

She didn't have to tell him she was ready to come. He felt her go rigid, heard her desperate gasps.

His balls drew up, and he thrust deep inside her, burying himself to the hilt.

Her internal muscles clenched, milking an ejaculation from him.

With a guttural, primal grunt, he came, deep, hot, claiming.

"*Fuck.* Master Logan!"

For a moment or two, long enough to be freaky, he had an absence of thought, of contentment. He wondered how long it had been since he'd felt this relaxed.

Eventually he became aware of his cock softening and her shifting to get more comfortable. "You're a magnificent sub," he said.

He took his time removing the alligators, gently squeezing her nipples until she stopped groaning and they returned to their normal size.

"I don't know whether I love or hate those evil little clamps." She frowned.

"You had them on when I arrived."

Her next comment was spoken into the bedspread.

"Repeat that."

"I wasn't able to climax without them."

"I'll keep that in mind." Along with every other detail about her.

He unfastened her wrists then helped her stand before turning her to face him.

She threaded her arms around his neck and buried herself against his chest. There was nothing that could have been more perfect or a bigger symbol of her trust. "I'm not finished with you yet," he warned like he had last week.

Jennifer looked up and gave him a bratty smile. "Bring it. Sir."

ENTICEMENT

Dedication

For anyone who has ever loved someone who has served in the military. YOU are my hero.

Chapter One

What the fuck?

Pierce Holden narrowed his eyes and propped a booted foot behind him on the upscale honky-tonk's wall, wondering what the hell he was watching, and why the hell it mattered to him.

Ella Gibson, his little sister's best friend, was standing at a bar-high table along with a couple of other people, leaning forward, her chin propped on her hand. Tonight, her brown hair — longer than he remembered from the last time he'd been back in Colorado for a couple of days' leave — framed her face and hung down her back.

A soft, oversized gray shirt slid from one of her shoulders, showing off her creamy skin, and her black skirt was several inches shorter than it should have been. If she bent over any farther, her ass cheeks would flash the whole world.

Why that thought bothered him, he couldn't say.

Her long, muscular legs were bare. Since it was the middle of May, she only had the barest hint of a tan. Her cowboy boots were black with hot-pink angel wings embossed on the backs of them. *Angel wings.* That was rich, when she was dressed like sin.

Randall W. Thurston, Jr. walked over to the table and offered her one of the glasses he was holding. If Pierce's guess was right, it contained whiskey. Neat. Absently, he wondered if Junior had sprung for the expensive stuff.

The two clinked their glasses together, and she smiled up at the slick attorney.

She took a sip then wrinkled her nose and shook her head.

Alcohol was never part of Pierce's approach. He liked his subs to be sober. So much so, in fact, that he made it a requirement.

Pierce tipped back the longneck bottle and took a deep drink.

From what his sister had said recently, Ella had gone through a breakup a couple of years ago. It had devastated her enough that she'd avoided dating for more than a year.

Seemed to him as if she was on track to make a full recovery.

Pierce wished she had better taste in men. He wondered if she had any inkling that Junior was a Dom. If so, and she was still talking to him, she either hadn't heard the rumors about him, or she was reckless.

From the outside, Junior appeared acceptable. The man had a fancy degree from a prestigious school. If he hadn't already made partner, no doubt the announcement was forthcoming. He wore wingtip shoes that were glossed to a military shine. Pierce would be willing to bet the man hadn't polished them himself. Maybe it was a chore he gave to a submissive. His suit was tailored and expensive. Unlike Pierce's haircut, which was the result of a once-a-week pass with his own set of clippers, Junior's hair lay perfectly, no doubt styled at an expensive salon.

The white, veneered smile couldn't hide the fact the slick lawyer had cheated on his wife and helped a man get away with murder—both sins in Pierce's structured world. None of that surprised him, though. Years ago, at a play party hosted by Joe Montrose, a good friend of his, a Dungeon Monitor had stopped a scene when Junior had refused to honor a sub's safe word.

The band trailed off, and after the applause died away, they strummed the opening notes of *Came Here to Forget*, a song that couldn't have been more apropos.

Behind Pierce, someone launched a cue at pool balls, shooting them across the green felt in an explosive boom. It was all he could do not to jump. Most men didn't have trouble blocking out the sounds of people having fun at a bar, teasing each other, calling out which pocket they were going to sink the solid into, but to him, and to countless others who'd been under heavy artillery fire, the surge of adrenaline was inevitable.

Even when he was away from combat, he was always aware, always on guard.

To calm himself, from the noise as well as the sight of Ella about to walk into dangerous territory, he took another drink of the all-American lager. Nothing fancy. Serviceable. Affordable. And with an alcohol content below that of popular microbrews.

Across the room, Junior drank his whiskey in a single swallow then slammed the empty glass down on the tabletop and signaled for the waitress.

Ella placed her barely touched drink back down and rose, lifting the heels of her boots from the scarred wooden floor as she leaned forward, her body language flirtatious, in order to catch something Junior was saying. Her leg muscles flexed in a way that appealed to Pierce's baser nature, and that damnable skirt rode up just a little more.

Fuck.

Instead of looking at her face, Junior glanced down her shirt.

Prick.

"There's something about Randall that I don't like," Morgan said, joining him.

Pierce turned toward his little sister and saw a ferocious scowl on her face. "That he's a cheat?"

"Yes. That. But it's more than that." She shrugged. "I'm not sure. Something about the way he looks at me. It's hard to explain. Like he wants to devour me. Creeps me out."

"Is Ella dating him?"

"No. At least not that I've heard. And she would have said something. He's a member of the *country club*."

The way she looked down her nose and emphasized the last two words told him a couple of things. Junior belonged to the same club as their parents. And Morgan also believed that Junior was a pretentious ass. "Have you told Ella what you think?"

"You can bet I intend to. I don't even know what he's doing here. The Neon Moon doesn't seem like his kind of place."

"Slumming with us."

"Hard to imagine, isn't it?"

"Anyway, I need to go," she told him. "Mom and I have mani-pedis at the nail salon tomorrow morning.

And I'm sure mimosas will be involved." She rolled her eyes. "God help us all."

Their mother could be dramatic at the best of times. Factor in a little alcohol and she qualified for an award.

After shaking her head, Morgan glanced back at Ella and the other people at the table. "I'll let them know I'm leaving. How about you?"

He shook his head. "Think I'll stay a while. Finish my beer."

"Are you kidding me? You're always the first one to hit the exit at these gatherings, not the last." She reached forward so that she could put her fingers on his forehead, pretending to take his temperature. "Who are you and what have you done with my brother?"

"Funny." But she was right. He left the bar scene to others. If he hadn't wanted to avoid spending time with his parents and talking about plans for tomorrow's party, which his mother hoped would make the society page, Pierce wouldn't have accepted the invitation to meet Morgan and a few of her friends at the Neon Moon—not that he'd spent much time talking to them. And until he'd seen Junior make a move on Ella, Pierce had been planning to go back to the hotel before eight, get in a quick workout, maybe a soak in the hot tub and a few minutes of mindless television. "Go home, Morgan."

"Don't forget Mom and Dad are expecting you to arrive in time to help set up tomorrow. By noon? Please?"

"I'll be there." Their parents were celebrating their thirtieth anniversary, though with the coldness with which they communicated, he had no idea how they'd made it that long. Determination, maybe.

Stubbornness, for sure. And without a doubt, it was all for show.

His mother had started planning last year and had reminded him of the invitation at least once a month. A few weeks ago, she'd resorted to strategic measures and had enlisted Morgan's help. His little sister had said, "It would help me if you came." His parents, he could resist. Morgan? Never. "Twelve hundred hours," he acknowledged in military time.

"It would be easier if you just stayed at their house, you know."

In the bedroom that was part shrine and a total reminder that he'd failed to fulfill the dreams his mother and father had had for him? Last he'd been in there, a college acceptance letter still sat on the desk in mute condemnation. In his final days of high school, he'd destroyed his parents by enlisting in the army then heading to basic training without saying goodbye. "I'm fine at the hotel."

"You sure? It's a long drive."

"Less than half an hour." In military terms, that was nothing. And the small place had a hot tub to soothe his muscles and a workout area to burn off the nervous energy that built up every time he was forced to interact with his family.

"Take pity on me? I could use the buffer," she admitted.

"You've gotten everything you're going to get out of me, no matter how much I love you. But I'm happy to let you stay at the hotel with me."

"Mom would kill me."

"She'd get over it."

"I've never been as brave as you, Pierce."

"You're just easier to manipulate."

"That's not true." She wrinkled her nose. "Is that true?"

He didn't respond.

"I hate that you're right."

"Go," he said.

"Fine. See you tomorrow."

"Don't let Mom have too many mimosas," he warned. "It's going to be a long day. She needs to pace herself." He watched Morgan walk up to Ella, and Junior's smile faded at her approach.

Pierce didn't have to overhear the conversation to see Ella smile and indicate she was staying.

His sister whispered something into her ear.

Ella's back went rigid for a second. She glanced at Junior then back at Morgan. Then Ella reached across to squeeze Morgan's hand, as if reassuring her everything would be okay.

The waitress returned with another round for the table, and Morgan took that opportunity to excuse herself.

With a last wave in his direction, she left the bar.

Pierce watched Junior down his second shot, and Ella scooted her glass to the side.

The Blake Shelton song playing in the background was replaced by an older ballad. A number of couples made their way toward the parquet dance floor. Seeming to take advantage of the new intimacy in the place, Junior moved nearer to Ella and skimmed his fingers across her bare shoulder.

In Pierce's mind, a line had been crossed. An urge to protect drove him.

Junior might have helped a client get away with murder, but Pierce sure as hell wasn't allowing the creep to put his hands on Ella.

Pierce slammed his drink on a nearby table, strode toward Ella then angled his body between hers and Junior's. "Dance?" he suggested.

"I'm talking with Randall."

"Were. You were talking to him. And you're done."

She scowled. "What?"

"Dance with me."

"Do you have any idea how rude you're being?"

"As a matter of fact..." He tipped his head to one side and grinned. "Yeah. I do."

"Ella?" Randall asked, craning his head to the side.

"Now," Pierce said, refusing to budge.

"It's okay," she told Randall with a forced smile. "I promised Pierce I'd dance with him."

It shocked him how easily the lie had rolled off her tongue.

"Shall we?" With a show of male dominance, Pierce placed his fingers on the small of her back and looked at Junior, sending a *stay back* message.

Aware Randall's gaze was fixed on them, Pierce smiled. Junior loosened the tie that Pierce would have liked to choke him with and signaled for the waitress instead of talking to the other people at the table.

"What in the hell is your problem?" Ella demanded, looking up at him.

How had he never really noticed how petite she was? He'd always seen her as his little sister's friend, not as a woman in her own right. To be fair, he hadn't spent a lot of time with her since he'd moved away. In the intervening years, she'd become not only attractive, but stunning. Her hazel eyes were wide and, fuck it all, her lips were an inviting shade of red. No wonder Junior was hot for her.

Thanks to a woman he'd dated for a while, Pierce knew the basic two-step. Nothing fancy, but enough to get Ella alone and not embarrass either one of them. He pulled her toward him. His arms fit nicely around her, despite the rigid way she held herself away from him. The overhead lights reflected off the coppery tones in her hair. And, this close, he drank in her scent, that of sunshine and promise, an intoxicating, perhaps lethal combination that he suddenly wanted to sample.

"Pierce?"

Jolted, he shook his head.

"I asked you a question," she said. "I'm not in high school anymore."

"So I've noticed."

"I don't need rescuing," she finished.

Despite her heated words, she moved flawlessly, following his lead. All of a sudden, he wondered if she'd be just as perfect in other ways, too. Rather than getting into an argument, he countered with, "What do you know about Junior?"

"Junior?" She frowned, her eyebrows drawing together. "You mean Randall?"

"Yeah."

"He'd hate it if he heard you call him that."

"I'm counting on it."

She scowled at him. "I'll ask it again. What is your problem?"

"I don't like him hitting on you."

"And?" She blinked. "What I do and who I do it with is none of your business."

"I'm making it my business."

She laughed. "Sorry to disappoint you, Pierce. You're my best friend's big brother, but that doesn't give you any right to stick your nose in my business."

"Someone has to look after you."

"No. Really. They don't. As I mentioned, I'm a big girl now. I can think for myself, choose who I want to hang out with. But thank you for your concern." She gave him a dazzling smile.

He just wished it wasn't as fake as it was big. And that it hadn't walloped him in the solar plexus. "What is it about him that you like?" he asked, again trying to keep her off balance so that she could hear what he had to say. He needed to get her past her annoyance first.

"He's a good conversationalist."

Pierce schooled his reactions so he could keep a straight face. "He must have been talking about one of his court cases. Maybe how he impressed the jury. Or found the best witnesses. Give him a spellbound audience and he'll go on for hours."

She frowned.

"He was boring you, wasn't he?" Maybe that was why she'd been shifting from foot to foot, the hem of her skirt swishing with every move. "Tell me I'm wrong," he encouraged.

For a few seconds, he watched her struggle to suppress a grin. Being diplomatic, she didn't respond to his challenge. Instead, she gave a different answer. "He's successful."

"That's easy when you get into a good law school on a legacy admission."

"Just because his dad and uncle went there doesn't mean anything."

"Oh? Any idea what his GPA was? Does he talk about that? Or the fact he had a cushy job lined up at his father's firm?"

"Okay, that's enough." She pursed her lips in what he imagined was supposed to be a fierce manner.

It just made her adorable.

"I appreciate your concern," she went on. "But I was having a good time until... Wait. Crap. Did Morgan say something to you? She doesn't like him."

"This is about me, not Morgan."

"In that case, we have nothing left to say. Thank you for the dance. I'll be getting back to Randall now." She started to pull away.

"You know he's into BDSM?"

She faltered, then she missed the next step.

Pierce pulled her close and eased her back into the dance. "So you do know." He was stunned and delighted.

But she seemed appalled. "Oh, my God. What did Morgan tell you about me?" Twin lines of scarlet embarrassment stained her face. "She promised to keep it secret."

"Is that what this is about? Do you need your ass spanked, Ella?"

"And what if I do?" Her words were laced with bravado and her eyes flashed with challenge fed by the brush of anger.

"Then I'm happy to oblige you."

"You're..." She trailed off then glanced around, as if to make sure no one was looking at them.

"Right here. Now, if you want. I can take you out back, or to my car, even to the ladies' room, if you're desperate."

"This conversation is inappropriate."

"Is it? Is that why you haven't pulled away or slapped my face?"

"I just said that you're my best friend's big brother."

"So?"

"Could you be any more obtuse?"

"Enlighten me," he said easily.

"We are so not having this conversation."

"But you are willing to have it with Junior." That thought pissed him off and tension crawled up his spine. "You know nothing about him. You're willing to let him tie you up, maybe lay a belt to your gorgeous backside."

"Okay, Pierce. Since you did so much work to get me out here, I'll play along. What do *you* know about BDSM?"

"Is that an honest question? Or are you issuing a challenge?"

She took a small breath. Her indignation seemed to have vanished. "I'm curious."

"I've practiced it for over ten years."

Her eyes widened.

"I've been to clubs, to play parties, and I own an assortment of toys that would keep even the neediest, greediest sub happy. I prefer a flogger to anything else, but I'm competent with and happy to use a cane so you can have a few marks to remember me by. Would you like that? On the backs of your thighs?"

Her breathing became shallow.

Oh, yes. No doubt the petite spitfire wanted exactly that. His arousal spiked, hard and fast. He kept her against him because having her near was so fucking right. "You could show up at my mom and dad's anniversary party tomorrow in a short dress and spend the evening wondering whether anyone could see the strokes of ecstasy that I'd seared into your skin."

She still hadn't run—she hadn't even blinked. So quietly that he had to strain to hear her above the band, she asked, "You're a Dom?"

"I answered your question. Now it's your turn. What do you know about BDSM?" Why did the thought of anyone else marking her infuriate him?

"I know enough," she replied.

"If that's true, my questions shouldn't unnerve you."

"If you were a man I was considering as a Dominant, they wouldn't," she said.

"I'm telling you this, Ella. If anyone's going to tie you up and beat you tonight, it will be me. Is that what you wanted to hear?"

"I... We can't."

"Because?"

"Beyond the obvious? You're in the military. I've had enough of men who move along when they're assigned to a new duty station."

He winced at that. His special operations team was deployed more often than most other members of the army. The assignments tended to be shorter, but also more frequent, up to six times a year. And he wasn't based in Colorado. All of which were strikes against him in her eyes, he was sure.

"I understand what you're saying." Less than a year into his military experience, he'd made the decision not to become involved in a long-term relationship. He dated casually and enjoyed scenes with subs, but he was honest about his lack of availability and his aversion to commitment.

One woman he'd cared for had been convinced they were meant to be together, and she'd expected him to change his mind, especially once mutual friends had announced their engagement. When he hadn't proposed at Christmastime, she'd given him a tearful ultimatum.

He'd held her while she'd cried, and he hadn't flinched when she'd slapped his face before leaving. That night, for the first and last time in his life, he'd gotten drunk.

Ella glanced back toward the table. Her other acquaintances were still gathered around, but Junior wasn't there. She frowned, and Pierce watched her scan the room, looking for him.

Ella noticed him a moment later. Junior was at another table, drink in hand, leaning toward a woman with his gaze focused on her chest.

Pierce hated for the fucker to hurt her, but he had to admit to being glad that she'd seen his real nature before she'd become involved with the bastard. "I'm sorry," he said.

She pasted on a sunny smile, as fake as it was brave.

The song ended. The guitarist said the next song would be a line dance. People—most of them women—abandoned their drinks and partners, grabbed a girlfriend by the wrist and headed toward the dance floor.

Since he had no interest in boot-scootin' across the floor, Pierce walked her back to the table.

Junior was still occupied, so Pierce took the man's spot.

He faced Ella, which seemed fine since the other people at the table were deep in their own conversations. "Do you want to continue our discussion here or somewhere else?"

"There's nothing to discuss." She lifted her water glass with a shaky hand and drew a sip through the straw.

But the look she sent him from beneath her lashes told him his words had gotten to her and that she was thinking about what he'd said.

Junior returned. With a scowl, he snatched up one of Ella's untouched whiskeys and gulped the shot in a single swallow.

"Want me to call you a cab?" Pierce offered.

Junior straightened his tie. "I'm fine."

"From what I've seen, you've had more than enough. The bar's going to be cutting you off. And you don't want to get picked up for drunk driving. Daddy wouldn't like it."

"Can I give you a lift?" Junior asked Ella, ignoring Pierce.

"I'll give her a ride home if she needs one," Pierce responded.

"Why don't we ask the lady?"

"Why don't we?"

They both faced Ella to see the lady's jaw was set. She drew in a deep, heavy breath. "I have my own car. I'll see myself home, thanks."

Pierce gave a feral grin. "This is where you say goodnight, Junior."

"Fuck you, Corporal Holden."

"Staff Sergeant," he corrected easily, ignoring the obvious insult. Figured the pussy needed to get in one shot to feel better about himself. Pierce didn't blame him. "Proud to serve my country so that others can sleep well at night, whether they deserve to or not."

Junior rapped his knuckles on the table twice. "I'll be in touch, Ella."

Once he was gone, she turned her furious gaze on Pierce. "I can't believe you sent him away."

"You can thank me later."

"Thank you?" she echoed. "Are you kidding me? Do you have any idea how influential his family is?"

"Doesn't concern me."

"Does anything?"

"Yeah. But not cowards like Junior, who use intimidation and coercion to get what they want. Rats who think they're above the rules." He shrugged. "Predictable in their patterns and behavior."

"Do you always live recklessly?"

"No."

"But you like danger?"

"I wouldn't say that, either."

"Then...?" She angled her head, as if she was genuinely interested in his answer.

"All my risks are calculated. It's the best way to stay alive."

The waitress hurried over with a bill and a scowl, watching as Junior walked out of the door.

"He'll take that," Ella said to the woman.

Pierce frowned as he accepted the bill. A glance at the bottom line proved the fucker had indeed sprung for the expensive shit.

"The price of chivalry," Ella said with another of those sunny smiles he was already starting to dislike.

He dug his wallet from his back pocket.

"Hope it was worth it."

"*You* are." He gave the server his credit card. "I would have paid ten times that amount to have you alone."

The server accepted with a grateful nod, pressing the card against her chest. He'd have picked up the tab, regardless. No way would he have left Ella or the hardworking server to cover someone else's bad behavior.

"So, back to the topic at hand. How much do you know about BDSM? Dabbler? Practitioner? Just curious?"

"I wanted to know more about you," she countered.

"I'll tell you anything you want to know." He paused. "But not until you answer my question."

"Uhm... I'm more than curious."

Those scarlet streaks were back on her cheeks, brighter than ever.

The music trailed off and the band announced a brief intermission, leaving the bar somewhat quiet.

She leaned toward him, obviously so they wouldn't be overheard, and his reaction was raw, unwelcome. He couldn't remember the last time he'd been this turned on. Ever since Karen had stormed out of his life, he'd channeled his energy into his job and training for marathons. "So you've had some experience," he surmised.

"The last guy I had a serious relationship with was a Dom. It was my introduction." She toyed with her straw.

"And?"

She swirled the straw around and around. He wondered if she was ever going to answer.

"Do you want me to be honest?"

"Nothing but."

She stared into the bottom of the glass before looking up. "I miss it."

"What parts?"

After glancing around to ensure others were occupied with their own conversations, she admitted, "Nothing as much as the physical contact."

"Impact play?"

"Yes." She nodded. "There's something exhilarating about being pushed, about pushing myself."

"So you *do* need a spanking."

"Pierce..."

"I'm happy to give you one."

Her mouth opened a little. He couldn't look away. That damnable, kissable red lipstick was ready to drive him off a cliff.

"I can't tell whether you're kidding or not."

"I don't say things I don't mean, Ella. Not when it's important." He met her gaze, held it. Something vibrant flared in her eyes, something that hadn't been there a few minutes ago. The spark of temptation? If so, he was ready to ignite it. "You're as safe with me as you want to be."

Chapter Two

Pierce Holden, a man she'd had a crush on for years, *was* serious. He'd looked after her and Morgan, making sure they'd arrived home safely after prom. Another night, he'd driven them home from a party when they'd been out too late. Someone had spiked the punch, something they hadn't figured out until much later in the evening when Morgan had slurred her words and Ella had burst into an uncontrollable fit of giggles. When they'd realized someone had put alcohol in their drinks, they'd been too scared to call their parents.

Every time she'd seen him, Ella had thought he was big, strong, serious, and oh-so fucking handsome. She recalled the way he'd dressed—in tight jeans, tighter T-shirts, and scarred, black boots. With his fast cars and faster motorcycles, he'd liked danger and adventure, not conformity. He'd never fit his parents' idea of the perfect son. He'd moved out of the house during his senior year in high school, worked in an automobile repair shop that his father hadn't owned, and paid his own bills.

To her, he'd been larger than life, a man who knew what he wanted and wasn't afraid to go after it.

On more than one occasion, she'd gone to bed and fantasized about him pushing her against a wall and kissing her. But he'd never been anything other than damnably, unfailingly polite.

Tonight, though...

At first, the way he'd taken charge of the situation had annoyed her. She'd been enjoying the conversation with Randall. The man was from a well-respected, old money Denver family. He was a member of the country club where she worked. And she'd heard rumors from a woman in the accounting department that he was into BDSM. So when he'd walked over to her table and offered to buy her a drink, she'd been thrilled.

But when she'd been in Pierce's arms on the dance floor, she'd been captivated by the power of his touch and his breathtaking scent, danger mixed with spice. When she'd missed a step, he'd been there, steadying her. By slow measures, her resistance had vanished.

And when she'd seen Randall flirting with the other woman and realized he'd had way too much to drink, she'd had to admit Pierce had probably been right to intervene.

He might have saved her from making a big mistake.

But she was certain that standing here talking to him might lead to an even a bigger one.

"I promise you, Ella, I will meet all of your needs. Maybe a few you don't even know you have." His deep, rich, rumbly voice sent shivers up her spine.

Erotic thoughts careened through Ella, driving her mad with excitement. The idea of him flogging her naked body flashed through her mind, impossible, and so tempting she ached to say yes, even though she shouldn't.

One-night stands and casual hookups weren't for her. She became too attached too quickly, and breakups devastated her.

Over the past two years, since she'd found out that Lance had had another girlfriend—another sub—in Killeen, Texas, Ella had concentrated on building her savings account, buying a small condo, working her way into a management position and avoiding potential hurt. Now that she was taking the first steps on the dating path, she was focused, searching for a solid, stable man and a long-term relationship that would lead to marriage. If a man showed no interest in that, she moved on after the third date.

"You were willing to tell Junior what you wanted," Pierce reminded her.

She rubbed her bare arms, trying to get rid of the sudden chill that raced through her. "He doesn't frighten me," she admitted. *At least not in the same way.* All day, every day, she dealt with men like Randall. She understood how to soothe them, inflate their egos, make them feel good. She had no clue how to deal with a man as complicated as Pierce. "You make me feel as if I've been swept up in a tornado."

He regarded her intently and she noticed the tiny grooves etched next to his blue eyes, lines that hadn't been there years before. Life experience, she knew. The result of events and challenges she could never imagine. From Morgan, Ella knew Pierce wasn't just military. He was in some special operations unit. She'd guessed it was involved with counterterrorism. And the last time Ella had asked his mother how he was doing, Mrs. Holden had smiled and offered another mimosa.

Even to his own family, he seemed to be something of a mystery.

That should be reason enough for her to stay away from him.

So why couldn't she stop looking at him?

Over the years, he'd become more hardened. He was still lean, with the physique of a swimmer or maybe a runner. He wore a short-sleeved navy T-shirt that showed his well-defined biceps. Jeans that were too soft to be new fit his thighs and hips snugly, invitingly. And his boot selection hadn't changed over the years. They were black and battle-scarred.

His dark hair was cut short, severely buzzed on the sides, a bit longer on the top…just enough for her to grab onto.

Ella blinked in a vain attempt to shove away the unwelcome thought.

He carried himself with ease, and with the confidence that came from knowing he could take care of himself and any situation he found himself in. Everything about him radiated control and determination. She had never been more flustered in her life.

The waitress returned with Pierce's credit card and the receipt, shattering the tension and allowing Ella to breathe again.

She caught a glimpse of the total amount he'd paid. Randall's whiskey had cost twenty times what she'd thought it would, and remorse ate at her. She had no right to stick Pierce with someone else's bill. "Look, Pierce. I shouldn't have done that." He added an obscene amount as a tip, and remorse morphed into guilt. "Let me pay you back." She grabbed her purse from the hook beneath the table.

He raised a hand to halt her.

"At least half?"

"I've got it."

"You didn't need to."

"I sure as hell wasn't leaving it for you."

The band took the stage again and began tuning their instruments, making conversation more difficult.

"Would you like to go somewhere quieter?" he asked. "A coffee shop? Maybe take a walk in the park? It's a nice evening."

"Are you staying with your parents?"

"No. I'm at a hotel near Parker and Arapahoe. Not too far from here, and close to Mom and Dad's."

"But not too close," she said.

He nodded.

What had happened that had caused him to leave home? And more, why had he stayed away? Was it his job or something more?

She told herself it didn't matter, shouldn't matter. But she couldn't tamp down the curiosity. "There's a Starbucks on Parker Road," she said, decision made. "I think it's open for at least another hour." It would be busy with students and couples on dates, but not too noisy to talk. On the other hand, this conversation might not be one she wanted others overhearing.

What was she thinking?

A rational part of her brain urged her to thank him for bailing her out and make an escape. Her heart thundered a warning. Adrenaline swamped her stomach in short, furious waves. All her instincts screamed that he was a man who could—would—devastate her. But sensual longing and sexual need went through her like lightning, obliterating everything else. "I also have coffee at my place."

He raised an eyebrow.

"Uhm, I mean, if you're interested."

His blue eyes flared with intensity and her insides did a flip-flop.

"Do you want me to follow you there?" he asked.

"Actually, I could use a ride."

"You told Junior you had a car."

"I lied."

"Was it your wicked plan all along to get me to drive you home?"

"What if it was, Staff Sergeant?"

"It worked." He grinned. "And you can call me Sir."

* * * *

Like everything else, the rental car suited Pierce. It was gloss black, American, all muscle and restrained power. Dozens of images flitted across the movie screen in her mind. Her naked and kneeling. Him undressing her. Her running her fingers over his chest. Him tugging his belt from its loops.

Ella shifted uncomfortably.

"Cold?" He looked at her while reaching for the temperature control.

"I'm fine." *For someone who's lost her common sense.* She was under no illusions. Pierce was suggesting a scene, nothing more. No whispered promises. But on Sunday or Monday, he'd be returning to active duty.

The only thing he was offering was the one thing she'd promised herself she'd avoid.

She told him to take a right turn, then he followed the rest of her directions and snaked the rental car through the streets until he reached her home. Fortunately, the unit next door was for sale, which meant she had no neighbors.

If he made her scream the way she was fantasizing about, that would be a good thing.

Enticement

Once he'd parked, he walked around to her side to help her out. Pierce closed his hand around hers firmly, but not too tightly. He held her for a few seconds longer than necessary. The combination of his gentleness and reassurance made her apprehension vanish. She just wished her nervousness would go along with it. The idea of getting naked with a man for the first time, especially one who might be tying her up and spanking her, left her shaky.

"Everything okay?"

"Fine." Her voice was a little high-pitched.

But after a few seconds, he nodded and let her go.

Until that moment, she hadn't realized she'd stopped breathing.

"Nice place," he said as they walked up.

"Thank you. I'm rather proud of it, honestly. It's close to work and I don't have to do any of the outside maintenance." The exterior was a type of stucco, the color of red clay. Cheery blue shutters provided a homey touch that had made her fall in love with it. In a way, the contrast of colors had reminded her of a trip she'd once taken to Santa Fe. To add to the feel, she'd planted lavender in southwestern-style pots on her front porch.

She flipped on a light when they were inside, and she wondered what it looked like to him, a man who oozed solitary, masculine style.

The townhouse was two stories, with a wide-open floor plan. The focal point of the first-floor room was a fireplace. The white-painted mantel above it overflowed with framed snapshots. Some were of her with friends, others with her mother. Ella's absolute favorite—occupying the center spot—was a faded picture of her with her late father. She'd been three, sitting on his shoulders waving a flag at a hometown

Fourth of July parade. He'd been smiling, and she'd been giggling. It was the last picture of them together.

The remaining space was filled with dried flowers in vases and a few vacation souvenirs, including a conch shell she'd hand-carried back from the Caribbean.

Every time Morgan visited, she complained that the living room was cluttered with too much seating, but Ella liked entertaining and having company. She had blankets and pillows stacked on the sofa and the chairs. And because she liked to read, end tables held books and magazines. Two torch-shaped lamps added atmosphere.

She had numerous potted plants in every corner and hanging from hooks in the ceilings. Almost all of her artwork highlighted the importance of family and friends, of memories and enjoying the moment. She figured now that he'd seen the inside, there was no way he could doubt how different they were.

"Nice place. Homey."

"It drives your sister crazy. Too much stuff. I'm surprised it doesn't bother you."

"After living in barracks and my spartan apartment, it's a nice change."

Surprising her even more, he moved toward the fireplace to look at her knickknacks and photos.

"Your mom?" He pointed at a photo.

"Yeah. She lives in Colorado Springs, but I don't see her as much as I'd like. She's too busy with her job, social engagements, volunteer work, that sort of thing." Ella shrugged. "I have to call her a month in advance to get on her calendar."

"Is this your dad?" He picked up the framed snapshot.

"That was a couple of months before he died in a car wreck."

"Sorry for your loss."

"Thank you." She wrapped her arms around herself. "I'm not sure people heal from something like that. Of course, we were forced to go on, but it shaped who I am, my view of the world. All of a sudden, I didn't feel as safe. But it has helped me to focus on what really matters to me."

"Relationships."

Which was another reason why a one-night stand was so difficult for her. She nodded. "And how precious every moment is. I spend as much time as I can with the people I care about."

"Did your mom remarry?"

"No. She threw herself into taking care of me, making sure I had the same kind of upbringing I would have had if Dad hadn't died. He left life insurance, but she still worked two jobs to keep the house so I didn't have to go to a new school. When I went to college, it was as if she'd been reborn. So many men, so little time. Last we talked, she was juggling three."

"Three?"

"Until recently, she was seeing four. But she broke up with the preacher."

"She was dating a preacher?"

"For a short time. It turns out they had different expectations about certain carnal things." She grinned. "She got tired of him praying for her soul. She thinks it's just fine, thank you very much."

"I like your mother already."

"She's a character. There's nothing I can't tell her."

He replaced the photo.

Ella led the way to the kitchen, and he took a seat at the granite-topped breakfast bar.

"Can I offer you coffee?" Nerves assailed her. "Or I have beer." To distract herself, she opened the refrigerator and pretended to survey the contents. "Wine? Soda?"

"Just the conversation."

"Water?"

"That'd be great. Thanks."

She grabbed two bottles, closed the fridge then turned toward him.

Pierce wore an easy grin, as if he sensed her nervousness. Her hand shook as she slid one across the countertop to him.

He nodded a thanks and set it aside, unopened.

She uncapped her bottle and swallowed a long drink. To keep much-needed distance between them, she took a few steps back to prop her hips on the counter next to the fridge.

"Tell me about your BDSM experience." His voice was half invitation, half unyielding command.

He didn't waste time. She toyed with her bottle as she answered. "The last man I was involved with, Lance, introduced me to it. We went to a few play parties, but it was an occasional, kinky kind of thing. I'd dress in leather when we went to clubs, we'd have scenes when we got home. That sort of thing."

Pierce nodded. "So you didn't live together?"

"No. He was stationed at Fort Carson, and had his own place with a couple of buddies. He'd come over maybe once during the week, and at least every other weekend." In retrospect, she realized she should have recognized the warning signs, but she'd been in love. She'd convinced herself he was busy, working hard or in the field on maneuvers. And she'd allowed herself to believe that he'd one day figure out they were meant to be together.

"Any other relationships?"

"That included BDSM? No."

"You didn't go back to play parties? Clubs?"

She shook her head.

"You told me earlier that you miss it. So why haven't you looked before now?"

"Do you have a questionnaire you'd like me to fill out?" Ella demanded.

"Just curious," he said easily. "I want to know you."

Funny. She quizzed her dates in the same way, probing, wanting to know as many details as possible in the shortest amount of time. She wasn't sure she liked being the focus of that attention, though. "No. It seemed odd for me to go by myself. The idea made me uncomfortable. I wanted to be with someone who could offer guidance." She deliberated for a couple of seconds before adding, "I talked to a couple of men online who said they were Doms. But I was never comfortable meeting them. They seemed more interested in hook-ups or exchanging kinky emails and pictures than in having a real relationship." Ella had nothing to lose by being honest with him. "I only started dating again recently. For obvious reasons, BDSM isn't something I mention when I first meet a new man."

"A real man won't be scared of your needs. If he is, he's not worth the investment of your time."

He could be right. "I went out with an accountant once," she said. "I made a joke about spanking…to gauge his interest. He dropped his butter knife on the floor of the restaurant. And then he shushed me."

"He—"

"Told me to shush." She nodded. "All the dramatics, too. Pressed a finger to his lips, just in case I hadn't understood the word. And he looked around to be sure no one else had heard me."

"I'm guessing you didn't appreciate that."

"As much as I would have enjoyed him throwing his drink in my face. Which is what he did, figuratively. I did learn that the life expectancy of a one-hundred-dollar bill is nine years. That's always good to know, right?"

Pierce smiled.

Despite the sexual tension crawling through her, she'd never enjoyed a man's company more.

"That explains why you were talking to Junior."

She nodded. "Tonight... I guess he met a client at the Neon Moon. And then when he was leaving, he saw me and recognized me from the country club."

"I know you work there."

"Morgan has a big mouth." Ella scowled. "Anyway, yeah. I figured he was safe."

"He's not."

"Could you make your dislike any more obvious?"

"What safe word do you use?" Pierce asked, rather than responding to her question.

"Stop."

"That works for you?"

She leveled her gaze at him. "I know red is more common, and if it's the safe word at a party or club, of course I'll use it. But I'm the type of woman who means *stop* when she says it."

"Respected," he acknowledged. "And for slow down?"

"I've never needed one," she admitted. "In fact..."

With seemingly never-ending patience, he waited.

Ella appreciated that Pierce made the discussion easy, with no more sexual charge than if they were discussing the weather. It made it possible for her to separate her feelings for him from the details of a potential scene. "I always wanted more."

"Did you ask for it?"

Heat crept up her face again. "Once or twice. But I guess I'm the kind of woman who tries to be grateful for what I get." Not that it had mattered in the end.

"What was it you wanted?"

"Something longer, maybe. A few times, it was over just when I was getting into it. And... There was a woman at one of the parties who talked about subspace. I wasn't sure whether she was joking or not."

"What do you think now?"

"I looked it up. A lot of people say they've achieved it. But I'm not sure I've been to the point that I had enough pain to tip me over the edge. I don't know." She searched for an explanation and came up empty. "Maybe I haven't been in a scene that lasted long enough. Or I haven't been able to empty my mind. Who knows?" She shrugged. "Or I could be lacking something."

"I doubt that." A smile tugged at his lips, and somehow that made him seem even more threatening. "But we could find out."

She slid her bottle onto the counter so she wouldn't drop it.

"Not that it should be the objective of a scene," he said. "Your satisfaction should be the goal."

"And yours?"

"Comes from seeing yours."

Without planning, the thought on the top of her mind tumbled out. "And sex?"

"Are you propositioning me?"

"No!"

"I was hoping you were."

Suddenly, she was wishing she had.

"It's up to you," he told her. "I have no expectations of sex. To me, BDSM is about the scene, the focus, the exquisite manipulation of pain so it becomes raw pleasure."

His words made her arousal spike.

"If you're agreeable…" He swept his gaze over her, taking his time, lingering.

Silently he'd reassured her of his meaning. He desired her, and whatever happened was up to her. "I don't sleep around," she told him.

"Neither do I."

She blinked. "What?"

"Surprised?"

"Flabbergasted," she admitted.

"One-night stands are awkward. I never know what to say. I hate leaving in the middle of the night. Worse, I don't want a woman getting out of my bed and finding her way home after dark. Having breakfast together is my preference, but that can lead to more intimacy."

She recalled being at a man's house years ago, and experiencing the same dreaded morning after. No toothbrush, limited makeup, a tight dress from the night before. She'd cooked him eggs and bacon when she'd have preferred granola and tea.

"I prefer to stick to scenes."

All of a sudden, ice went through her. "Do you have a girlfriend? Someone at home?"

"No. I'd never do that to her. Or to you. I've seen too damn much heartbreak to intentionally inflict it on someone else."

She raised her hand. "Recipient. Though I suspect Morgan told you that, too."

"What happened?"

Ella noticed he had neither confirmed nor denied her guess.

"I believed things were more serious than Lance did."

"Was he your Dom?"

"Yes. And it turns out he had a girlfriend in Killeen." She might as well get it all out in the open. "I'm embarrassed to admit that I missed obvious signs because I liked him and the play."

"Ouch. I'm sorry."

"It's okay. I'm wiser now. I'm grateful I found out before I invested any more time or energy into the relationship. That's my story. And since I'm being so straight with you, I do miss the scenes." *Miss them?* Obsessed about them was more like it. Last night, she'd dreamed she was being flogged. The Dom hadn't been Lance, but more of a compilation of a several men she'd seen at parties. She'd woken up horny, and using her vibrator had only given her temporary relief.

"What about you?" Ella folded her hands across her chest. "I mean... You have needs, right?"

"I masturbate."

"Lucky hand."

"I can show you how I like it done."

"Or I could watch." What the hell was it about him that removed the filter from her mouth?

"That's hot," he said. "Do you have toys that you like to use?"

She squirmed as things became more serious. "A few."

"Show me?"

"They're in my bedroom."

"You can get them or I can come with you."

"I…ah… Let me get them." She pushed away from the countertop and had to pass him to get to the stairs.

So fast that she didn't see him move, he snagged her wrist, stopping her. He turned her to face him.

"This is a good time to practice," he said.

"Practice what?"

"Proper responses." His eyes had darkened like they had in the bar when he'd taken her onto the dance floor. The softness that had been there a moment earlier had vanished, ice into vapor. "'Let me get them, Sir,' is what I want to hear."

Ella gulped for air, once again wondering what the hell she was thinking in agreeing to scene with Pierce. He was nothing like Lance. Pierce seemed much, much more serious in his approach to BDSM. And most other areas of his life, she surmised. Her voice soft and obedient, she repeated, "Let me get them, *Sir*."

"Very nice."

Rather than releasing her, he threaded the fingers of his free hand into her hair, bunched it then eased her head back a couple of inches, nothing that hurt, but enough that she couldn't look away.

"You didn't tell me a word that means you want to slow down."

"I told you I've never needed one."

"You've never been with me."

Her knees started to buckle, but he was there, giving silent support.

"You said you wanted more from your previous Dominant. I intend to leave you satisfied. And that may mean you'll be taking more than you've ever received."

I hope. "In that case, I'll use yellow."

"Go get your toys."

Almost imperceptibly, he tightened his hand in her hair.

"Yes, Sir," she replied.

"But first, I'm going to kiss you, Ella."

"About time."

"Oh?" He raised his eyebrows and tipped his head to one side.

Though his expression was fierce, she wasn't intimidated. "About time, *Sir,*" she corrected saucily.

His grip was as firm as it was intractable. "I've been wanting to do this all night. Open your mouth for me, Ella."

She wasn't sure whether she complied or whether he didn't wait, but their tongues were entwined. His was hot, searing. He sought her submission, and she gave it.

He groaned as he penetrated her deeper. Never had she been kissed like this. Pierce tasted of determination and promise that she hoped he could fulfill.

She met his kiss with desperate hunger. She'd yearned for something this intense.

Pierce released her wrist and placed his palm on her ass, nudging her up onto her toes to change the angle for a greater possession.

With her back arched, she wrapped her arms around his neck, holding on, trusting him to care for her.

The kiss was as demanding as it was stimulating…everything she could have hoped for. It had the potential to make her lose her heart if she wasn't careful.

She wondered how was she supposed to go back to an ordinary kiss—an ordinary man—after this?

Slowly, and simultaneously far, far too fast, he eased away.

Her mouth was swollen from his passion. But she wanted him with a hunger she was afraid she wouldn't be able to deny.

He took his time helping her to stand upright, and he released his grip on her hair.

It was then she realized he hadn't done anything more than kiss her. He hadn't slid his hand up her skirt, run a finger over her slick pussy or even cupped one of her breasts.

She knew he desired her. The blaze in his blue eyes was unmistakable. Instead, he was restrained.

The man had brought her to the edge then left her there. He was smart. And maddening.

"Hurry back, Ella. You've got five minutes or I'm coming up."

"Yes, Sir," she whispered. Ella was aware of his gaze on her backside as she dashed up the stairs.

Once she was inside her bedroom, her thoughts became a jumbled mess.

Aware of the clock ticking, she closed her eyes for a moment to clear her brain. After blinking a few times, she knelt to drag out a large plastic box from beneath the bed.

None of the contents had been touched since she'd played with Lance, and seeing them made her heart race.

She was getting the BDSM scene she craved, with a man she had a crush on.

The first thing she removed was a crop with a big red heart on the end. It had seemed like a fun piece when she'd bought it, but she couldn't imagine how ridiculous it might look in Pierce's strong hand.

Since he'd said he would be the one to tie her up and beat her ass, she took out two lengths of hand-spun silk rope. Then, just in case he wasn't familiar with how it worked, or preferred not to take the time it required, she selected a couple of pairs of soft handcuffs.

Then she paused and sat back on her heels.

She had a paddle with wicked holes in it.

Earlier, he'd mentioned stripes that might embarrass her at his parents' anniversary celebration. Right now, she craved some.

But the paddle wouldn't leave the kind of marks she wanted.

Though she'd had limited experience with a cane, she pulled one out of her box. It was rattan, thin, frightening. She thought about Pierce and how much she trusted him.

After drawing a breath to give her confidence, she placed it on the floor next to the rope and cuffs.

She put back the paddle, but decided to offer him the ridiculous crop.

After sliding the box back into place, she crossed to the far wall. The bottom drawer of her dresser was full of lingerie and a leather outfit she hadn't worn for several years.

Since he hadn't said anything about whether he wanted her naked or dressed, she grabbed the A-line leather skirt and matching shelf bra. Wondering what his reaction would be like, she hurried as she changed.

"One minute!" he warned.

"Yes, Sir!" she called back. Adrenaline rocketed through her.

Forcing herself to concentrate on what she was doing, she slipped her feet into a pair of tall, red stilettos, bending to adjust the ankle straps. She gathered up the toys she'd selected then gripped them tightly before taking a steadying breath and heading down the stairs.

Halfway down, she paused. Pierce was standing with his back to the fireplace, his arms crossed over his chest. His commanding presence overwhelmed her.

"Holy…" He trailed off.

Ella gripped the banister as he perused her, from her shoes, to the skirt and shelf bra.

Even across the distance, she saw his blue eyes flare with desire. "Damn. You're a lovely woman, Ella, with perfect instincts."

His approval sent shockwaves through her, leaving no doubt that her choice of outfit had been the correct one.

"Come here."

She walked toward him, her spiked heels echoing off the wooden floor.

In the time she'd been upstairs in her bedroom, he'd been busy. He'd scooted the couch and lamps back at least a couple of feet, rolled up the rug and moved it over near the back sliding door, leaving a large, open area, with the coffee table in the middle. She also noticed that he'd placed their water bottles on the mantel.

She stopped in front of him, and her pulse skittered in apprehension. "I'm not sure what to do," she admitted. She'd only been with Lance, and the BDSM had evolved over time.

"Communicate," he suggested. "Enjoy yourself. Relax with it, with me. Talk me through the toys you brought down. Lay them out on the coffee table. Tell me why you selected each item."

Ella knelt to spread out her toys, and when she looked at him, she read approval in the set of his jaw. Emboldened, she said, "I brought rope and cuffs because…"

He waited.

"Because you said if anyone was going to tie me up tonight, it would be you. Not everyone is into rope bondage, so I brought cuffs, too."

"Silk?"

She nodded.

"And the crop?"

Her whole body heated, so Ella knew she was blushing. "I know it might look ridiculous, but I kind of like the way it feels."

"Where?"

Oh, God. "On my nipples."

"Good to know." He picked it up and smacked his open palm. The sound echoed off the ceiling, making her jump. "And your pussy?"

"I've never tried that."

"You're willing to?"

"Yes." She sounded more breathless than confident.

"What are your hard limits?" he asked.

"The usual ones that are banned at parties. No permanent markings, no breaking of the skin, nothing that will send either of us to jail."

He nodded his understanding. "So tying you up and beating your ass is fine?"

Yes, please. She shuddered. "Isn't that why we're here?"

He picked up the cane, ignoring her sassy comment. "How much experience have you had with this thing?"

"Not much at all." Lightning bolts of awareness went through her. "But I'm curious."

"It's not a beginner's toy."

"But you can choose how much force to use, right?"

His lips twisted in a wry smile. "I imagine I can."

Pierce's words jolted her, reminding her of the differences in their lives. She had ordinary experiences—working, trying to buy a house, pay her bills, get ahead at work, thinking about a relationship—while he defended the country's freedom, did things he'd never talk about. *Yeah.* No doubt he could wield a cane with the intensity she might be able to tolerate. "Was that stupid to say?"

"No." He shook his head. "Whatever you want from me, I want to deliver. I like that you're trusting me." Pierce tested the cane, slowly at first.

She stared as he flicked it back and forth.

It lumbered through the atmosphere without a tremendous amount of force.

Then he moved it again and snapped his wrist.

The cane cut the air with a scary swish. She sucked in a breath and met his gaze. Handled like that, the rattan would leave a mark, sear, ache. She fucking wanted it…on her ass and on the backs of her thighs as he'd mentioned.

Transfixed, she watched him arrange a few pillows into a stack on the couch.

"Like this?" He tapped the top one a few times, without leaving an indent.

If she were smart, she would say yes.

"Or this?" This time, he let the rattan fly.

It landed with a thwack that dimpled the material.

She shivered. "Somewhere in between?"

He demonstrated again, leaving a precise line of marks across the pillow's surface.

"I should have realized that you knew what you were doing."

"A cane isn't to be treated lightly. I want you to understand that I will give you what you want. I'll warm you up, watch your reactions."

"Yes." She was already imagining.

"So beyond the obvious, what else is on your limits list?"

Ella was still staring at the rattan.

"Ella, please. Look at me. This is important."

She refocused. "I don't like to be left alone during a scene, especially if I'm in bondage. It's more upsetting than it is sexy."

"Tell me more."

"One time, Lance tied me up and left the room while he did some gaming. I think he didn't want to scene that night, but he humored me since I had asked. He didn't think he was being a jerk. It wasn't meant as punishment. He was just trying to meet my wants as well as his own. But I got a few muscle cramps."

"Were you hurt?"

"No. Pissed."

"I give you my word that I will be there for you at all times. I can't imagine needing to leave you, but if I did, it would be for a moment. And I would tell you where I was going and when I'd be back. First, I'd ensure it was okay with you and see to your comfort."

Reassured, she nodded. "Thank you."

"Anything else?"

"No humiliation. I just... I don't like to be called debasing names." She couldn't find the words to help him understand.

"You don't need a reason. You just need to tell me the rules."

"It's a hard limit."

He dropped the cane onto a couch cushion before taking two steps toward her and offering his hand.

She slid hers into his, feminine to masculine. Trust to strength.

"Humiliation isn't something I'm into. I think you are too perfect, too precious to debase in any way." He didn't release her. "If it were your kink, we would have negotiated something to ensure I got you off. But honestly, Ella? It would have been one of the most difficult things I'd ever done."

Damn. She so wished this could last more than one weekend. Wished he wasn't military. Wished she was the type of woman who wouldn't be hurt when he walked away.

"Just for clarity, are gags humiliating for you?"

"I've never been gagged."

"Are you willing to try?"

"As long as we have a safe signal, yes."

"Understood." He nodded. "Anything else you want me to know?"

"I'm willing to have sex with you, Sir. If you want to. I have condoms in the master bathroom, under the sink." She couldn't believe she'd admitted it. Couldn't believe how much she wanted it. Pierce and his quiet, relentless strength had gotten to her, chasing away her normal doubts and inhibitions. He was the devil incarnate. And she was ready to book a one-way ticket to hell.

Chapter Three

Pierce had meant it when he'd said that Ella was perfect.

To him, she was. More innocent than she'd like him to believe. Beautiful. Sassy. Brave. And with a dose of sexual appeal that walloped his senses.

Over the years, he'd played with a lot of women. They'd all been experienced in BDSM and, like him, knew what they wanted. He'd never made promises or created false expectations.

But because of who Ella was and what she was risking, he was doubly conscious of the weight of his responsibility to her.

He intended to give her everything she craved. All while protecting her. "Show me your body. I want to know every inch of it, where you're sensitive, and how you like to be touched." He released her hand. "We'll start with your breasts."

She locked her gaze on his as she pushed her breasts together.

"How do you like your nipples to be touched?"

Her breaths came in rapid bursts and her hazel eyes darkened.

She stroked her thumbs across her nipples, and they hardened, the rose color deepening.

"Do you like it this gentle?" he asked.

"No." She took his hands and put them on her breasts. "More," she whispered. It wasn't a demand, but a soft, sensual request.

He increased the pressure until she sucked in a breath. "How's that?"

"Enough to make me horny," she said.

The admission was more direct than he'd expected, and it made him grin. Damn, he liked learning about her.

He rolled each of her nipples back and forth, using a bit more pressure each time.

She curved her hands around his wrists. Then she closed her eyes.

He kept a close, close watch on her while he squeezed each tip.

She bent her knees and leaned toward him for support.

"You do like nipple play," he mused, easing his grip.

"I had no idea I could like it this much."

"Then I think it's time you showed me your pussy."

Her nostrils flared, and the tremble that went through her might have been missed by someone who wasn't paying attention.

"Lie on the coffee table." He cleared away the toys. "On your back." She uncurled her fingers and he asked, "Did you wear panties, Ella?"

"I guess you'll find out. Sir."

He moved quickly, taking a seat on the couch, snagging her wrist then tugging her over his lap.

She squealed, more from shock than fright, he imagined.

Ella pushed her fingers against the hardwood flooring to keep her balance. He clamped one arm across her back to hold her steady, and he raised his knees a couple of inches to tip her toward him so she wouldn't fall.

Her hair trailed wildly, the copper highlights like flames. Her skirt rode up, exposing her thighs. And those shoes—bright red—seemed to be an invitation to fuck. He was man enough to know he'd masturbate to this image a dozen times, maybe more.

"Damn, woman. If I had ever seen you like this when I'd been home on leave, I'm afraid my army career would have been over."

"AWOL?"

"Most definitely."

She gave a sound that was part giggle, part triumph.

"Vixen."

"Am I wearing panties, Sir?"

"You like to live on the knife-edge, delicious little sub?" With the way she'd behaved at the club, sticking him with a three-figure bar tab, it shouldn't have surprised him that she was a bit of a tease. Her sassy personality was a bonus, but that sure as hell didn't mean he'd let her conduct pass unpunished.

He flipped up her skirt.

She was bare.

No panties, no pubic hair. Waxed. And slick. He knew that without even touching her. *Fuck.*

This woman...

His woman...

"How many spanks do you deserve?" He rubbed her skin. "Not just for your sass, but for distracting me from exploring your body?"

"You are exploring," she pointed out. "Sir. And I think the punishment should be mitigated by the fact I'm not wearing panties."

"You do, do you?"

"If Sir's hard dick pressing against his sub's tummy is any indication, he's not terribly disappointed." She squirmed beneath his touch. "If the sub may be bold enough to say so."

"She may not."

"Oops."

"Spread your legs."

Instantly, she complied.

"Farther. Turn your toes in. In the absence of any other instruction, always assume that's my wish. How are you with anal?"

"What?" She tried to wriggle onto her side to look at him. "Now?"

"As pleasure. As punishment."

Ella tightened her ass cheeks.

"You didn't list it as a hard limit."

She didn't respond right away.

"I'll take that as agreement, then?"

"I'm not sure about the punishment part. But maybe for pleasure."

"Do you own a butt plug?"

"No."

"That answer was a little too fast."

"Well… A small one."

"You've added a few strokes for the lie, Ella." Damn, she delighted him.

He teased her pussy, stroking her labia. She dug her toes into the floor, lifting her hips, trying to influence him.

"Ella. Ella. I know what you're doing."

She stilled immediately and he pulled his hand away. "Go get the toy. Bring some lube, too, and I'll consider whether or not I'll use it when I shove the plug up you."

She crossed her legs.

"That's not turning your toes in," he said. He dropped his knees and helped her to stand.

"Sir..."

"The plug, Ella."

"Yes, Sir," she mewled.

He watched as she walked up the stairs, taking her own sweet time, exaggerating the sway of her hips.

When he'd agreed to Morgan's desperate pleas for him to come home for the weekend, he hadn't been expecting this. He might accept a few more of his pesky sister's invitations after tonight.

Ella moved around upstairs, and it seemed she was taking more time than necessary. "If you touch that pussy, I will cuff your hands for the rest of the night!"

She called something back. It might have been, "Yes, Sir." But it easily could have been something else.

Within a minute, she was standing in front of him. The slender piece of silicone wasn't much thicker than his forefinger. It would do. For now.

He extended his palm and she gave him the requested items.

"Are you—?"

"Over my lap."

She looked at him.

He raised his eyebrows. "Do you need me to repeat my order?"

"No, Sir."

She stared at the plug for a few seconds before doing as he'd asked.

"We'll continue the exploration of your body," he said. "Reach back and spread your buttocks."

"I'll fall."

"I won't let you." He put his free palm flat against the middle of her back.

"It's been a long time since I did anal," she said.

"If you want me to use lube, you'd better do as you're told and quit stalling."

She lifted her hands from the floor for a couple of seconds, but then she quickly dropped them again.

Pierce waited.

Then she reached behind her with a little more confidence and spread her cheeks, giving him a glimpse of her tiny, tight anal whorl.

"I'm going to keep this in you for the rest of the night," he warned. "Not all physical punishments are about spanking."

"I was afraid of that."

He waited.

"Sir," she added in a faint whisper.

He reached for the lube, flipped the top then drizzled the viscous liquid over the plug. "Relax as much as possible," he informed her. "It's going in, and it's up to you how much of a struggle it is. Bear down." He pressed the tip against her hole.

"I..."

"It's a third of the way in already." He pulled it back a little until she drew a breath, then he pressed forward again.

As the thicker part of it started to breach her, he fucked her with it, creating a rhythm she could cope with but with the progress he wanted.

"This sucks," she protested. "I don't remember it being this uncomfortable."

"Good."

"What?" She moved around, and he took the advantage to sink the toy all the way in.

She yelped.

"You're there." Pierce settled the base between her cheeks. "I like the way it looks. I think I'll make you wear it to my parents' party tomorrow."

"You wouldn't."

"Yeah. That settles it. And a short skirt or dress."

"What have I gotten myself into?"

"I'm rather enjoying it."

"Because you're diabolical."

"Getting more so by the minute. I want you face up on the coffee table." He helped her to stand.

"I thought..."

"That you'd get rewarded with an orgasm?"

She scowled at him.

"I've got a dozen planned for you. How many of them you receive is up to you."

"Is this my incentive to behave?"

"I don't know." He lifted a shoulder. "Is it?" Either way, he was fine with it. He enjoyed being inventive with her punishments almost as much as he liked playing with her to begin with.

He went into the kitchen to wash his hands, aware of her gentle sounds behind him as she moved the toys to the couch and got into position.

When he returned, she looked exactly as he'd envisioned. Her feet were on the floor, her hands dangling at her sides, her tangled hair in that wild mess, her eyes wide, mouth parted, chest rising and falling in shallow bursts, her nipples hard and begging.

In this position, she was open to him, vulnerable. Perfect and compliant. Almost as good as actual bondage. "Show me your pussy."

"Yes, Sir." She brought her hands forward and spread her labia.

"Touch yourself."

Ella dipped a finger into her pussy then circled her clit.

He loved watching the nub swell and turn a dusty pink color. "Keep going."

With a soft moan, she closed her eyes.

"More. Give me a show."

After a few seconds, she began to move her hips. She made faster, tighter circles on her clit. Her breathing became more erratic.

He let her continue until she lifted her hips, tightened her buttocks and slid a finger inside herself. "That's enough."

She pursed her lips but didn't protest. Nor did she move her hand. "Ella," he warned.

"Just a minute. I've been out of my mind since we were at the Neon Moon."

"I said stop."

"But, Sir…"

Pierce could smell her arousal. Was there anything sexier than a woman waiting for a man to pleasure her? "Is there a reason you're being a deliberately disobedient sub?"

That got through to her. She froze and opened her eyes.

"That's better. Now let your arms drop to your sides."

Ella sighed.

With her body exposed and her breaths even, he took a couple of steps toward her then bent over to stroke between her folds.

With a keening moan, she arched toward him.

"So your clitoris doesn't need as much stimulation as your nipples?"

"Not at all. But since I was touching myself, I'm already aroused."

He pressed his thumb to her clit while sliding a finger inside her wet cunt. "And this... Is this what you want?"

"Oh."

"Oh?"

"Yes. Yes, Sir. That's what I want. Thank you."

Her pussy clenched around his finger. Because of the plug in her ass, she was tight, and he was certain that had to make his movements more invasive.

How long had it been since he'd been with a woman this responsive? If he wasn't careful, he might become addicted.

She fisted her hands.

"How close are you to an orgasm?"

"Seconds, Sir."

He moved his thumb even faster and inserted a second finger then started fucking her hard. "Wait for my permission."

"I... No. That's not—"

"Wait." He touched a finger to her G-spot and saw her lift off her heels, silently demanding more.

"Sir!"

"You may come."

His woman—his sub—convulsed. She screamed, arching, seeking. Pierce watched, giving her what she needed until her shoulders relaxed again. Then he took his hand away from her. "I think I've learned a few things about you," he said. "And you've earned more of those orgasms. Now we can play."

"Now?" Ella repeated. Her body had never been more soft or supple, and her mind was at peace in a way it hadn't been since Lance had broken up with her. "Then I'm not sure what it is that we have been doing, Sir." She was already so content she'd be happy to snuggle into his arms. Maybe they could make love before they drifted off to sleep.

"Ella, I haven't even started with you."

His face appeared more relaxed than it had earlier. Tension was no longer grooved next to his eyes. It seemed he'd shut out everything but her.

Pierce picked up the cuffs. She wrinkled her nose. "I don't think I'm going to like this."

"Maybe you will." He took his time securing her wrists. As she'd come to expect, he double-checked that the bonds weren't too tight and that her shoulders were comfortable. Then he attached the cuffs to her ankles. "Damn. These shoes…"

She suppressed her grin.

With his thumb, he made a tiny circle on her right ankle. "I may take them back to North Carolina with me."

"And masturbate to the sight of them, Sir? Remembering me?"

"Ella, there'd be no forgetting you. Ever."

He secured her feet to the coffee table legs.

She lay there, a bit uncomfortable and helpless. There was nothing more thrilling than being this man's captive.

His motions exquisite and tender, Pierce rubbed her breasts and her tummy before flipping the hem of her skirt out of the way so that her thighs were exposed.

She watched him intently, fascinated by the way he studied her. His deliberateness ignited her senses.

Then he picked up the crop.

Ella had been afraid it might appear ridiculous in his masculine hand, but it didn't.

Then she noticed his gaze was focused on her pussy. "Uhm, you can't mean to use that on my..."

"Pussy?" he supplied.

The pretty bright red heart had seemed fun at the store, but now it terrified her. "I'd meant for you to use it on my butt, Sir." Someplace where there was plenty of padding.

"I'm sure you did."

He stood over her and trailed the edge of the heart down her chest then over her belly before dipping between her legs.

Ella tried to keep still and failed. Even though she'd just orgasmed, her nerve endings reignited. She'd never been with a man who understood her or her body this well.

He tapped her breasts, her nipples, her legs, her pussy. Terror vanished as if it had never been there. "Oh..."

Then he smacked the inside of her thigh hard. It didn't burn—it was a dull, achy, fabulous thud.

He caught her again, on the other thigh.

Before she was ready, he brought it down on her already-throbbing pussy. She screamed, clenched her ass cheeks—making the silicone shift inside her—then thrust her pelvis forward, offering her body...her trust.

"*More.*"

"That's a perfect response."

The hurt had been exquisite, maybe because he'd already tormented her pussy so much.

He moved on to her breasts, cropping them, hitting her nipples, making her tremble with the need to come again. Pierce rained kisses of torment down her belly, then again between her legs, not just her clit, but all of the exposed, sensitive flesh.

"What do you want?"

"My clit," she pleaded.

"Be clear."

"Spank my clit with the crop, Sir." She couldn't believe she'd asked for that. Couldn't believe how much she needed it.

"How many times? Just once?" He tapped her lightly.

"Sir!" Frustrating. Maddening. She looked up at him, but he wasn't watching her face, he was focused on her pussy.

"How many, sub?"

"Five, Sir? Six?" *A dozen.*

Just when she was afraid he wouldn't give her what she had been begging for, he parted her labia.

Common sense urged her to backtrack, tell him she'd changed her mind. But raw desire crowded every thought from her brain. "Do it."

Pierce lowered the heart then pulled back and gave her a stinging slap.

She yelled. It burned. It stung. And she ached with the need to come. "Pierce. Sir. Sir, sir, sir."

"Your pussy is bright red, swollen."

"I need…"

He placed the crop on her stomach then crouched to lick away the pain, soothing her, driving her mad.

Tension coiled in her body. "I have to come."

All of a sudden, he stopped.

"What?" She shook her head and pulled against the restraints. "Sir?"

"I like having you this aroused."

"You can't leave me like this."

"No? Having you on the edge will make it easier for you to take the cane marks that I intend to give you."

Cane? Fear wound through the arousal, making her vibrantly alive.

"It's a kindness, if you want to think of it that way." After he released each cuff, he took a few seconds to rub her skin to ensure her circulation was fine.

"Everything's fine. Except for the fact I'm stuffed full of a plug and I need to come."

"You said you didn't have a gag?"

She clamped her mouth shut.

He grinned.

"Let's go upstairs." He offered a hand, and she accepted it.

Even just a few minutes on the wooden surface had left her a little sore.

He picked up the toys and the water bottles before following her up the stairs. The unnaturally high heels forced her to be careful. Between them and the plug he'd mercilessly shoved up her ass, her movements were slow and somewhat exaggerated. She'd never been more aware of being a submissive, never been more aware of her femininity.

This experience was so much more than she could have ever imagined.

"Condoms?" he asked when they reached the bedroom.

"I'll get them." She hurried into the bathroom. Unsure how many he'd need—just one? Two?—she decided to grab the whole box.

He was sitting on the foot of the bed, arms folded.

After placing the box on a nightstand, she stood in front of him.

"Strip for me," he said. "But leave the shoes on."

"You definitely have a thing for them."

"Wasn't joking that I might take them home." There was no teasing in his voice.

Ella reached behind her to unhook the shelf bra. She would have let it fall to the floor, but he reached out a hand to catch it.

Then she unzipped the skirt. She shimmied her hips and the material dropped to the carpet. Then, being bold, she hooked it with her shoe and lifted it.

He took the skirt from her foot. "You'll be the death of me."

Maybe they could meet in hell.

"How does your pussy feel?"

"You had to mention it," she replied.

"And your tight little butthole? In fact, don't answer. Spread your legs then bend over and grab your ankles." He moved behind her. "Let me see for myself."

Pierce, relentless and dominant, pushed on the base of the plug. She grunted in an unladylike way and grasped her ankles tighter so she didn't topple over.

"Looks gorgeous." He turned it back and forth several times, like a corkscrew inside her.

She gasped. It hurt, and at the same time was erotic.

"You may stand."

Even as she did, he stroked his fingers over her pussy.

She clenched, on the verge of an orgasm again.

"Turn toward me."

When she did, he tweaked her nipples, much, much harder than he had earlier, and she cried out. It wasn't so much from the pain as the shockwaves of awareness.

Just when she was ready to plead with him to release her or let her come, he dropped his hands.

"Sir…"

"I want you face down on the bed, Ella."

He picked up one of the lengths of silk.

"Wrists crossed above your head."

"Yes, Sir." Her heart doing a slow thud, she crawled onto the bed and into position.

"I'm going to tie you up," he said. "And give you eight strokes with the cane. You might not think you can endure. But you can. You will. And the reward you earn will make you so damn proud."

Ella buried her face in the mattress. She wanted it every bit as much as it terrified her.

Expertly, he tied the rope, ensuring it wasn't too tight and that she couldn't pull free.

"What's your word for slow?" he asked again.

"Yellow." And before he could prompt her again, she added, "And stop is my safe word."

The mattress sank under his weight as he sat next to her.

He ran his fingers down her spine, between her cheeks, across the backs of her knees.

Then he secured her feet. Unable to resist, she tested his work, pulling, wriggling.

He said nothing.

"I didn't need to worry about your competency with the rope."

"Ella, I know at least twenty ways to tie a knot so that you can't get away, no matter the material—silk, hemp, bamboo, nylon. In a pinch, I can use a pair of your stockings. And I'd be willing to bet I could figure out how to keep you in place with just your pretty bra."

"What other mad skills do you have, Sir?"

"Let's find out."

She thought he might begin right away, but she realized she should have known better. He paced himself, refusing to rush.

He smoothed his hands over her skin before rubbing vigorously. He massaged her deeply, and she knew it was to ensure a good blood flow. No doubt the man was a master at what he did.

"I know you're not all that experienced and it's been a while since you've played, I'm going to give you a few warm-up taps. They won't count toward the eight strokes I promised you."

"Yes, Sir."

As he delivered the first few, she exhaled. She'd suspected he would know how to use the cane, but this exceeded her expectations.

They weren't as hard as she'd feared they might be, but much harder than she'd anticipated.

"When the caning begins, none of the marks will be a third more harsh than the previous one. To manage it, breathe. Remind yourself you wanted it. Surrender. To the extent possible, keep your fists unclenched, your fingers spread, your body relaxed. Going through an ordeal is ninety percent mental. Perhaps more."

"Is that something you have experience with?" she asked. "From your military training?"

"It's about the story in our heads, Ella. If we are convinced we can't do something, then it will never happen. On a forty miler—that's what we call a forty-mile march—you concentrate on each step, not the entire journey, otherwise the pack, no matter the weight, would be unbearable."

She nodded then moved around, getting more comfortable, preparing herself.

"You're delectable, Ella. I love this sight of you. Bound, exposed, hot for me. If you were mine, I'd keep you like this as often as possible."

Sincerity laced his words, filling her.

"The caning is about to begin. Eight strokes. None a third more intense than the previous one."

She swallowed the sudden lump of fear that had formed in her throat.

"Ready?"

"Yes." She drew a steadying breath. "Yes, Sir."

A frightening whistle rent the air hundredths of a second before the rattan marked her right ass cheek. "Oh my God!"

The pain went on and on, radiating, getting more intense.

She squirmed, trying to get away, but from what, she didn't know.

"Gorgeous." He rubbed the ache, and it began to fade. "That was one," he said.

There were seven more to go?

He grabbed a handful of her left butt cheek and squeezed tight. Then, as soon as he let go, he seared her with another stroke.

Her body went rigid.

Just like it had last time, the pain worsened, going on and on. It was relentless, eating at her resolve. After about thirty seconds, the agony vanished, leaving behind a satisfied glow inside her. Damn it. She liked that.

He worked his hand beneath her pelvis then found her clit and began to tease her.

"Oh, Sir!" Between the pain from the stripes and the way she was already aroused, prickles of sensation rushed through her.

"You'll get a second orgasm," he promised as he removed his hand.

She whimpered.

"You have to earn it. As I told you, your pride will make it all the more spectacular."

This time, he laid the cane across both of her butt cheeks.

Ella screamed.

He gave her no time to recover. Instead, he placed another just below it and an additional one above it.

Desperate, aching, she gyrated her hips against the bedsheet, seeking to get away, hoping to grind out a forbidden climax.

"You've got three more, my brave little sub."

Could she do it? Did she want to?

Earlier she'd bravely—maybe brazenly—told him that she'd never come close to needing a word for slow down. That she wanted to be pushed. This was testing everything she had—her reserve, resolve, determination.

He worked his hand beneath her again and zeroed in on her clit. He teased her then slid two fingers inside her hot pussy.

Moaning, she tried to lift her body to give him greater access, but the bonds kept her from gaining any leverage.

Pierce thrust his fingers in and out. "You are so fucking wet, Ella."

The pain from his stripes morphed into need—clawing and consuming.

"The next ones will be harder to take," he warned. "I'll give you those marks you want, and they will be a testament to your bravery. Then tomorrow at the anniversary party, you'll show them to me."

And if they left her that far out of her mind, she wanted it.

"Cry. Moan. Scream. Curse. Whatever you need. Unless you're at yellow?"

A few minutes ago, she might have been. But now... "The way you're tormenting me makes me believe I can take anything."

"Would you like a gag?"

She shifted. "Do you want me to have one?"

"I prefer the sound of your screams to silence."

"Then no, Sir."

"Get to eight, wear my stripes, and I will reward you," he whispered into her ear.

She turned her head to meet his gaze, gaining strength from the depths of his glacial blue eyes. Oh, she wanted what he was offering, all of it and even more. She'd made her decision about sex, even if she had to suffer the emotional consequences later. "I want you to fuck me, Sir," she said.

"Now?" He frowned. "Are you stopping?"

"No."

"So me fucking you is the reward you want?" He feathered across her clit without using enough pressure to get her off.

She'd never been more sexually frustrated than she was in this instant. "Yes."

Adding to the frustration, he stopped toying with her. He plowed his hand into her hair and tightened his fist, pulling her head back enough that he could kiss her, fast and hard, heating her mouth, making her taste his power.

He completed her. Owned her.

"Your responses make me happy."

Slowly, he released his grip.

She inhaled. Tonight…this…Pierce… It was everything she could have hoped for. And more. "Please finish the caning, Sir."

"Nothing would make me happier."

He rubbed her thighs, giving her a clue of his intention.

Ella steadied her breathing and tried to keep her muscles relaxed.

"That's it."

He arched downward, caning her in the middle of her right leg. The tip seemed to bite in.

She screamed, undone by the radiating pain. "Fuck!"

Pierce smoothed his palm across the mark and the heat began to dissipate.

Before she'd finished processing the pain, he repeated the stroke, with the same kind of precision, on the other leg.

Despite all her intentions, tears filled her eyes. She laced her fingers together, trying distract herself. "Pierce, I…"

"One more. The choice is yours, though. Would you like to stop? I will adore and appreciate you no matter your decision."

"No." God, her voice ached from the anguish, filled with tears. "I want it." She had to know. She wasn't doing it for him, but for her.

His hands were on her, all over—her legs, the backs of her knees, her buttocks, her shoulders. He massaged and soothed. And all of it promised a completion that she had to have. She'd never be satisfied if he ended it here.

"Last one. No more than thirty percent harder than the previous one," he repeated.

Again the cane tore through the air before searing her as it landed well below her buttocks.

With a scream, she bucked. The motion forced her sensitized pussy against the bedding, and an orgasm clawed at her. "Pierce. Sir!"

"I've got you, Ella. I've got you." It took him less than thirty seconds to unfasten her ankles, and he spread her legs apart.

He pulled the plug out a little and fucked her with it. It was too, too much. And at the same time, it wasn't enough.

Pierce sank two fingers into her now-saturated pussy. At the same time, he grabbed the silicone by the hilt so he could pound both of her holes.

"Orgasm any time you're ready."

The pain, the sound of the cane and her emotional response to his brilliant dominance overwhelmed her

Sobbing, she shattered completely, the climax obliterating her.

"You're so perfect." He soothed her with his words, with his touch, and with a kiss on the top of her head.

Then... It was over.

She was somewhere else.

"Ella?"

She blinked, and everything around her wore a silvery, shimmery halo. Exhausted, she yawned, then she closed her eyes, surrendering to the feeling of bliss. Every part of her throbbed.

"How're you doing?"

Pierce's voice reached her as if from a great distance. Even then, it sounded fierce and protective, something she could rely on.

He moved his knuckles across her cheekbone.

Startled from the floating sensation, she opened her eyes.

"Welcome back."

She was in his lap, snuggled up to him, one side of her face nestled into his soft T-shirt. Without her awareness, he'd managed to untie her wrists, plump the pillows, remove his boots and sit on the bed, legs stretched out. "Uhm…what?"

"Subspace?" He smoothed her hair.

With a hand on his chest, she pushed away so she could look at him.

Pierce shrugged.

"Do you think?" She wrinkled her nose. "That's not what I expected. I guess I thought that was something that happened while you were being flogged or beaten. Endorphins, like a runner's high."

"The caning was substantial."

"And so was the orgasm."

"You're welcome." He grinned, and it was so disarming that she smiled back, more satisfied than she remembered being in a long time.

"We could do it again to test your theory," she suggested. "See if I can reach it again."

"Are you brave? Or reckless?"

"Both?" She settled again, enjoying the reassuring pounding of his heart. "That was nice."

"Nice?" His lips twitched. "If that's all it was to you, I'm going to have to work on my skill set."

She laughed. "Nice is good."

"Good?" he said, sounding even more scandalized.

"Fabulous, even."

"We're getting somewhere."

"Spectacular."

His arms were loose around her, but the bond was tight enough to keep her in place. She loved it. The caning had been more wicked than anything she'd ever endured. True to his promises, with his approval and encouragement, he'd made each stroke manageable.

When she imagined a perfect Dom, he behaved like Pierce had. It would be so easy to fall for him, or at least this part of him.

Ella told herself to separate her emotions from reality. They had agreed to one night together, then he'd be leaving again. God knew how long it would be until she heard from him again. *If* she heard from him again. That thought crashed into her and she forced herself to refocus. She could worry about that tomorrow. Right now, she wanted to experience everything she could. "You promised me sex," she reminded him.

"I did, didn't I?"

She crawled from his lap. "Should I undress you?"

"Was that a hint that you would like me to hurry?"

"Well..."

He climbed from the bed and stripped off his shirt in a single, upward motion.

Holy hell. From his strength, she'd known he was in shape, but she'd had no idea how honed his muscles were. His abs were hard and flat. He was lean. Rugged. Capable. He had a frightening, jagged scar on his left side, below his ribs. She shook her head to clear it. Just another reminder of what he did for a living and of her earlier, internal warning to avoid getting involved with military men.

He removed his belt, jeans and socks and stood in front of her wearing nothing but tight, navy-colored boxer briefs.

She couldn't look away.

He pulled off his underwear, and the size of his cock made her eyes widen.

"Well, Sir."

"Well, sub?"

Meticulously, he picked up his clothes and placed them in the order he would re-dress.

He donned a condom then said, "Come here."

Long and enticingly, he kissed her. Within seconds, she was hungry for him all over again.

She stroked his dick and he moaned in response.

"I've got to have you."

Ella wanted him every bit as fiercely. "Yes."

As she was coming to expect, with him being such a considerate lover, he made sure she was on the verge of coming before ordering, "I want you on the edge of the bed, with your knees as far apart as possible."

"Sir?"

"I'll show you."

He helped her into position, her ass lifted high, face on the mattress.

"Is this a yoga position I've never heard of?" she asked, afraid of losing her balance, hyperaware of the plug and the fact he'd be able to penetrate her deeply.

"Yeah. I call it the Holden Reverse Half Squat. You might want to practice it daily."

"Is that a threat, Sir?"

"It might be, if you don't do as you're told." Adding emphasis to his words, he smacked her right butt cheek.

"Ouch!" She tried to move away, but he trapped her hips.

"Behave." He adjusted her position slightly, leaving her ass and pussy even more exposed. "Cross your wrists."

Once she had, he clamped his hands over them, pinning her in place.

"I'm going to fuck you from behind so I can look at my marks on you."

Ella wanted him to be as proud of her as she was of herself. "Do me."

His thick cockhead pressed against her entrance.

She looked back but couldn't see him. She was helpless... He could do as he wished, and she shivered deliciously. "Sir."

Chapter Four

Pierce traced his thumbnail over the startling red cane mark on her right ass cheek. Nothing left a stripe like rattan. The sight of it on her delectable, creamy flesh thrilled him.

Ella wanted to please him, and that had made their scene all the more spectacular. He'd watched her every movement, calculated the mental and physical cost of each thing he did to her, wanting to give her the BDSM experience she craved.

And in return, for the first time in his memory, a woman had sneaked past his defenses.

"Sir?"

"Admiring my handiwork." It was the first excuse he'd been able to find.

"I think I will get to enjoy it for the next few days. Something to remember you by."

Her reminder that this was temporary gave him an unwelcome jolt. He wondered if she'd said it on purpose to keep her emotions safe, or whether she meant it more as a warning to him.

Responding, he kept things as light as she had. "One should hope you don't forget me or the caning anytime soon, sub."

"Fuck me, Sir. Please."

He curled his hand around his sheathed cock and teased her still-heated cunt with it. Since the plug was in, the fit would be tight.

Pierce bent his knees in order to slide in a little deeper.

"Yes," she whispered.

He stroked in and out, his cock ready to burst.

This woman, accommodating and challenging, was a joy to fuck.

Finally, hunger driving him, he sank his dick all the way in.

She expelled her breath in a rush.

"Are you doing okay?" Her strength surprised him. No doubt, she was the type of woman he needed to be with.

"Fine."

"Good. Then keep your hands in place." He released his cock to grasp her hips and imprison her.

He slid in and out slowly, repeating the process dozens of times before he shortened the strokes.

"I think you're too big."

"It's just right." He dipped a hand between her legs to heighten her arousal, wanting her to have at least one more orgasm.

"So damn full," she said, voice muffled.

So freaking tight. He wasn't sure how long he could hold off.

Schooling himself, he shook his head and withdrew his cock.

"Sir?"

"I want to look at you."

He rolled her onto her back. "Put your legs on my shoulders."

"And this is the…?"

"Holden Salutation."

She grinned and propped her feet on his chest. "Gonna need some help with this one, big boy," she teased.

Fun. That was something unique to her, making it unlike any other sex he'd ever had.

He lifted each of her legs and placed her calves on his shoulders. The spiked heels added an element of risk that he enjoyed.

After placing his cock at her entrance again, he surged forward, sliding in.

She yelped. "I think you'd better rename this one the Holden Holy Hell position."

"No worries. We'll practice until you get it." He placed an arm across her knees and saw that her hands were curved into the bedding.

Her eyes drifted closed as she gave herself over to him.

He leaned forward to play with her nipples, then moved upward to run a finger across her bottom lip, wanting her to know how much he appreciated her.

"Oh, Sir."

"Go ahead and take it."

Her pussy pulsed and he gritted his teeth to avoid ejaculating that instant. She used his shoulders for leverage to change the angle slightly.

She opened her eyes when she came, and he liked the way heated cognac seemed to spill across the hazel.

It — *she* — could become an addiction.

After she'd ridden out her orgasm, he allowed himself to climax, a sensation that seemed to come from the depths of his balls, emptying them in a satisfying way that masturbation never could.

A final shudder nearly toppled him and he shook his head.

By slow measures, he eased himself from her pussy. "Bend your legs." Before she could protest, he plucked the plug from her ass.

She sucked in a deep breath.

He walked to the bathroom, cleaned up, then returned to her with a warm, wet washcloth.

She reached for it.

"I've got it," he said. Then he added, "Let me."

"I…"

"The correct response is 'yes, Sir'."

"Yes, Sir," she replied, the words more dutiful than agreeable. He didn't mind, as long as she did what she was told.

"Your pussy is nice and red. We should keep it that way." After washing her, then going into the bathroom to rinse the washcloth, he turned off all but one lamp before climbing into the bed. He lay next to her and pulled her close, her soft ass against his pelvis, his arm around her waist.

He needed time to unwind, but he could hold her while she rested.

"What's that against my ass?" she asked a few minutes later.

It seemed neither of them could sleep. "What do you think?"

"I'm just surprised. You can't be ready again?"

"Seems I am." He grinned. When she didn't respond, he continued, "It can wait. *I* can wait." No way could she be ready for more.

"You're accustomed to controlling your body's needs."

"A necessary habit, yeah." He smoothed her soft hair, realizing he liked being in bed with her. How long had it been since he'd done something like this? On some elemental level, he'd missed it.

"You lead a dangerous life."

"It can be," he agreed. "Not always." And in the times it wasn't, he trained hard, ensuring he stayed sharp mentally as well as physically. He couldn't let himself or his team down.

"So why do you do it? Why did you join? I thought you were going to college. Then all of a sudden you were gone. Without ever saying goodbye."

He adjusted her position so that she faced him and he could look at her eyes, the hazel color soft in the dimness. Even so, her face was expressive. He tracked the furrow that ran between her eyebrows. "I wanted to map my own future."

In an ironic twist, once he'd joined the military, he'd had less of an opportunity to chart the course of his life. But it had gotten him away from home, from his father's relentless control.

Long before Pierce was born, Gerard had decided Pierce was going to earn his business degree from a respected undergraduate program in the state before attending a prestigious grad school in Pennsylvania.

Gerard had expected his oldest to intern at the corporate headquarters. He'd started by franchising automotive repair shops, then moved on to ice cream parlors. By the time Pierce was in high school, Gerard had opened a few short-term, payday-type loan stores. Pierce hoped his father had moved onto something less usurious.

Enlisting in the service had been Pierce's best option to flip his family the bird.

His father had been furious at the news. He could have arranged, through his cronies, for an admission to a military academy. At least that way, the Holden name wouldn't have been tarnished. As if enlisting in the army was in any way dishonorable.

"And you stayed in because...?"

Over the years, he'd harnessed his restlessness. He'd honed himself into a lethal, precise machine. He'd been trained to think in terms of targets and situations, not about people and places. At times, Pierce wondered about the cost to his humanity.

Aware that she was still waiting for an answer, he said, "Turned out I was pretty good at it."

"I'm sure. When you focus on something, you're pretty intense."

"Do you have any complaints?"

"No." She tightened her ass cheeks. "Not a single one."

"Good."

"So no plans to get out?"

"I live in the moment." Or he had. And deployment always loomed on the horizon. "I don't look past the next mission." For the immediate future, that meant the beautiful woman in his arms.

"Any regrets?"

"About?"

"The decisions you've made?"

Not until now. "I don't deal in regrets..."

She frowned.

"But if I did, I'd regret not fucking you all night long when I had the chance."

"I'm a firm believer that we shouldn't live with regrets, Sir."

"Are you?"

With a grin, she reached for his dick. With firm, long motions, she stroked him to full hardness. "We have plenty of condoms, Sir."

"Are you sure you're not too sore?"

"Even if I was, it would be worth it."

He dropped a kiss on the top of her head.

While he grabbed a condom, she sat up against the headboard and wrapped an arm around her upturned knees. Her mussed hair flowed over her shoulders and she was watching him intently.

She looked so damn hot, and he was willing to concede that there were things he'd missed out on when he'd chosen not to pursue a relationship. "I want you on top of me," he said, "so I can play with your nipples to be sure you get off. But first, come here and put the condom on my cock like a good sub."

Ella crawled across the bed to him. She wasn't just good. She was perfect.

She took the package from him, ripped it open then placed the latex over his cockhead. "Like this, Sir?"

As she rolled it down, she squeezed and stroked his shaft, taking her time and looking up in a way that told him she knew exactly how enticing she was.

And if he weren't as disciplined as he was, no doubt he'd spill his load all over her hand.

When she was finished, he seized control again, scooping her up. She squealed, and he sat on the bed then pulled her into his lap, facing him. "There's a punishment for that intentional teasing."

"Oh? Is there?" She batted her eyelashes. "Wait. I mean, I didn't do anything on purpose, Sir."

"No? How many strokes did you give me with your hand?"

"Only as many as it took to get the condom on the right way. I wanted to ensure a good fit."

"How many strokes was it?" he asked again.

"Five? Ten, maybe."

"Last chance to be honest."

She gave a heavy sigh as she rested her palms on his shoulders. "Twenty or thirty, Sir."

"We'll go with thirty. My new favorite number for you."

That attractive little furrow buried itself between her eyebrows again. "Thirty what?"

"Strokes. I want your cunt on my dick. Stroke yourself up and down thirty times." He paused for a beat. "With your hands clasped behind your back."

Her mouth dropped open. "I'm not sure I can figure that out."

"I have confidence in you."

"So you're going to sit there and let me do all the work?"

"All of it," he affirmed.

"I thought you were a gentleman."

"Not at all," he agreed.

"So you want me to fuck you. Is that it?"

"You were pretty good with your hand. Now get on with it."

She released one shoulder and angled her body in order to reach his cock. Then she guided it toward her entrance. She was already slick, and her hot pussy wrapped around him.

"Hands behind you," he reminded her.

It took a couple of seconds for her to adjust her knees and body weight so that she could obey his order.

Slowly she began to move, first with short strokes, then longer, more confident ones as she found her balance. She flexed her hips and abs, undulating in a mind-blowing way.

Thirty? He wondered if he would survive punishing this woman.

When she was halfway through, his chest tightened. "Arch your back," he instructed, his words jagged. "I want to play with your nipples." And wanted to distract himself.

With soft moans, she continued to move against him even as she pulled back her shoulders to give him greater access.

"How many strokes so far?" The number was at least fifteen or twenty.

She responded, "Ten."

His Ella was far too clever. *Brat.*

"I need to be sure I've been taught a lesson, Sir."

There wasn't enough time to do that with her.

He gripped her nipples and tugged. Her internal muscles contracted in immediate response, which was hell on his restraint. "Keep going."

She lifted and lowered herself a dozen times before saying, "Fifteen, Sir."

Pierce gripped her hips so that he would have more control over her. He lifted her higher, then guided her all the way down. "Like that."

"Oh… Yes, Sir." She closed her eyes and tipped back her head, following his lead while he squeezed her breasts.

Her breathing became choppy, matching his own.

"Sir…"

He knew her orgasm was imminent. His wasn't far behind. "Keep going. Don't come. Next time, you might want to keep the count a little more accurately. How many are we at?"

"Twenty-nine?" Her voice held a hopeful, desperate quiver.

"We'll start from seventeen."

"Not sure that I can last to thirty, Sir."
"You can."
"I need to come."
"Fight it."
"But—"
"Count out loud." It would distract her and give him an endgame. Through his army career, he'd met numerous challenges, few more grueling than the hellish sandstorm where they'd taken a hit. He'd called on his training to get through. He could manage this.

As she continued, he realized that harsh, tough things were easier to endure than the softness of her body.

"Eighteen."

By the time she reached twenty-three, he closed his eyes to shut out the ethereal vision of her sensual response. Instead, he concentrated on the numbers she called, counting backward from seven to confuse his brain.

"Twenty-four."

Six more to go.

"Twenty-five."

Her pussy clenched him.

Five.

He breathed, but even the air smelled of her, filling his senses, making him think of sunshine. It would be something to remember during endless nights under siege.

She moaned, moving faster.

"How many, sub?" He had to remain in control, even when his grip on reality was fraying.

"Twenty-nine, Sir."

"Twenty-eight," he corrected. "Another two."

She grabbed onto him, and he opened his eyes. Her mouth was parted, her chest heaving.

He squeezed her nipples even harder.

"Now, Sir? Now, now, now?"

"Come for me, sub."

She did, in a heated rush, screaming his name, clenching then collapsing onto his shoulder.

With his eyes closed, having made certain his woman was taken care of, he set his back teeth. He gripped her hard, holding her prisoner as he pressed up inside her tight cunt.

Pierce surged and pulsed, hot cum spilling from his cock. The orgasm was every bit as powerful as the previous one.

Replete, he wrapped his arms protectively around her. "I can't get enough of you, Ella." It surprised him to realize how much he meant it.

"Me, too. I might be sore tomorrow, but it would be worth it."

He held her for a long time before helping her from his lap and onto the floor.

"I've never shared a bathroom with anyone," she admitted, crossing the threshold in front of him.

"Get used to it."

"I'm not allowed to have secrets from you, Sir?"

He met her gaze in the mirror. "When we're together, you're mine."

Her hazel eyes held a smoky look. "Yes, Sir," she acknowledged.

Possession spiked through him, something he'd never experienced with another woman.

After they'd cleaned up and returned to the bedroom, she opened a drawer to pull out a T-shirt and a pair of shorts.

"What are you doing?" he asked.

"I wear pajamas to bed."

"Not when you sleep with me."

"Naked?" she asked.

He nodded. "Naked." Then, not giving her time to voice an objection, he continued "I'll keep you warm. Now get over here."

Together they remade the bed.

She spent an unholy amount of time punching her pillow into shape.

Another person might annoy him with the routine. From her, he thought it was quirky, adorable.

Rather than making her move, he snuggled up behind her to keep his promise.

And he woke up a dozen times through the night to ensure she was warm.

* * * *

Ella rested her shoulder against the doorjamb and enjoyed the gorgeous view.

Pierce Holden—*the* Pierce Holden, her best friend's big brother and her lifelong crush—was in her kitchen, measuring coffee grounds into the filter. He was shirtless. His jeans looked baggy, so if her guess was correct, they were unsnapped.

Without her saying anything, he turned toward her.

Breath vaporized in her lungs.

"Morning," he said.

She couldn't respond.

The sight of him rendered her speechless. In the bright light, his scar was more prominent, a visible reminder of the peril he faced.

She drank him in—his muscular arms, honed abs, trim hips, lean legs. His bare feet spoke of the intimacy they'd shared and his comfort at being in her home and life.

But his eyes... He stared at her, more directly than any man ever had. Pierce wasn't looking at her—he was *seeing* her. Ever since he'd swept her onto the dance floor, he'd allowed her no secrets. He scared her, thrilled her.

When she'd awakened, alone in the bed, she hadn't known whether or not he was in the house. For a minute, she'd been convinced she was alone. A pang of grief had stabbed her until she'd shoved it away. She'd reminded herself that they had agreed to a scene, nothing more.

Then the welcome sound of running water had reassured her...until memories had rushed back. She'd recalled him putting a plug up her ass and the caning that had forced her to scream and pushed her to the boundaries of her endurance.

Then, unsure whether he'd left any marks, she'd rolled onto her side and used her fingertips to seek out bumps. That had been when she'd realized how sore her body was. She'd made a mental note to go back to her yoga classes. Barring that, a bath in Epsom salts would be nice.

She'd sat up, realizing she was nude and that she hadn't gotten cold. And that was when she'd remembered the powerful orgasms he'd given her.

The sight of his shirt and belt draped over her dresser had sent relief swimming through her, and she'd collapsed against the pillows.

If she'd experienced grief when she'd thought she was alone, how would she react when he left for good?

"You're dressed," he observed.

"Nothing more than the robe," she said. That part, she'd thought through.

Because she wasn't sure of her own emotions, and dreading the morning-after, she'd decided that being naked would leave her exposed. It was possible he'd want to put their BDSM scene behind them, maybe pretend it hadn't happened. Part of her wanted the same thing. Another more insistent part wanted it to continue. For the first time, she'd had a scene that had left her satisfied. Now that she'd experienced it, she wanted it to continue.

"Do you have any marks?"

"I think so. One or two."

"Show me."

So he wasn't just a Dom in the bedroom or for a scene. Obediently, she turned. Then, with her fingers shaking, she pulled up the robe.

"Nice."

She allowed the material to fall before facing him again. His eyes had darkened a shade, the blue turning the color of a mountain lake. "I don't think it's a good idea to permit subs to wear clothing at home."

"You don't? Subs in general? Or me in particular?"

"Everything is about you, Ella. When you're naked, it's much more difficult for you to forget that you're my submissive."

"I couldn't, regardless." How could she?

"Boundaries define relationships." He raised an eyebrow. "Evidently, I wasn't clear. Take off the robe, Ella."

With a nervous gulp, she unknotted the belt then shrugged the material from her shoulders.

"See what I mean?"

He extended a hand and she offered him the robe, which he placed on a counter.

"Any doubt about the nature of things now, sub?"

Even his words were enough to make her cunt wet.

"No, Sir."

"Turn around," he said, his firm, uncompromising voice cutting, bringing her back to the moment, just as it had last night. "Spread your legs then put your palms flat on the floor."

Part of her knew it would be smarter to refuse, just have coffee and move on with her life. Every moment she spent with him brought her closer to a broken heart.

Yet his tone compelled her, urging her compliance.

Then she acknowledged the truth. It was much more than his tone that made her giddy. In spite of the risk, she wanted this and his boundaries every bit as much as he did.

She slowed her breathing and got into the position he'd said.

"You have two marks," he said, scraping his thumbnail across one.

It seared anew, and Ella wobbled.

"Wear something short to the party. I want you to remember last night."

As if she could do anything else.

"I've been thinking about how beautiful you look."

"Is that all?" she asked, unable to resist.

"And maybe laying leather across your ass." He grinned. "It's a little more personal since the belt belongs to me." He ran a couple of fingers between her legs.

It took all her self-control to remain in position.

"Fetch it for me."

He dropped his hand, and she froze.

Her motions jerky, she pushed up to a standing position. "Yes, Sir."

Before she could turn, he captured her shoulders. She looked up at him, noting the firm set of his jaw.

"Any man who would keep another woman on the side when he could have had you is a fool. Your honesty, your transparency, the truth of your emotions is humbling. He didn't deserve you."

Though she'd told herself the same things, hearing it from someone she admired and respected was a powerful aphrodisiac.

"Now hurry. I'll add extra strokes if you stall."

She fled up the stairs, aware of him watching her.

Nudity made her uncomfortable, but there was no doubt how right he was. It did reinforce their dynamic. There was something thrilling about her seeing her lover's eyes narrow with desire when he looked at her.

After grabbing the belt, she returned to him.

He was seated on the coffee table. The sound of the coffeemaker hissing and sputtering in the kitchen added a surreal air to the atmosphere.

"This is for your pleasure," he told her.

"Pleasure?" She frowned skeptically at the leather in her hands. "Mine?"

"And something for me to remember every time I put this belt on. Over my knee."

His legs were rigid. She couldn't fill her lungs and balancing was almost impossible.

Pierce clamped one leg over hers, imprisoning her lower body. She tried to put her hands on the floor, but her fingertips only brushed it.

"Your ass was made for spanking," he said.

She tensed.

He stroked her gently.

Tension eased, despite the low-level fear churning in her.

"Perfect."

He gave her a dozen or so gentle hits and chased away the apprehension. She should have known that Pierce wouldn't give her more than she could endure.

Over time, he increased the pressure, and her body seemed to be glowing.

Everything except pleasure and being one with him fled from her brain. Her body became supple.

"Such a pretty sub," he said.

"Oh, Sir." She squirmed as arousal built. "I want…"

"Talk to me."

"Harder."

He gave it to her, not with the ferocity she expected, but a solid, steady, rhythmic beat that took her on that journey inside herself where floating and happiness combined.

She hadn't realized it had ended, but when she blinked, she was against his chest, comforted by the power of his arms.

"You've made it ridiculously difficult for me to get on a plane after tonight's party, Ella."

For the first time, she was tempted to suggest he stay. But she couldn't. Didn't dare. They had an agreement. And she was going to be strong. *Damn it.*

She composed herself, smoothing her hair and reaching for the smile she'd perfected while working at the country club.

He helped her to stand and held on to her waist.

Ella told herself to pull away, but she couldn't make her body obey her brain's orders. "The coffee sounds as if it's finished brewing."

"It does." He seemed as reluctant to let her go as she was to move.

It was as if they were both aware of how little time they had together, and how much each moment mattered.

"Cream and sugar?" she asked.

"Black."

She shuddered. "I forced myself to learn to appreciate it. A lot of times cream and sugar are luxuries."

Another reminder of his self-discipline and the difference in their lifestyles.

Pierce followed her into the kitchen. The man consumed her, from the way her skin bore his marks to the way she inhaled his scent. He'd rearranged furniture, even made himself at home in her kitchen. Intuitively she knew it would take time for her life to become ordinary again.

He'd already placed two mugs on the counter. One was blue, glazed and had a brown moose etched on it. A friend had brought it back as a souvenir from an Alaskan cruise.

The second was one she'd bought on a whim after a bad day at work.

He read the inscription aloud, "I was supposed to be a princess. Seriously. Someone better fix this shit." He traced the gold-colored tiara. "This true?"

"Some days, I wish it were."

"Use it often?"

"No." She shook her head. Then she corrected the lie. "Well. Maybe."

"Maybe?"

"Almost every day."

Pierce filled both mugs. It had been a long time since a man had been in her kitchen. And she didn't remember one ever making her a cup of coffee. She was pretty sure it was the first step toward becoming a princess. If so, she wondered where she collected her tiara.

She added a couple of teaspoons of sugar and a dollop of French vanilla cream to her cup then closed her eyes for an appreciative sip.

When she opened her eyes, he was staring at her. "What?" she asked.

"How do you expect me to keep my hands off you when you do that?"

"Do what?" She looked up at him as she blew on the coffee.

He plucked the mug from her hand and slid it onto the counter.

Heat blazed in his blue eyes, thrilling her and making her molten.

Before she'd realized his intention, he had her back against the cold stainless steel refrigerator.

He grabbed her hands and pinned her arms above her.

Shockwaves of awareness ripped through her.

"Spread your legs, princess."

She did *not* need to be told twice. Ella opened for him.

He fished a condom from his front pocket. She wasn't quite sure how he managed—maybe through the force of his willpower alone—to open the package, lower his zipper and roll the condom down his thick cock.

"Impressive *staff,* Sergeant."

"It's amazing how resourceful I can be when something matters."

"And?"

"And fucking you right now matters more than anything."

He lowered his head toward her and devoured her mouth in a searing, sensational kiss that made her forget her own name.

"On your tiptoes, Ella."

She did as he ordered, helpless to do anything else. Pierce pried her knees a bit farther then bent so he could position himself at her heated entrance.

"You're ready," he said unnecessarily. "Hot. Wet."

"Yes, Sir." Everything about him aroused her. "Fuck me." He must have showered while she'd still been sleeping, and she breathed in his crisp, clean scent, that of spring and seduction.

He pushed into her, impaling her, giving no quarter.

"God, yes," she moaned.

"I could hold you like this all day."

He filled her.

How long he kept her like that, she had no idea. Their gazes met. For a moment, something ghosted across his eyes. *Regret? Doubt?*

While she was still puzzling it out, he began to move. The pressure caught her unawares and she glanced away, severing the connection, the moment lost.

"The minute I get done fucking you, I start thinking about it again. I've been waiting for you to get out of bed. I'd have given you five more minutes, but that's all."

It required all her abdominal strength to take him in this position. He demanded more from her than she'd given anyone else.

It was soul-searing.

He found his rhythm in short, sensual strokes.

She leaned her head on his shoulder, realizing he was supporting her with his body weight.

He overwhelmed her.

With his free hand, he reached behind her neck and tugged on her hair.

He claimed her with another kiss, this one brutal, stealing her breath. Everything he demanded, she gave. Everything she offered, he returned. It, he, this...exceeded her dreams, and an orgasm began to unfurl deep inside. "Sir?"

"Yeah," he said, the word graveled.

Her body went rigid.

"That's it. Squeeze my cock."

She clenched her internal muscles. He rewarded her with a guttural moan, and she rode a wave of exhilaration. Big, strong, special operator Pierce Holden was weak, for her.

And then...

She splintered from the inside out.

"Fuck..." He tightened his grip on her wrists, holding her in place as he surged up, his cock becoming harder with each abbreviated thrust.

His breathing was heavy and heated against her ear. There was no place she would rather be.

She lifted her heels from the floor, leaning into him, trying to accept more from him.

"*Fuck.*" He went still for a second then groaned deep in his throat.

He tightened his hand in her hair.

She adored the way he did her, possessed her.

Her calf muscles were quivering by the time he slid from inside her. She had never been more tender than she was right then.

"I want all of you, Ella."

For her, he was like an addiction. The more she got, the more she wanted.

By slow measures, he released her hair, then her wrists.

She lowered her arms then shrugged away the tension she hadn't noticed until now. After making slow circles on skin, he rubbed her shoulders.

"I think I need a warm bath. I'm starting to fantasize about that as much as I am you."

"You've earned it. I'll make breakfast."

"You don't need to leave?" God, did that sound as desperate to him as it did her?

"I have to help my parents set up. At least that's what Morgan says. But Mom hired caterers. I suspect the command performance is more of a way for them to spend time with me." He shrugged. "I need to get in a workout and a run before I head over there. But I've got time enough for all that."

"Pancakes?" she asked hopefully. "I have a mix."

"Do you have flour? Eggs? Milk?"

"You don't need a box?"

"Just the ingredients."

"There's a cookbook in the cupboard above the stove." She pointed.

"Bacon?"

Her mouth started to water. "I like to eat a big breakfast on the weekends, but I'm too lazy to go out and get it."

"Then it will come to you."

"This can't be real. Pinch me."

"How hard? And where?" His grin made her shudder. He stepped back and she realized his jeans were still around his ankles. "You drive a man to distraction."

"No apologies for that, Sir."

"I suspected as much."

She refilled her mug then hurried upstairs to soak in the tub as he moved around, opening and closing cupboard doors and the refrigerator, clattering pans and dishes.

He didn't ask questions. And if he cursed, he did it under his breath.

Was the man competent at everything?

Within twenty minutes, he shouted that breakfast would be on the table soon.

She took her time climbing out of the bath before drying off. Then, self-consciously, she left the towel draped over a rack in the bathroom.

He was right. Being nude made her hyperaware of her submissive role.

After fluffing her hair, she pulled back her shoulders.

Then, on impulse, she went into the closet and slipped into the high heels that he liked.

When he saw her walking down the stairs, he dropped the spatula.

In that moment, she realized she had as much power over him as he did over her. She looked at the floor so that he didn't see her triumphant grin.

He'd set the table with napkins, placemats, even her nice silverware. He'd added a bottle of pure maple syrup and two glasses of orange juice.

"Pretty fancy," she noted, watching him transfer the bacon onto a platter. "I figured you would have opted for paper plates and plastic utensils."

"And I guessed a princess would appreciate a nicely set table."

"I could get used to this shit. Seriously." She moved a small pile of bacon and a huge fluffy pancake onto her plate.

He put the remaining food on his own plate.

Watching him eat was impressive. Fast and efficient.

In contrast, she wasn't halfway finished when he went into the kitchen to fetch the coffee pot to refill their cups.

He sat back to watch her.

"You're making me nervous."

"Oh?" He took a drink, unconcerned.

She swirled the last bit of pancake in syrup. "This was amazing."

"I cook when I have the chance."

"I'm surprised."

"I like good food. Don't have the temperament to go out much." He shrugged. "So I'm self-taught. Television shows, mostly."

"I pictured you as a man who watches sports or history, maybe even military. But a cooking channel?"

"I have big knives."

"Of course you do."

"And a barbecue."

"Like that old saying, men will cook if danger is involved?"

He lifted a shoulder.

Having him at the head of the table, broad and so tempting, while she wore nothing, made the meal and conversation surreal. "You know, Sir, this whole lack of clothing thing is distracting." How was she supposed to keep her hands off his inviting chest?

"If I was here longer, you'd have more of an opportunity to get used to it."

"A robe would make it easier."

"Things that are worthwhile aren't often easy."

"Is that another of your philosophies?"

"Never thought of it that way." He slid his cup onto the tabletop. "But, yeah. Like the caning you took last night. The end result was that you were proud of yourself. I thought you were spectacular."

"And I had a world-class orgasm." She popped the last bite into her mouth. "Worthwhile."

He gathered the dishes and carried them into the kitchen.

"I'll wash the dishes," she said, trailing behind him. "Since you cooked."

He nodded and folded his arms, resting his rear on the counter.

"Uhm, don't you need to get ready to go?" She rinsed the plates.

"Nope."

She opened the dishwasher and bent to pull out the bottom rack. "You're staring."

"Yes. I am."

"You're being lecherous."

"Dominant," he corrected.

"Dominant? How is gawking being a Dominant?"

"Ensuring my sub is paying attention to details."

"Lecherous," she reasserted when he ogled her ass.

"Maybe. And maybe I'm thinking of a way to fuck you this afternoon at my parents' party."

"No." She dropped the dishrag she'd been holding. "Nope. Absolutely not. Not happening."

"Want to bet?" He came up behind her, snaked an arm around her waist and brought her back against him.

Resistance vanished when he pressed his hardness into her.

Unable to stop herself, she rested her head in the seductive spot just below his shoulder.

"And do you know what else, Ella?"

"Hmm?"

"You're going to like it."

"*If* it happened, no doubt I would like it."

"By this afternoon, you'll be ripping my clothes off me."

She wiggled around, tipped back her head and met his gaze. "You're on, Sir."

He propped the pad of his thumb beneath her chin then captured her mouth in a kiss that devoured her. All of a sudden, she was no longer convinced she could resist him.

Chapter Five

"I want you to wear this one to the party." Pierce plucked a hanger with a little black dress from Ella's bedroom closet and offered it to her.

Her eyes were as wide as they were scandalized. "It's way too short. It's the kind I wear when I go out with my girlfriends. I've never even worn it to work."

"It's exactly the right length. It covers everything important."

"But…"

He perused her gorgeous body, from the fiery highlights in her hair to her painted toenails, and all the delicious, uncovered skin in between. Pierce knew he'd fantasize about this scene in future…a lovely sub, naked for her Dom. "I think it's perfect." It wasn't inappropriate in any way. Since the temperature would be in the low nineties, warm for May in the Denver area, plenty of women would be in similar dresses. "What were you planning to wear?"

She pulled out a blue, flowy thing that would cover everything, even, he imagined, her toes.

"You don't like it?"

"It's fine. For another occasion. Such as..." He searched for an appropriate word. "Winter."

Ella frowned. "It's one of my favorites."

"The other one will be easier to manage when we have mad, passionate, crazy sex."

"Would you stop?" She rolled her eyes. "We are not doing the wild thing at your parents' house."

"Have you seen the way I look at you?"

"Yes." She hesitated. "And with your military training and all, you have excellent control. So it should be easy for you to behave yourself."

"I think you've confused control with stamina." Pierce couldn't recall ever having such playful banter with a woman. He should have left an hour ago. "I could fuck you all day. But resist you? Impossible." Though he was running out of time, he had no regrets. Instead, he wished he had another hour with her. Ella was more than the perfect sub. She was a sharp, beautiful woman he enjoyed being with. There was no tension, no pretense.

He told himself it was because this was a short-term agreement. But he wished he could be sure of that. "Wear the dress. For me?"

"I'll consider it." Before he could give a fist pump, she added, "No matter what I wear, there will be no wild, crazy, passionate—whatever adjective you want to use—sex."

"Wild, crazy, passionate and *unforgettable* sex."

"I've told you—"

"It's not happening," he interrupted, repeating her words. "No way. Not ever. Uh-huh. I heard you. Every word." He grabbed the dress, tossed it onto the bed, then snagged her wrists and secured them behind her at the small of her back. Then he exerted enough pressure to force her onto her tiptoes.

"If that's true, then tell me what else I said."

"I quote… There's *absolutely* no way we are having sex at my parents' house."

"That's right, mister. I'm glad you understand, Staff Sergeant Holden. Sir. No sex at the party."

He captured her lips.

She tasted of sweetness and sass, laced with the inevitability of her surrender.

He explored her mouth, communicating in no uncertain terms how much he desired her. Pierce slipped a hand between her legs, teasing for a brief second. Then he squeezed one of her ass cheeks, hard.

She leaned into him.

"I'll see you this afternoon," he promised as he ended the kiss.

"What?"

He released her wrists then took a step back.

"Wait. You can't do that."

He grinned.

"Leaving me turned on like this is mean."

"Let's consider that stage one in my devilish seduction plan. I'm calling it Operation Fuck Ella Senseless at the Party."

"Operation…?" She gasped. "I'm warning you, Staff Sergeant Holden—"

"You'll be ripping my clothes off," he reiterated.

"I won't."

"Oh, you will. It's a promise." He traced his thumb across her bottom lip. "Do you want to start now? Get a little practice in?" The idea of Ella removing his clothing, one item at a time, made his dick hard.

She placed a hand on his chest. "Do we have time for me to take your clothes off, Sir?"

Not unless he was going to be late.

His bold submissive pulled her hand away and reached lower to grab him through his jeans.

He allowed her to, enjoying every second of her teasing. Moments before he was going to need to unzip and shove his erection into her mouth, he stopped her.

Her eyes were wide, darkened to the color of a fine, aged brandy. *Perfect.* He wanted her obsessed with thoughts of him.

"Are you stopping me, Sir?"

"Yeah."

"But you..." She licked her upper lip. "Don't you need me to take care of that problem?"

"The killer erection, you mean?" He grinned. "Nice try." Damn, he liked the fact that touching him had aroused her. This woman was his match. Now to convince her.

"If leaving me turned on is stage one, what happens next?"

"You'll find out soon."

"I'm not sure I like your tactics." She pouted, her perfectly plump lips tempting him to turn his back on his promise to his sister.

"Ella, Ella, Ella. You haven't begun to see what I have planned for you." He wanted to go caveman on her, claim her, whisk her away, lock her up, keep her naked and submissive. Make her his.

The thought made Pierce's testosterone surge.

His entire life, he'd shaken his head at friends who made decisions based on the reactions of their cocks. But now, he was a poor, miserable, besotted man, humbled like any other mere mortal.

After another kiss that left him restless, he released her. "Don't even think about playing with yourself."

"I wasn't."

"But now you are. And you're noticing how hard your nipples are, how tender your breasts feel. You might even be aware of a tingle in your clit. No doubt you're aroused, and that's made worse by the fact I won't allow you to do anything to relieve it."

"You're an ass, Sir."

"Unapologetic. Unrepentant." He kissed the top of her head. "Before I go, we need to exchange cell phone numbers." So she wouldn't have an excuse not to contact him, he programmed his information into her phone then called himself so that he could save hers.

"That's tricky."

"No need to see me out."

But she grabbed a robe, fastened the belt tight then walked outside with him.

When he looked in his rearview mirror, he saw her on the front porch, her right hand lifted in farewell. Despite their banter a minute before, her lips were pressed together, as if she was fighting back emotion. He fucking didn't like that sight. He'd rather see happiness and excitement on her features. The joy of *hello*.

When he turned at the next stop sign, he shook his head to clear it then focused on the road ahead.

Figuratively, he didn't look back. Ever since he'd been a teenager, he'd charted his course, planned the future he wanted, set goals to get there then went after them with unwavering determination.

And now, he wanted Ella.

His cell signaled an incoming message. Could be from his unit or a friend. Then he grinned. Maybe, just maybe, it was from Ella. At a traffic signal, he checked the phone.

As he should have expected, it was Morgan, reminding him to be at their parents' house at twelve hundred hours.

He replied that he wouldn't let her down then dropped his phone back on the console.

The next time he stopped, he picked up his phone again and proceeded to step two of Operation Fuck Ella Senseless at the Party — give her sexy orders.

Skip the underwear.

By the time the light turned green, there was still no response.

The woman had more reserve than he did. With a grin and to be certain he remained in her thoughts, he sent another.

Remember that I also told you to wear a butt plug.

After parking in front of his hotel, he rode the elevator to his room, where he changed into a lightweight gray Denver Broncos T-shirt and shorts before heading down to the workout room and a treadmill.

Running indoors, with the air conditioning chilling the air, was a luxury he didn't often manage. To stay sharp, he almost always chose to run outside. He had to work in heat and humidity, relentless wind, blazing sun or soul-sucking cold.

He turned off the television and set the treadmill for a brutal pace so that he wouldn't get lost in his own thoughts. Exercise that was too easy allowed his mind to wander. The more challenging the workout, the sharper his focus.

Still, images of Ella crept in around the edges of his mind. And when he inhaled, he imagined he could smell her, femininity curled around demand.

He wished for a moment that his life could be simpler, that she was the type of woman he could whisk off to North Carolina. A few of the guys he knew managed a relationship, even a marriage. But he doubted any of those women had been as adamant as Ella about not being involved with a military man.

Not that he blamed her.

He cranked up the speed, breaking a sweat, but not dislodging thoughts of her. How the hell did they even stand a chance when they'd be half a continent apart?

Even if they weren't, she wanted a life much different from the one he had to offer. He'd miss dinner most evenings.

The buzzer sounded, signaling he'd put in forty-five minutes, though it seemed like less.

He brought the speed down to a jog then a fast walk for a couple of minutes.

After his breathing and heartrate were normal, he sought out the free weights.

A woman in a halter shirt and form-fitting workout shorts sauntered in and caught his eye in the mirror. He nodded back. While he acknowledged she was beautiful with pulled-back blonde hair and a quick smile, she did nothing for him. Unlike the seductive hazel-eyed submissive he'd had up against the refrigerator a few hours ago.

No doubt. He had it for Ella Gibson. Bad. And she was worth whatever he had to go through to get her.

He finished his repetitions then re-racked his weights and heading for the stairs to take him to his third-floor room.

The knowledge that he was going to see her again soon was enough to arouse him. Even though he'd had more sex in the last sixteen hours than in the last two years, he jacked off beneath the cold spray of the shower, imagining rubbing his ejaculate all over her breasts.

Temporarily sated, he dressed in jeans and a casual polo shirt before packing his duffel bag.

His phone rang. This time it had to be Ella.

He glanced at the caller identification. His grin faded. Logan Powell.

He and Logan had been friends for years. They'd met in the service. And he didn't remember Logan calling before.

Pierce swiped the answer key. "Holden."

"Are you ready to quit playing army, yet?"

Like most men he knew, Logan didn't waste time on unnecessary pleasantries — things most people might consider manners. "What you got?"

"I'm planning to get married."

Pierce let out a long, slow whistle. "Does the woman know?"

"Well…" Logan cleared his throat.

Which meant he hadn't yet proposed. "You'd better get with it before she figures out you're an asshole."

"Knew I could count on you to be the first in line to congratulate me."

Pierce imagined his friend flipping him the bird.

"I'm going to need to expand the size of the office," Logan continued, as if the previous exchange hadn't happened.

"Ask Montrose for help. He's a logistics man." Pierce knew little, and cared even less, for administrative responsibilities. He was a tactics and assault specialist.

"We're considering combining forces. We could use a few good men."

Pierce paced to the window, thumbed aside the curtain and took a cursory glance outside. Didn't matter whether he was in Africa, the Middle East or the US. Habits were habits, and he never kept drapes or blinds open. "What do you have in mind?"

"We'll be doing some executive protection."

"I don't babysit or bodyguard." He'd trained for it. Hated it. Everything would be fine until an ambassador's wife wanted to host a tea party that would jeopardize a dozen lives, behaving as if she still lived in the Hamptons and that scones were available on any menu. "Nice talking to you. Regards to Montrose. I'll call him on my next visit."

"And we're working with friendly forces overseas."

Code for official government-sanctioned operations. American and allies. All of which would be denied if something went tits-up.

"There's some homegrown work out there, too."

Which meant counterterrorism efforts on United States soil. *Now* he was intrigued.

"The running track at the high school near your parents' house," Logan said.

"On my way." Without waiting for an answer, he hit the *end* button.

After showering, Pierce packed his duffel bag, checked out of the room then drove to the park.

Logan was already on the track, at the farthest point, running at maybe a five-mile-an-hour pace. The man must have been close by when he'd placed the call and confident that Pierce would agree to the meeting.

Before Ella, he might have told Logan to look him up in the future, another ten years or so, after he'd retired with full military benefits. But now? Couldn't hurt to listen. He could always say no.

He locked the vehicle. Since no one was close, he dropped the keys near a bush, stretched his muscles, more to be sure that he was alone than because his muscles needed it, then hit the track at a jog. Figured it would be three minutes, maybe a bit less, before Logan drew up alongside him, long enough for both of them to be sure they had no eavesdroppers.

Habits. Ingrained in both of them.

Took Logan one minute, seven seconds to fall into step. The pair could have called out a cadence to the synchronized rhythm.

Neither said a greeting.

"Resources are stretched stateside," Logan said.

Budgets and politics. Always a wicked combination. The feds didn't have the time or resources to check out every lead and perform the numerous tasks their fearless elected leaders demanded of them. And no matter who was at the top of the food chain or who was in the White House, or how much information each department said they shared, details slipped by. Connections were missed. And shit got real.

"Takes skilled people who know what they're looking for to sort through things."

During the time he'd been training to be an operator, he'd spent three days in Washington DC outwitting the FBI. Hadn't been easy. But it should have been more difficult. "Not sure why we're still talking. I don't do admin." Pierce had resisted promotions for that reason. He liked field work. He had no desire to train others. No urge to fill out more paperwork than necessary.

"We could use some team leaders. Recon."

"I'm good at stopping stuff." Barging in while others sat in a situation room and waited for updates. "But I have no patience for tedium. I think you're talking to the wrong person." No matter how tempting.

"It wouldn't be what you're used to," Logan agreed. "But you'd be on US soil."

"How often would I be home?"

"Where's home?"

Good question. Until Ella, Pierce had never considered moving back to Colorado. But now... "You have operations outside of Colorado?"

"We do. And we're working on expansion. We've been focusing on the West, California, Las Vegas. We haven't moved into North Carolina yet. Not saying we wouldn't if it mattered to you. But we would need admin, a leader. Someone to get us started."

Pierce shuddered.

Logan laughed.

"Denver area," Pierce said.

"We're looking at a lot of surveillance, gathering intel. Not the adrenaline you're accustomed to."

"You saying I may never throw another flash-bang before going in with live ammo?" Boredom was not something he thrived on.

"Yeah. Could be you'd prefer a root canal to my type of job offer."

"Heard you were shot at a few months ago."

"You sound more interested all of a sudden."

To some that made Pierce a freak. Not to Logan, he knew.

"Got a little too close. My cell phone took the worst of it."

So the position wasn't entirely without risk.

Logan named a salary range that was above Pierce's current paygrade. He'd been planning to hang around the army long enough to retire. This offer was enticing, though, and he held back a whistle.

"You'd still be serving your country."

Pierce realized Logan thought the offer wasn't good enough. That wasn't the case. In fact, Logan's figure held a comma Pierce hadn't been expecting.

Since he was overseas so much of the time, he hadn't spent a lot of money. His savings and new income level would enable him to continue his retirement plans while caring for Ella. Not in a way that Junior could, certainly. But paying the bills wouldn't be a problem. "We'll continue to talk."

Logan nodded. "Job's ready anytime." He stepped up the pace, leaving Pierce behind.

When he returned to the parking lot, there was no sign of another vehicle. After grabbing his keys and opening the door, he checked his phone.

There was no return text message from Ella.

Turned out she might be as stubborn as he was. That would make things interesting.

Time to up his game and move to step three of Operation Fuck Ella Senseless at the Party — denial.

Stroke your clit thirty times. Don't come. If you have to stop so you don't come, that's fine. But the number is thirty. No less. No more. And the correct response to my direct command is, "Yes, Sir."

He tossed the phone into the console then stuck the key in the ignition and drove to his parents' house, analyzing the conversation with Logan, thinking about Ella. Pierce arrived less than ten minutes late.

Is this still step two?

The response I'm looking for is, Yes, Sir.

He was grinning when he entered the house through the French doors in the back.

His father stood in the kitchen, a cup of coffee near his elbow. Instead of greeting his only son, Gerard checked his Yachtmaster Rolex, a watch he wore even though he was terrified of the water. "Your sister said you'd be here at noon."

"Good to see you, too, Dad." *For the first time in three years.* Pierce extended his hand.

As if he had something to prove, Gerard exerted extra pressure when they shook.

"You look well," Pierce observed. Even though the party wouldn't start for hours, Gerard was already dressed in a white shirt. A blue tie was knotted at his throat. He wore a casual blazer and chinos. And, of course, deck shoes to match his nonexistent boat.

Perhaps Gerard had just come from the office. Despite the fact it was Saturday, that was a distinct possibility. Most men opted to work from home on the weekends, but Gerard seemed to use his downtown Denver office as a refuge.

"You are planning to shower and change?"

"Not to worry. I've got extra clothes in the car. Went for a run with Logan Powell." He crossed to the coffee pot and pulled out the metal carafe to shake it. Liquid sloshed around. He didn't want any more caffeine, but grabbing a cup gave him something to do. "He's working with Joe Montrose now."

"Oh." Gerard nodded.

"Thinking about joining them."

"Does it pay better than the army?"

"A lot of things do." The fact he would still be serving his country mattered to Pierce, though. "To some people, it's not all about the money."

Gerard said nothing.

Pierce poured a cup of coffee. Even though it was tepid, it was strong.

"When you're ready to grow up and take a real job, you have a place in my business."

He took a drink, regarding his father over the rim. *Good to know nothing ever changes.* "Don't have the required degrees."

"You still have time for education. Night classes. Online. That type of thing. If getting smart matters to you, you can figure it out."

"Generous offer, Dad."

"Your mother would be pleased to have you in Colorado."

Pierce's thoughts were with one woman, and one woman only. "I haven't made any decisions yet. There's a lot to consider and work out." He took another sip, then put the cup on the limestone countertop. "What needs to be done?"

"It's time you get out of the army. Before you get seriously hurt."

As if the punctured lung hadn't been significant. "Thanks for the concern about my well-being."

"You've had a long enough rebellion, Pierce. Tell me you're ready to join the firm."

"No." Not even for a second.

His father sighed. "At some point, Pierce—"

"I will stop being a disappointment," he finished the familiar refrain.

Gerard shrugged. "Today is not that day, is it?"

He gritted his back teeth. "What does Mom need help with? Brawn can be handy."

"The caterers have most things handled."

No doubt. Laurel Holden left nothing to chance. "So why did I need to be here early?"

"I'm sure your mother will want to move some tables once she arrives home. Last-minute changes. She's worried about how everything will work when the band starts."

"Band?"

"Not a big one." Gerard shrugged. "And there'll be a small area for people to dance. But the catering company will handle the setup."

Pierce nodded.

The soft sound of a car engine rumbled in the distance, and he walked to the window then nudged aside the blinds so he could glance outside without being seen.

"Oh, for Christ's sake," Gerard snapped. "Are you going to behave as if you're in a spy thriller all afternoon?"

"Yeah. Probably."

Morgan parked their mother's sleek black sedan in the circular driveway. And Laurel remained seated until her daughter opened the door to help her out.

Dutifully, Pierce opened the front door to await his mother's grand entrance.

"Pierce! My darling, darling boy! You're home. Home at *last*." She offered a cheek.

As he bent forward to give her the air kiss, he was engulfed in a puff of gardenias and lilacs. The subtle floral blend was her signature, something she'd worn every day since he was a child.

She missed a step as she moved away, and Gerard cupped her elbow.

Pierce met Morgan's gaze. She shrugged, silently saying, yes, mimosas had been served at the nail salon.

Morgan closed the door behind them.

"Where are my babies?" Laurel demanded, facing her husband. "Didn't you pick them up?"

"Babies?"

"The dogs," Morgan supplied.

"Dogs?" Since when did his mom have more than one?

"Gerard," she wailed.

"Sorry, darling." He took her hand. "I was called into the office."

"Which means you passed the groomer's shop on your way home and left them there!" She snatched her hand back. "My God, Gerry. You're a beast." She checked her watch and shrieked. "You could have said something. Anything. They close in half an hour. We can't leave them there. Damn you. I want a divorce."

Some things never changed. His mother wanted a divorce at least once a week. Pierce believed she meant it, too. But she liked her life, her house, her status too much to change it. He couldn't recall his parents ever being anything other than tolerant of one another.

Was it any wonder he'd avoided relationships?

And his sister, too.

"Cancel the party, Morgan," Laurel said. "This time, I mean it. I'm through. I have had enough of your lack of respect, Gerry. You made a promise and didn't keep it. Again."

"We have plenty of time," Morgan soothed. "I'll go and get the dogs while you relax."

"Relax?" She pressed a ring-laden hand to her forehead. "While I'm worried about my babies and company is coming? And there are a million things to do? Gerard Holden, you *promised.*"

"I'll go with you, Morgan." Pierce fished his keys from his pocket.

After quick goodbyes, he and Morgan escaped.

"We should take the SUV," she said when he headed for his vehicle. "It's set up for the dogs."

He followed her to the garage and selected the keys from a hook. And then he saw what she meant.

The back two rows were folded down and the floor was covered with a mattress, along with numerous blankets and toys. "How many dogs are we talking about? She has one, right? Fifi."

"You should be grateful you're out of touch. She's got four of them."

"Four? Who the hell needs four dogs?" He scrubbed a hand across the top of his head. "How do you manage four dogs? Isn't that like a ton of poop? And food?"

They slid into the SUV and Morgan fastened her seatbelt without interrupting his rant. When he fell silent, she responded. "Mom's been getting a new one every year. It's her birthday present to herself. To be honest, I think she does it to annoy Dad."

"That's hard to imagine." He slid her a glance then reversed the SUV out of the garage. He maneuvered around his mother's sedan, Morgan's sports car and his own rental before turning onto the quiet two-lane road.

She gave him a general idea of where to find the groomer's shop in the historic Parker area.

"Since I've been out of touch, update me on you."

"Not much to say." She shrugged.

"Work?"

"It's good."

Could she be any more noncommittal? It occurred to him that he had lost touch, not just with his parents, but with his little sis. And at one time, he'd known everything about her, bailing her and Ella out of trouble, holding her while she sobbed over another breakup, helping her come up with an explanation for an F in algebra. "Love life?"

"Nonexistent."

"By choice?"

Morgan answered in a monotone voice, "No."

"Sorry."

"I keep busy with friends. And I'm going to a speed-dating event soon."

"Speed dating?"

"You know, you go into a room, sit down at a table with a man for a few minutes, see if anything clicks. If it does, you exchange information. If not, you move to the next table after a buzzer signals that time's up."

"Sounds intriguing."

"He said with sarcasm."

"I guess it's better than online?" he asked.

"Yeah."

They arrived at the groomer's less than five minutes before closing time. A woman with dog on a leash nodded at him. He bent to pet it, and the vicious fur ball bit him.

"Lucy is scared of strangers." The woman with hair sprayed so stiff it could have served as a battering ram in a no-knock raid, offered no apology. Instead she scooped up the still-snarling animal and walked out of the door.

"Are you okay? I am so sorry." The blushing receptionist grabbed an antiseptic wipe and offered it to him.

"It's superficial. Nothing to worry about."

"You said that when you were stabbed," Morgan said.

The receptionist's mouth dropped open. "You were stabbed?"

Sliced open was more like it. "It wasn't all that bad."

"You were in a hospital for how long?"

"More of a vacation, really." He told himself that any time he wasn't being shot at, life was easy. But it wasn't true. At times, nightmares gripped him, and he saw the cold darkness in the assailant's eyes, contrasting with the warm smile. The juxtaposition startled him so much he would awaken with a gasp.

It *had* taken a while to recuperate from the collapsed lung. The worst part hadn't been the injury. The worst part had been the fact the rest of the team was out there, doing the job while he was in a bed.

Another woman emerged from the back with four standard poodles.

"Thank you, Lisa," Morgan said, taking the leashes.

"All of those are ours?" His mouth dropped open. They were all white. They looked identical.

"Beautiful job," Morgan said.

"Bikini clip, for the summer."

"What?" Pierce asked.

"There are a number of different ways to groom them," Lisa explained. "Mrs. Holden wanted this so they'll be cool for the party. They'll grow out fast, so she can show Farrah in a couple of months. So by fall, for sure."

He shook his head. How soon until he could get back to his unit?

Each poodle had a ribbon on top of its head. And the color matched the collar, which matched a leash. "How the hell do you tell them apart?"

"Fifi, Bon Bon, Walter and Farrah all have different personalities," Morgan assured him. "Can you hold them while I pay the bill?"

He accepted the leashes as if they were a grenade.

She signed the credit card receipt.

He grimaced when he realized he'd gotten all the leashes intertwined. War was easier than dealing with this wriggling, squirming, prancing bunch of canines.

"You hold Walter, and I'll get the other three."

It would help if he knew which one that was. "Blue?" he guessed.

"Teal."

Of course.

She took the fuchsia leash from his hand, dropped it then worked it free from the tangled mess.

She continued with the pink and purple leashes until she had control of three dogs.

Lisa, failing to hide a grin, opened the door for them.

He used the key fob to open the vehicle then opened the back hatch.

"Walter goes in first."

"Why?"

"You tell me. It's an alpha thing. I figured you'd understand."

"You're right. I got it."

Walter jumped in and then turned around for Morgan to unclip his leash.

"Won't he get out?"

"They love going for rides in the car, so no."

His sister was remarkable, addressing each of the animals in a slightly different tone of voice and using finger commands to indicate what she wanted to happen.

Walter herded each of the other dogs into place as Morgan loaded them in.

"They're complicated as hell."

"Wait until Mom gets another one for her birthday."

"Are you kidding me?"

"She has a deposit on a puppy."

"Another one?" He shook his head. "I'd think one was too much damn work."

"They're highly intelligent, can work out strategy, but yeah, energetic. They have a woman who comes and gets them every day, sometimes twice if Mom is busy. I think having a bunch of them probably isn't any more difficult than just having one."

Fifi licked his forearm then sat, looking at him with wide, bright, unblinking eyes. Her tail was the only part of her body that moved.

"It's love."

Unable to help himself, he stroked the animal behind the ear. Absently he wondered how long it had been since he'd taken time to do something like that. He was out of touch with the smaller pleasures in life, and he was no longer certain that was okay. Being sure the animals were inside, safe, Pierce closed the hatch.

He and Morgan slid into the front seats, then he started the engine and checked the rearview mirror. He saw nothing else other than electric-colored ribbons, wagging snowball tails and an endless sea of white.

He eased forward, and one of the balls of fluff stumbled sideways. "Sorry." Was he really apologizing to a dog? Maybe he should have let Morgan drive.

He turned onto Main Street, and he cringed when something warm and wet slurped up the back of his neck.

"I told you it was love."

He put up a hand for protection. It didn't work. The dog pressed her wet nose against his ear. "Make her stop."

"Aww. She loves you."

He slid Morgan a fierce scowl that made grown men take a step back.

Morgan snickered. "Just drive. They'll all settle down."

He looked at the poodle in the rearview mirror. "No licking the driver."

Fifi woofed and wagged her tail.

"I mean it."

She woofed again.

"Isn't she supposed to do what I tell her?"

"Of course." Morgan nodded. "Just like all females."

Maybe he was losing his touch. He still hadn't received his anticipated 'Yes, Sir' from Ella.

As he accelerated, the animals jostled for position and two of them pressed their noses against the windows. Fifi, however, sat behind him, chin on his shoulder. "I'm glad we brought the SUV. I had no idea. How often do you end up doing this?"

"At least once a week. I don't mind, really. The dogs are always a welcome distraction when spending time with Mom and Dad."

"What's the deal with them?"

"Neither of them are happy."

"They never have been, as long as I remember."

When they arrived home, his mother was stretched out on the upholstered chaise longue in the great room, a throw draped across her feet and a compress to the back of her neck.

Gerard was seated in a leather armchair with a notebook computer on his lap. He didn't glance up.

"My babies!" Laurel kicked off the throw.

The four dogs pranced over to her. Walter took the lead, and Fifi was last. She glanced back at Pierce with her wide, soulful eyes.

"You are all so pretty. All your ribbons are perfect. You'll be the belles of the ball. Well, except Walter. You'll be the stud." The ice pack tumbled to the floor.

Silence hung suspended.

"Aren't they adorable, Gerry?"

As Pierce could have predicted, Gerard mumbled, "Adorable."

"Gerry! Did you even look?"

He gave a half-wave to match his half-smile.

"What kind of computer is that?" Pierce asked. The sleek, titanium-looking case appeared to be both purple and blue and somewhat translucent at the same time. It had a distinctive logo on the back, part wave, part lightning bolt, all linked together. "Is that a Bonds?" Pierce walked over for a better view.

His father slammed the lid closed and placed it on the end table next to the chair. Then he covered it with a magazine about financial success. "Your mother said something about making sure the bar is set up on the patio in the correct place."

"I don't know anything about where it should go."

"Neither do I." Gerard pressed his lips together.

Laurel framed Walter's head with her hands and studied him while talking to her husband. "You know what to do. Make sure it's as close to the house as possible, at an angle so that our guests have plenty of room to walk around."

"Yes, dear."

"Morgan, be a love and fetch me a mimosa. The other one is wearing out."

"Wearing out?"

"Off. Whatever." She narrowed her eyes and waved at her daughter. "Less orange juice than the last one."

Interesting, no matter how ill she claimed to be, her lipstick was always perfect.

Pierce followed his father outside.

The bartender was already there, organizing glasses, arranging bottles of wine and beer on the top in rows, orderly enough for Pierce to appreciate. There were parts of the military that suited his personality. Precision was one of them. "Is there anything ready?"

"Yes, sir. I can get you a beer."

"Isn't it a little early?" Gerard asked.

"Is it?" Not when he was expected to endure hours with his parents. If Ella were here, things would be different. Pierce turned to the bartender and gave her a big smile. "What do you have in a can?"

"I've got a pale ale from a brewery in Lyons."

"I'll try it."

The woman set it on the bar, popped it open then pulled out a glass.

"The can is fine."

Gerard shuddered. "Put it in a glass."

"Can won't get broken." He grabbed the beer then wandered over to a nearby tent.

One person was lining up chafing dishes. Another was placing three big bags of tortilla chips inside an enormous silver bowl. A third person was setting up cold packs.

He lifted the lid from one of the dishes and found it empty.

Gerard walked over to join him, a glass of something strong in hand. Whiskey, Pierce guessed.

"We have some fried chicken inside, if you can't wait until the food is served."

Pierce turned toward his father. "Breakfast was a long time ago." And he'd had plenty of exercise since then. "But I'm curious about your computer."

"Ordinary machine. Came out last year. Outdated now that the new models have been released. You can buy one yourself. There's a store in Cherry Creek. Since you won't have time before you leave again, you can order one online."

"Good to know." He leveled a stare at his father. For the first time, Pierce noticed the grooves etched next to Gerard's eyes, the ridges trenched into his forehead. "Anything you need to talk about?"

For a moment, Gerard said nothing. But he didn't snap an answer like Pierce expected.

Indecision warred in Gerard's eyes.

Perhaps for the first time ever, Pierce noticed that his father's eyes were the same shade of blue as his own. It startled him. And he wondered, with a frisson of discomfort, if they were alike in other ways as well.

Gerard opened his mouth then closed it before shaking his head. "No."

"Okay. You have my number if you change your mind." Pierce suspected both of them would be shocked if Gerard used it. "About that fried chicken?"

They walked inside. Morgan was just closing the fridge.

"Your brother's hungry." Gerard continued to the great room.

Surprise. "I can manage." Pierce opened the refrigerator door. "I don't expect you to wait on me."

Enticement

"As if I would. It's in the green bowl." She picked up the champagne flute. "There's potato salad in there somewhere, too. Oh, Mom wants us to move our cars. The driveway is reserved for guests."

"I'll move them. Mom's, too?"

"Please. Hers can go in the garage."

"Where are your keys?"

"With all the others."

After glancing at the poodle-shaped wooden key hanger next to the back door, he nodded. "Consider it done."

"Thanks for being here."

"Wouldn't miss hanging out with my pain-in-the-ass sister."

She flipped him the bird behind her back as she exited the room. He grinned. She'd done that often while they were growing up, always out of sight of their parents so she could appear to be the perfect child. They were grateful to have one.

His phone dinged and he pulled it from his back pocket. Was it finally Ella?

Yes, Sir.

Air whooshed out of him. Until this moment, he hadn't realized how much the little minx had been winning the battle of wills, and how much he despised that fact.

He waited for a second message. Anything.

A minute later, he figured one wasn't coming.

Maybe he should have told her to call while she was rubbing herself. That would have been better.

Next time.

He typed in a response.

Did you do what you were supposed to?

I was about to. Sir.

Fuck. Maybe he shouldn't have asked. This morning, issuing commands had seemed like a good idea and easily accomplished. Now, though? He wasn't as sure. He'd never played with a sub who left him confounded and horny.

Text me when you're done, Ella.

Are we still on stage one?

What do you think?

I don't know. Yes? Since I'll still be needy if you don't let me come.

It's step two. Saying sexy things, including giving you orders that remind you who your Dom is.

Increasing the stakes, Staff Sergeant?

You were warned.

He prepared a plate of food for himself then took a few drinks of beer while he waited for her to respond.

Done, Sir.

His cock hardened.

You make me so damn proud. How was it?

I think I will walk funny for a while. How about letting me have an orgasm?

How about...no.

She sent back a frowning emoji. He grinned and replied with a picture of flowers and a smiling face.
Right away, as if she'd had it queued up and waiting, she replied with a red devil.
He grinned as he responded.

You're not helping your cause, princess.

She sent back an emoji that showed a smiley face that was blowing a kiss. Because he couldn't stop thinking of her, he sent one more before eating.

When will you be here?

She didn't answer right away. He hoped she was already on her way.
Pierce finished his meal then cleaned up the kitchen before grabbing all three sets of keys to move the vehicles like his mother had requested. He parked his at the farthest spot on the property, near the fence line. Far enough to be almost considered a neighboring city.
After the sedan was in the garage and the sports car outside beneath a light, he pulled out his phone. Ella still hadn't responded.
It wasn't until he was back inside that a ding signaled her message.

I don't know. An hour. Maybe two.

In other words, she was stalling, and she wasn't already on her way.

Drive safe. Let me know if you need anything.

With a frown, Pierce returned to the rental car to grab his belongings, including the garment bag he'd left hanging from the hook in the back. Avoiding his parents, he hung up all the keys then carried his beer upstairs to the guest bedroom.

As he showered, he imagined Ella in that dress, with no panties, a plug up her ass, marks on her legs—*his* marks—and her clit throbbing from her teasing.

He stroked his hard shaft a few times, but he stopped after thirty strokes, figuring he would endure the same torture he was putting her through.

Seconds later, teeth gritted against the incessant demand of his dick, he shut off the shower then vigorously dried himself with a towel.

He shaved then dressed before heading downstairs.

"What the hell?" His sister dropped a set of sketches on the kitchen counter. "I didn't know you owned a suit."

Until last week, he hadn't. "I dress up all the time."

"Uh-huh."

"Have you noticed Dad behaving strangely?"

"More so than usual?" She shook her head.

"He seems secretive about his computer."

"He was probably working and didn't want Mom to know."

"I asked if I could see it."

"It's a Bonds."

As if that explained everything.

She shrugged. "You know Dad. He's always working on something new. And he never tells anyone what he's up to."

Their mom had never complained, as long as there was money in the joint account.

Pierce fished a handful of nuts from a small glass bowl.

"Do you ever stop eating?"

"Worked out earlier."

"I should have known."

"What are you looking at?"

"Mom's thinking of adding a pool and a guesthouse with a place to change downstairs and a small apartment upstairs."

"Four thousand square feet isn't enough?" He picked up the top sheet.

"It gives her something to focus on. And maybe she hopes you'll come home more if you have a separate place to stay. I'm going to get changed."

Fifi wandered into the kitchen and leaned against him. Fortunately, she didn't get any hair, or fur, whatever it was, on him.

The doorbell rang. A cacophony of barks erupted, bouncing off walls. Sixteen paws scrabbled over the wooden floor as all four dogs dashed to the foyer.

"Traitor," he muttered as Fifi dashed away.

After putting down the drawing, he wandered toward the door in time to see his mother glide down the staircase wearing a designer dress with pumps. Her pearls were as perfect as her smile.

The bell chimed again, reverberating as if they were in a cathedral.

Gerard held out a hand toward her. "Shall we, darling?"

She pressed her fingers to the palm of his hand, and they smiled at each other as if they were a happily married couple anticipating another glorious and successful thirty years.

His father opened the door.

Game on.

Chapter Six

Ella raised her hand to ring the doorbell of the Holdens' house—more of a mansion than a home—then dropped it again to smooth her dress, pretending she wasn't shaking.

More than once she'd been tempted to text Morgan and Pierce with an apology, saying she wouldn't be in attendance. She'd rehearsed a dozen excuses, from a headache to a sprained muscle, to a forgotten commitment. But the truth was, she didn't want to see Pierce.

Even though they hadn't spent a lot of time together, she was already falling for him. That had to make her either mad or stupid. She'd had enough of military men.

What they had shared last night and this morning had been so much more than hot sex. He'd known what she needed and had given it to her. She'd had an emotional connection with him that undid her. Raw need for him made her shove rational objections into a deep dark dungeon. It was as if her inner devil had locked the door and tossed the key over her shoulder with a satisfied wink.

But every time she'd picked up the phone to make her excuses, there'd been a message from him, and her resolve had crumbled.

As she'd slid into the dress he'd selected and struggled to get the damn plug up her ass, she'd accepted that she wanted what he was offering…the teasing, the orgasms, the sensual, trusting dynamic.

And, at least for today, her desire outweighed the inevitable pain she'd experience tomorrow.

Before doubt crawled through her mind yet again, she pressed the doorbell.

Barks exploded behind the door.

Too late now.

She curled both hands into a death grip around her clutch.

Mr. and Mrs. Holden opened the door, and Walter pushed through the opening to jump up on her.

"Down!" Mrs. Holden shrieked.

Walter didn't even look at his owner.

All her tension gone, Ella scratched him behind the ears. Nothing soothed like Walter's demonstrative, unconditional love.

"He never behaves like that with anyone but you." Laurel Holden shook her head. "Be a dear and don't encourage him, Ella."

"I'm sorry, Mrs. Holden."

Laurel grabbed the dog's collar and tugged him back. "If you make me ruin my manicure, you naughty, naughty boy…"

Ella petted all the dogs, ending with Fifi—well, the one she assumed was Fifi since she patiently waited her turn.

"Come in out of the heat." Gerard allowed his wife to struggle with the animals while he held the door open farther. "You could put up the childproof gates, Laurel."

"They will go mad if we close them off from our company."

"Better them than me." He smiled big.

"Did you say something?" Laurel turned big, unblinking eyes toward him.

Gerard closed the door. "Nothing at all, dear."

"I didn't think so."

Ella looked away so the couple didn't see her grin.

"You're welcome to put your purse on the bench," Laurel said.

The bench was a stunning, custom-carved piece that dominated the entryway, built into the wall with a row of hooks above a long, thin mirror.

"There's a bar outside," the woman continued. "And we'll begin serving food in about…"

Responding to the prompt, Gerard checked his watch. "Half an hour."

"Morgan's here somewhere."

As was Pierce.

Nerves turned her stomach inside out.

Just the thought of being the focus of his attention made rational thought impossible.

The doorbell resounded once more and the dogs again exploded in frenzied barks. Ella excused herself. She placed her purse on the bench then pulled back her shoulders in a fake sign of poise.

Knowing a glass of wine would help her relax, she walked through the house toward the back door.

She thought she was prepared to see Pierce. But the sight of him, near the fireplace, made her heart stop. She paused, her gaze riveted on him.

He wore a fitted dark-gray suit with a silver tie and snowy-white shirt. Ella wouldn't have believed it was possible for him to look any more devastating than he had in denim, but he did.

His slender but muscular body was spectacular and irresistible in the tailored silk. She wondered if the suit was stage three of his plan to fuck her senseless this evening.

As if sensing her, he turned away from the man he was conversing with.

His gaze found hers.

Even across the room, his arresting blue eyes blazed with intensity. A slow smile sauntered across his mouth, and sexual heat poured through her, notching up from simmer to a slow boil.

He perused her and a slow smile slid across his face. No doubt he was wondering if she'd inserted the plug and skipped the panties as he'd instructed.

Every noise in the room amplified in her ears as her nerves slammed into hyperawareness, fueling her need to escape.

Knowing he'd seek her out soon, she exited through the French doors onto the patio.

The temperature already hovered near ninety degrees, and numerous large, colorful umbrellas had been opened.

She ordered a glass of chardonnay from the bartender then headed toward the water feature that Mrs. Holden had installed last year, a stunning waterfall and pond. An aspen tree provided some shade, and she took a fortifying sip of the wine.

"So. Did you go home with him?"

At the sound of Morgan's voice, Ella spun. "What?" She glanced around the Holdens' patio, hoping none of the anniversary party guests had overheard her friend and praying that no one knew she and Pierce had spent the night together.

Morgan clamped her arm on Ella's elbow and dragged her closer to the waterfall for privacy. A small brown sparrow that had been splashing on top of a rock shook its wings then took flight.

"Details." Morgan kept her grip tight, as if afraid Ella would try to run away. "All of them."

"About...?"

"What happened last night after I left the bar?"

Ella's pulse picked up as she scrambled to find an answer that would appease her friend.

"You know what I'm talking about." Morgan rolled her eyes. "Randall."

Randall. So Pierce hadn't said anything. In relief, Ella exhaled. "There are none. I didn't go home with him."

"Thank God. I was worried about you. He gives me the heebies." Morgan shuddered with exaggerated movements.

Ella grinned. Though she hadn't been captivated with him, she'd been looking at him through a realistic lens, inventorying faults as well as strong points, trying to ascertain whether he was a man she would want to date and perhaps spend her life with. He might have been egocentric, but so were a lot of men she interacted with at the country club. It didn't mean they were bad guys. "What don't you like about him?"

"He didn't honor a sub's safe word at a BDSM play party."

The voice, masculine, calm, familiar, made desire arrow through her.

Pasting on a false smile, the one she wore almost all day, every day during the work week, she turned to face Pierce. She inhaled his crisp scent and memories crashed through her. Bravado fled, and her knees threatened to buckle.

"Ignore my big brother," Morgan apologized. "He says inappropriate things."

If Morgan had any idea...

"Ella." He extended a hand.

Having no choice, unless she wanted to make Morgan suspicious, Ella shook his hand. He held hers for too long, squeezed, but not too hard, just a reminder of how well he knew her and what they'd shared.

"I'm glad you could be here."

Since he didn't let her go, she tugged away from his grip. "I wouldn't have missed it." The lie fell from her mouth. Her voice hadn't wavered and betrayed her inner emotions.

"Is that true about Randall?" Morgan asked him. "I've heard things about him from some of my friends, but that's not one of them."

"It happened."

"Ick." Then Morgan propped her hands on her hips "Wait." With a fierce scowl, she demanded, "How do you know it's not just a rumor?"

"I was there."

"What?" Morgan screeched. "What were you doing at a BDSM club, anyway? And Randall is a Dom?"

"No. He's a fake. That makes him a menace."

"Hold on a minute." She narrowed her eyes. "Which club are we talking about? One in Denver?"

"None of your business, little sis."

"I need details, Pierce. And I mean it."

"What do you know about BDSM clubs?" He raised his eyebrows.

Ella took a drink of wine to hide her smirk.

"Mom's waving at you."

"Again?" Morgan sighed, glancing toward the tent where Laurel was standing next to the caterer.

"I think she wants another mimosa. Or something."

"Oh. God. I'll be right back."

"That was mean." Ella frowned at Pierce when Morgan strode off, steps certain over the uneven flagstone surface. "Your mom wasn't even looking this direction."

The smile on his face was unrepentant. "She's going to need something sooner or later."

"Still—"

"I wanted to be alone with you." He took a step toward her, crowding her space.

Tension unfurled in her, triggering the fight or flight instinct. She did neither. Instead, she froze.

Everything about this man fascinated her.

While she'd been at home, she'd told herself she could, would, resist him. But when he stood scant inches away, and they breathed the same air, her intention was crushed.

"I've been looking forward to seeing you again since I left your house."

"Planning your strategy is more like it." She kept her words light, hoping to wedge some emotional distance between them.

"Yeah." He raised one shoulder. "It might be time to move into stage three of Operation Fuck Ella Senseless at the Party."

"Wait." She pretended to be a woman in control, someone accustomed to this kind of raunchy flirtation. "What was stage two?"

"Saying sexy things. Reminding you who your Dom is."

"Do you behave this way with all the women you pursue?"

"I don't pursue women. Or I didn't…until you."

"Are you saying—?"

"That you're different? That I'm different when I'm with you? That I've never experienced anything like this before?"

She waited.

"Yeah. All of those things."

Ella couldn't breathe. This man. Every word was well chosen and perfect, further eroding her resistance to him.

"You look beautiful, Ella. As I knew you would."

When he spoke, he studied her, sealing the connection of their gazes, as if there were no other person on the planet who interested him.

"The dress…"

He'd made an excellent choice, she had to admit. It flowed nicely, but it was fitted enough that the gentle breeze didn't lift it.

Before she'd left the house, she'd raised the hem and looked in the mirror. It had taken some contortions to see over her shoulder and angle her head so she could ascertain whether he'd left a stripe on her skin. He had. One.

"And did you wear panties?"

Stage two, say sexy things. Even though she knew what he was doing, the strategy still worked. Her pulse became thready. Ella knew she'd reacted as he'd intended. "I skipped them."

He sucked in a breath. "And the plug?"

Distracting her, Walter dashed through the open French doors and headed toward her. He angled his tall, strong body between her and Pierce, as if trying to protect her. "Hello, Walter. Have you come to say hello again?"

She swore he gave her a doggy grin. Walter plonked himself down, one of his legs on her foot, as if he were a prince and had every right to sit wherever he liked. Ella placed her glass on one of the waterfall's rocks and scratched him behind an ear. "I think he's protecting me."

"It will take more than a dog to keep me away from you." Pierce's smile was feral. She shivered. "About the plug, Ella...did you follow my order?"

She took a breath. When he used that tone—command, wrapped in a sensual huskiness—she was undone. "I did."

"Yes?"

"Yes, Sir," she amended. As she said the words, something inside her shifted. Her voice became softer. She wanted to please, to surrender. Her reaction to him was as much physical as it was emotional.

She met his gaze. The approval and longing there made her glad she hadn't disappointed him. "I inserted the plug." Another in a long line of firsts for her with this man. Being both bare and stuffed for him was exhilarating. The way he pushed her past her inhibitions was liberating. And each time she did something new, it undermined her determination not to fall for him. Then she shocked herself by adding, "And I re-waxed my pussy, as well, Sir."

"Fuck." He uncapped a water bottle and took a long drink.

"Maybe you shouldn't have asked, Staff Sergeant?" *Stage two, Sir. Say sexy things.* She just had no idea how difficult it was to be bold this way. Teasing him turned her on.

"You're playing a dangerous game."

"Am I?" Maybe she was. Since they had such a short time together, it was worth it.

"You already know I intend to fuck you."

"And I've already said not that's not going to happen." She picked up her wine, and Walter nuzzled her free hand.

When Pierce spoke, his tone vibrated with a deep, soft rasp. "Did you stroke your clit?"

When she'd first read the text, she'd thought her phone might start to sizzle from the heat of his words. "I did. Sir."

"And?"

"It aroused me." He had to know that. "But not as much as the way you kissed me and played with me before you left my house this morning."

"How turned on are you right now?"

Ella tightened her grip on the glass.

"Scale of one to ten. One being tepid."

"And ten...?"

"Ready to come the second I slide my finger between your legs."

She shouldn't have asked.

"Eight?" he guessed. "Nine."

Nine and a half. "Five or six."

His lips quirked. No doubt, he recognized she was lying. "Shall we see, princess?"

"No!"

Walter jumped to his paws.

Scandalized, she glanced around the patio and exhaled when she realized no one was close enough to hear.

She petted Walter to soothe him. But Pierce's smile was broader than ever. Damn him.

"So what's the real answer, Ella?"

"Nine."

"Meaning it would take me a minute or two to get you aroused?"

She closed her eyes. "Closer to a ten."
"It's a ten for me."
"What?"
"I thought of you in the shower."
"Did you...?"
He waited.
"I mean..."
"Ask."
Walter sat again, and she angled her chin. "Did you jack off?"
"Yeah. But I didn't come. I fantasized about you, about seeing the mark I hope is on your skin, about the thought of you playing with yourself, about giving you everything you want."
One more time before he left. So tempting. So wrong.
Mr. and Mrs. Holden emerged from the house and stood near the food tent. Walter seemed to forget about Ella and dashed over to his owners. The other dogs gathered around him and jockeyed for position.
Morgan, composed and gorgeous, stood in front of the dogs, got their attention and signaled for them to sit.
As if choreographed, they all plonked down at the same time, looking regal and impressive.
After giving another hand signal, Morgan walked off to one side. A few people snapped cell phone pictures, and she wished she'd held onto her purse.
Mrs. Holden waved a hand, and her numerous rings winked in the overhead sun. "Thank you for coming to help us celebrate our thirtieth anniversary."
The crowd clapped, and a few whistles split the air, making Bon Bon tip her head.

Pierce moved into place beside Ella, as if they were a real couple. She liked having him next to her so much that it terrified her.

"Please help yourselves to food," Mr. Holden said. "Later, we'll have cake, a champagne toast, and a band."

The caterers pulled back the siding on the tent, removed lids and cellophane then left the area.

"Shall we?" Pierce extended a hand toward the tent.

Nothing could have surprised her more. "You need to interact with other guests."

"I will do that later. For now, I like watching you, imagining the plug in you."

While embarrassment gnawed at her, he grinned then picked up his water bottle as if he hadn't said something scandalous.

She gulped down the rest of her wine before handing the empty glass to one of the servers.

In the buffet line, he introduced her to several of his parents' friends, and as they walked toward a table, he rested his fingers at the small of her back. He'd done it at the bar, as well. She found it protective and possessive as well as endearing.

He guided her toward a table with a few empty seats. "Is this okay?" He pulled back a chair for her.

"You don't have to sit with me, Pierce."

He scowled. "Of course I do. I take care of my woman."

She appreciated seeing this side of him, interested in others and asking thoughtful questions, all while glancing over at her on numerous occasions and being sure to include her in the conversation.

When asked what his job was, he kept his answer vague, making it sound as if he spent his days buried in administrative responsibilities.

"Watch out for those paper cuts, Holden," one man said. He laughed at his own joke.

"Keep a first-aid kit in your desk drawer," another added.

Pierce took a drink of water then leaned forward to ask the person across from him how business was.

Not long after dinner, some people, especially those with kids, began to leave.

The catering crew removed some tables and rearranged others. At the same time that the band was setting up, two men brought in big panels that resembled wood but seemed thin and somewhat flexible. They laid them over the flagstones and taped the seams together to create a dance floor.

"You don't mind that teasing?" she asked him later, after the Holdens had sliced their cake and champagne had been shared.

He shook his head. "They don't matter in my life any more than they did ten years ago. You, on the other hand…"

The band started, playing a slow, easy-listening song made popular by Otis Redding decades ago.

"Dance with me."

Tonight, it was an invitation rather than the order it had been at the honky-tonk. "I can't believe you want to dance."

"I don't. But I want you in my arms, and I figure it's the only way you will let me put my hand on your ass."

She grinned.

"Is that true?"

From beneath her lashes, she looked at him. "It could be."

He stood then offered his hand, followed by his irresistible grin.

Instead of leading her in the direction of the makeshift dance floor, he surprised her by guiding her toward the privacy of the waterfall…which, she told herself, she should have expected.

Overhead, the sky was pink and orange, with beautiful swirling clouds, as the sun set behind the Rocky Mountains. The temperature had dropped a couple of degrees, so she didn't object when Pierce held her close.

As he had last night, he led, but not in a dance step that she knew. This was more of an intimate sway. Without being told, she responded, lifting onto her tiptoes to lean into him and wrap her arms around his neck.

"Perfect." He pressed one palm to the center of her back with his fingers splayed. Then he moved the other to her bottom. "I could keep you here forever."

A lump lodged in her throat. There was nothing she wanted more. The impossibility of it made her heart hurt.

The instinct for self-preservation urged her to pull away. But the yearning to be with him won. Ella reminded herself that once he left, she would hurt anyway. Might as well make it worthwhile.

They moved together, as if they were in a private, magical world created for the two of them.

"You've gotten to me, Ella. Being here with you instead of alone somewhere is torture."

"Good."

"You've got an evil streak." The words, said into her ear, sent a shiver skipping down her spine.

In exaggerated shock, she asked, "Do you want me, Staff Sergeant?"

"Is it obvious?"

"You left me wanting earlier." And the need had continued all day.

"I've warned you about your dangerous game."

She smiled, enjoying the banter. For the first time in her life, she rested her head on a man's shoulder, knowing she was safe, protected. For now, she wanted to savor the moment.

All too soon the music faded. They swayed to a stop several seconds later, when others were returning to their tables.

He tucked her hand inside his as he led her back to their chairs. She'd never been with a man as attentive as he was.

As he had earlier, he pulled back her chair. "Would you like another glass of wine?"

"No." She shook her head. "I need to drive home."

"Holden, there you are!" A tall, thin man with a receding hairline rushed over and stuck out his hand.

Pierce stood. "Harold Loughton? Haven't seen you in years."

"Since I was in high school."

The two shook hands.

"What the hell are you up to? I know your dad wants you to join the firm."

"May I introduce you to Ella Gibson? She's a longtime friend of Morgan's and mine. Ella, Harold Loughton. His father was in business with my dad. Harold went to work for the company after he graduated from college, if I remember?"

"Yep, yep. You're absolutely right." Harold nodded. "Good to meet you, Ella."

The man grasped her hand and squeezed with far too much enthusiasm. She extracted herself from his grip without responding to his greeting.

"Mind if I join you?" Without waiting for an answer, he grabbed a chair, turned it backward then sat. Harold bounced his right leg, radiating perpetual-motion energy. "You still at Fort Bragg?"

"Yes." Pierce uncapped his water and took a drink. She watched the way he looked at Harold. Cautious, questioning, distant.

"Aren't you bored out of your mind? Ready for some real work? You know, you could make a difference in the world. I'm still working for your dad's company. VP of Accounting. But I don't go around bragging."

"No?"

"Trying to keep all the money straight. He's expanding again. Enough work to keep an army busy. Get it? Keep an army busy. And you're an army guy!"

She wondered if the man ever took a breath.

"We could use someone to train store managers. I'm betting you've been taught some leadership skills. At least that's what some of the veterans we've hired say about the service. Platoons and units and all that."

"All that," Pierce echoed, sounding as if he were in agreement.

"Hey, I'm serious, man. We could use some brains at headquarters."

Since Harold seemed to be settling in for a long visit, she excused herself.

Pierce stood and squeezed her hand. "I'll find you."

"Don't worry about me."

"I'll find you."

Since arguing with him would serve no purpose, she nodded. "It was nice to meet you, Harold."

He lifted a hand in acknowledgment but continued talking to Pierce.

She visited with a few people as she made her way across the patio. Since Morgan was occupied, Ella decided it was a strategic time to leave. Better than saying goodbye to Pierce. *That,* she wasn't sure she had the strength to do.

After looking over her shoulder to confirm he was still talking with Harold, she found Mrs. Holden. Since the dogs were gathered around their besotted owner, Ella petted them all, giving Walter a little extra attention. He angled his head to make it easier for her to scratch behind his ear. Smart boy. "Thanks for inviting me. I had a wonderful time. The food was great. The band is fabulous. You throw the absolute best parties."

"I'm glad you could make it." Mrs. Holden pulled her shoulders back, preening at the effects of the compliments. "You'll have to join Morgan and me for mani-pedis some Saturday morning. They serve mimosas."

"I'd enjoy that." Before heading inside to collect her purse, she added, "Happy anniversary."

Ella's hand was curved around the front door knob when Morgan caught up to her. "Wait! Don't you even think of walking out of here without talking to me!"

She dropped her hand and turned to face her friend. "That was a great party, Morgan. Everything was perfect."

Morgan narrowed her eyebrows. "Did I see you dancing with my brother?"

"Yeah." She might as well admit it so Morgan would leave her alone. "It was a pity dance. He saw me standing there alone with only Walter for company." It hadn't happened in quite that order, but she didn't mind playing loose with the facts.

"That didn't look like a pity dance to me."

"I haven't got a clue what you're talking about."

"I know what I saw."

"You saw your brother being polite."

She cleared her throat. "As if. The words Pierce and polite don't belong in the same sentence. I'm telling you, this conversation isn't over. I want answers."

"There's nothing to tell. You need to get back to your guests."

Morgan's scowl grew fiercer, more determined.

"Go." *So I can get out of here before Pierce notices I'm gone.*

"I'm telling you…"

"You already made that threat. You need a new one." Ella grinned and hugged her friend. "Give me a call."

"Don't think I won't."

"Not ever," Ella promised. She fished her keys from her clutch then left the house, closing the door behind her with a decisive click.

She paused on the porch to draw in a breath. Then, before Pierce could come after her, she walked toward her car. Since so many people had already left, her car was isolated in the distance. The outdoor lighting was faint as she moved away from the house and no moon brightened the sky.

When she neared her car, she pushed a button to unlock it and turn on the interior lights.

She froze. Pierce stood next to the driver's door, arms folded, his expression unreadable in the dimness. She sucked in a short, uneasy breath.

"Did you think you could escape without me noticing?"

"I hoped," she admitted.

"Because…?"

"Please, Pierce. I can't do this."

"Do what? Leave without letting me kiss you goodnight?"

She took a shallow breath. "You're dangerous."

"What harm can there be in one kiss?"

The question hovered on the night air. Because she knew the answer, she remained silent.

"Come here."

Yes. In the end, it wasn't a battle. She dropped her keys into her purse then went to him. And now that she was so close, she could read him better, saw the set of his jaw and the hurt in his eyes. *Hurt?* How was that possible? She'd expected frustration, maybe even anger. But the raw flash of honest emotion made her wonder if this might be more than a simple weekend affair for him.

"Damn it. It's impossible for me to think of anything else when you're around."

The car's interior light faded, and the darkness seeped around them, leaving them shrouded in privacy.

Pierce put his hands on her shoulders and guided her around so that her back was to the car, using his body to shield hers. No casual passerby would see who he was with.

"A gentleman to the end."

"You're my woman."

As if that says it all.

He feathered his fingers into her hair and pulled back her head. Then he nudged a knee between her legs. "Open your mouth."

She surrendered...because she wanted to more than she wanted to hold on to her sanity.

Pierce touched her tongue with his own, in a seductive dance, and he tightened his grip. She was aware of the band still playing in the far-off distance, an upbeat song that electrified the night.

The kiss—his kiss—was hard and deep, devouring her, communicating the words he hadn't said, the promises he wanted to make but never would. It wasn't enough for her.

Ella returned his kiss and opened her mouth wider. She lowered herself so that her pelvis was a fraction of an inch above his thigh. He put his hand on her back for support.

The touch of her bare pussy to the rough material covering his muscled leg almost made her come. She groaned. She knew he had a plan to seduce her and was so confident of it that he'd told her all the stages. He'd aroused her, said sexy things, reminded her she was submissive. No doubt he had moved onto the third step, and so far, it was working.

Without shame, she rubbed herself against him.

He murmured something indistinct, but she recognized it as encouragement. She rocked her hips forward and her labia parted, exposing her clit. The plug shifted deeper, filling her more.

Pierce ended the kiss, leaving her mouth swollen, her lips parted. He pulled her hair harder, forcing her to arch her back. She gasped and shifted her position.

"That's it. Rub yourself on me."

Operation Fuck Ella Senseless at the Party... Heightening her arousal was part of his strategy, but it didn't matter. Need sucked rational thought from her brain.

He slid his hand beneath her dress and his palm warmed her flesh. She tried to say his name, but nothing more than a moan emerged.

He rained kisses down the column of her throat and ended at the tiny indentation at the hollow.

"Do it thirty times."

"I can't." *Shouldn't.* She would be begging him to fuck her soon and ripping off his clothes as he'd promised.

"You can." He held her in position. "It would be better if I fingered your hot cunt at the same time."

"Then do it."

He hissed, and Ella gave herself a mental fist bump. Getting that reaction from Staff Sergeant Pierce Holden was no easy feat.

He offered a finger and she sucked, pantomiming giving him a blow job.

"That will be quite enough."

When she didn't stop, he captured her chin.

"How far would you like to take this?"

A ridiculous, reckless part of her wanted to push it until she achieved the reaction she wanted. *Which was...?* A spanking? A fucking? Making it as difficult for him to forget her as it was going to be for her to forget him?

She sucked his finger deeper into her mouth.

"Oh, Ella." He exerted a small amount of pressure on her cheeks, and she was forced to release him.

He slid his hand between her legs.

"You may want to get busy. I told you to rub yourself thirty times. I meant it."

"Yes, Sir." She had to adjust her balance. And he jostled his leg, throwing her forward. Her breath whooshed out and she let out a loud *oomph.*

"One," he prompted.

She recovered her breath and he inserted a second finger. The sensation, with their hands bumping and the plug moving, overwhelmed her. Still, she sought more.

"Delicious sub."

Lost in their sensual, naughty, risk-taking play, Ella lost count of the times she'd stroked her clit.

He still had a hand in her hair, keeping her arched.

This image would fuel her fantasies for months.

Stunning her then, he added a third finger, splitting her apart. There was no way she could do this…

She struggled for breath.

"How aroused are you now?"

Dazed. This time she told the truth. "Nine point nine."

"That pleases me."

"Oh, Sir!"

"Now stop."

"What?" She blinked. "You can't mean that." *Again.*

One at a time, he eased his fingers from her and also loosened his grip on her hair. "It's your choice. We can leave it as is, and I can wish you a good night."

She waited. "Or?"

"We can finish it, and you can rip my clothes off in one of our vehicles. If you prefer, we can go back to your house."

"You have a plane to catch." Ella couldn't endure him walking out of her house a second time.

"It's a red-eye. I've got a couple of hours."

Holy fuck, she was so turned on, she was going to lose it if she didn't come. She could always say no, but the release he gave her was so different—*better*—than any orgasm she'd ever given herself.

All day, since he'd left her unfulfilled at home that morning, he'd created tension in her. He'd ratcheted it up with each calculated message he'd sent and the fact he'd made her stroke herself just to the point of orgasm before she'd left for the party.

But the truth was, being in his arms near the waterfall, with her head on his shoulder, had been enough, all by itself, to melt her resistance to him. "Where is your car?" It was larger than hers, making it more appealing.

"Over there." He pointed to a place even more secluded, beneath some tall pine trees.

"I think yours is a better choice."

He nodded.

"Give me a second. I want to get in my car."

He stepped to one side, and she opened the door to slip her purse beneath the driver's seat. Then she grabbed a package of sanitary wipes from the center console. "I think we may need these." She opened the foil package and pulled one out.

"Good call." He wiped his hands then snagged her wrist.

"Wait!"

Instead of doing as she said, he reached over her to flick the door closed.

"You read my mind, Staff Sergeant."

"As usual."

"So, if you are reading my mind..." Ella trailed off.

"You're planning to start by unknotting my tie and opening a few buttons, even though most women would choose to remove my jacket first. A few would even fold it or hang it from the hook in the back. But since you're as impatient as I am, you'll pull my shirttails out of my waistband without thinking about my jacket. Then when you do, you'll be hoping I manage it myself since you'll be busy working on getting my cock out and sucking it deep into your throat."

"Oh, God..."

"Is this still step two?"

"Either that or my keen imagination. Come on."

More than any man she'd been with, he made things fun.

With customary impatience, he led her to his vehicle. He, too, used his remote to open the locks, and she saw him scanning the surroundings, taking them in, looking for risk, ensuring her safety and modesty.

He opened the back door and tipped his hand sideways, indicating she should enter.

She slid across the soft leather seat, all the way to the far side.

Pierce took another look around, including a long surveillance of the main house and yard, then nodded. Once he was inside the car, he pushed the button to lock the doors.

He didn't advance on her until the light faded, but then…

He grabbed her waist and pulled her over to him. She yelped from the surprise, and he silenced the sound by yanking her over his lap. He bounced his right knee a couple of times, tipping her off balance, her ass in the air.

He flicked her dress aside. "Stay still."

When she didn't, he gave her a solid smack on the rear, driving the plug deeper.

The sound reverberated in the car and her ears. It satisfied, soothed and settled her.

"Follow orders. And when in doubt, 'yes, Sir' is always a good response. Didn't take you long to forget."

"Maybe I need constant instruction." She couldn't believe she'd said that. Why couldn't she resist goading him?

He reached into his jacket pocket. She realized he'd pulled out his cell phone. He turned on the flashlight app and looked at her naked bottom. A moment later, he groaned. "You do have a mark."

"And the plug. I think I told you that, Sir."

"Yeah." Using his free hand, he slid a couple of fingers in and out of her damp pussy.

She stilled. Maybe if he didn't have any idea how close she was, he would continue until she came...

Instead, he turned off the flashlight and dropped the phone back into his pocket then slipped his fingers out of her cunt. "Sir!"

He helped her up and guided her into place, straddling him. "What do you want?"

"You. Inside me. I think you've given me blue balls."

He laughed. "That happens to men."

"It means a person is in pain from the blood flow from not being allowed to come, right?"

"More or less. But if we're being technical, the term refers to what happens when the testicles—"

"So blue clit. Whatever. Call it what you want. Just get me off, now. Please."

Even in the darkened interior of the car, she knew he'd drawn his eyebrows together.

Taking the initiative, she shifted her weight. His legs were spread so that her swollen clit was elevated and exposed. "You were right."

"About?"

"The way I'm going to undress you." She tugged on the knot in his tie, loosening it. Then, patience gone, she lifted his collar so she could yank the tie up and over his head. She dropped the material, still knotted, to the floorboard before she began work on his buttons.

When the top three were undone, she sucked in another breath. She ran her fingertips across his chest, and the feel of his honed muscles sent shockwaves through her. "I want you."

"Not even half as much as I want you."

"This has to come off." She slid her palms beneath the lapels of his jacket. Always helpful, he leaned forward. "Good. Now shrug."

"You're bossy."

"Blue balls, Sir," she countered.

"We'd better take care of that."

"Yes, please."

He helped her with the jacket. She tossed it on top of the tie.

Losing all sense of control, she grabbed handfuls of his shirt and yanked it free from his trousers.

Her pussy throbbed with incessant need.

The sounds of their frantic breaths filled the car's interior.

She fumbled with the last few buttons, and he brushed her hands aside and opened the next one down. Since he was busy, she got to work on his belt buckle. In the dark, with desperation driving her, she kept losing her grip.

Finally, once she had it open and pulled through the loops on his trousers, she unfastened his waistband then dragged his zipper down.

He'd worn no underwear.

"That is so freaking hot, Sir." She took hold of his hard cock and stroked it. His balls were already tight. "You're as ready as I am."

"Have been for hours."

"Oh, my God. Condom? Tell me you have a condom."

"In my wallet." His fished it out of his back pocket, and since he'd lifted his hips, she took the opportunity to work his slacks down to his knees.

While he opened the wrapper, she returned to stroking his shaft. She became wetter just from touching him. "Fuck me, Sir."

"I think Operation—"

"You win. Now do me. Do me. Do me. *Do me.*"

"Are you asking for something, sub?" Even though he'd tried for serious, laughter lurked behind his words.

"Yes, please. Your beautiful dick, Sir."

"Where do you want it?"

"In my hot cu—" Before she could finish the word, he moved her from his lap and onto the seat beside him.

Then he slid a palm beneath her buttocks and scooted her a few more inches. "I want to be on top of you."

She grabbed the bottom of her dress and started to pull it up, but he stopped her.

"Leave it. If anyone comes, I want you covered." He loomed over her.

Since her vision had adjusted to the dark she could make out the ferocity in his eyes. She dropped the material.

"The next time I see you, I may cut your clothes off you." He pressed her down as he slid his cock into her.

"Sir." She sighed.

"Rub your clit."

It took some effort to work her hand between them, and she gasped when her nail abraded the swollen flesh. She'd never played with herself when having sex before, and a thrill zipped straight through her. Between that and the plug, she was about undone.

"Please tell me you won't make me stop at thirty."

"Keep going." He surged into her.

Pierce overwhelmed her. His gorgeous face dominated her vision, and she breathed in his clean, musky scent. "So, so, close, Sir."

"Come when you're ready, Ella."

Unsure whether her clitoris could endure any further torment, she pulled away her hand and surrendered to the dominance of his cock.

She wrapped her arms around his neck. Then she squeezed her eyes closed as the orgasm rocked her. Ella cried out his name, and he swallowed it with a sensual kiss at odds with the way he fucked and the force of her climax.

Everything he did created dissonance, intensifying her reactions. Her brain couldn't figure out what he was doing before he'd moved on to something else.

When she opened her eyes, she saw his were closed and his head was tipped back. She loved seeing him this vulnerable. It made her heart swell with love… Ella shook her head to force away the thought.

Pierce shortened his strokes, and she responded by tightening her pussy around him. He moaned deep in his throat. A frisson of satisfaction raced through her. She loved knowing she had some power over him.

The first spurt of his ejaculate caused his body to go rigid, and she tightened her grip on him.

"Damn," he said a long time later after dropping a kiss on her forehead. "I love being inside you."

His arms were shaking, and she realized that he'd held his body away from hers the entire time they'd been having sex. He had made certain he didn't crush her, even while she had been pulling down on his neck.

"I haven't done this in a dozen years. Wait. Make that more than a dozen years."

"It's a first for me."

"I popped your backseat cherry?"

She giggled as if she were a schoolgirl. "That's one way to put it."

"I'm honored. Proud."

"Gonna notch your bedpost?"

"Wouldn't be worth it." Where his voice had been gentle and teasing, it became serious. "You're the only woman who's ever mattered."

Ella wasn't quite sure how he managed it, but one moment she was beneath him, the next she was on top. It took her a second to figure out what had happened. "Do you have superhuman strength?"

"And reflexes." He pumped his arm.

"Of course. And reflexes."

"Always good for you to show proper appreciation for your lover." He studied her. "And Dom."

Her smile faded as reality plowed into her, dragging her under a wave of emotional devastation. He was neither. Could never be.

"Ella?" He frowned and tucked her hair behind her ear. "You okay?"

All lightness fled. "That was pretty intense." She meant more than the sex. Her words were honest, more honest than he might have realized.

He disposed of the condom in a napkin that had been in the glovebox.

She smoothed her dress into place, pretending everything was fine, that she wouldn't wake up tomorrow with her heart in a thousand jagged pieces.

He buttoned his shirt while she ran her fingers through her hair, trying to tame the wild mess. "Sure you don't want to move to North Carolina?"

For a second, her mind raced. Her heart wanted to seize the opportunity. "It's not the place that's the problem." Being by herself while her man was gone fifty percent of the time was.

"You're wounding my ego."

"Flex your muscles when you look in the mirror. That will help."

"No doubt."

Something threaded through his voice, as well. Tension? Was he trying to be as light as she was? As disingenuous?

To occupy herself, she picked up his jacket and tie and placed them on the seat next to her, then reached for the door handle.

"You don't want to talk for a bit?"

"People will have noticed you're gone. We don't want questions. And… I need to get home. I didn't get much sleep last night."

"Wait there."

He exited the rental then came around to her side to open it and offer his hand. Once the interior light was illuminated, she noticed he'd missed fastening a button. Unable to help herself, she fixed it.

"Thank you."

"You'll want to tuck your shirt in, Staff Sergeant."

"Is it okay if I leave the lipstick on my face?"

He kept hold of her until they arrived at her car.

She faced him, her buttocks on the car front fender. He took a step toward her and placed his feet on the outside of hers, trapping her.

"Thank you for tonight. For the weekend. You made my trip home more than tolerable."

"Thank *you*." Her voice cracked. "It was fun." *Damn it.* Ella prayed he couldn't hear the threat of tears in her words. She wanted to be casual, as if she were the type of woman who did this all the time and that it hadn't mattered to her.

"I want to see you again."

She shook her head. "As I said, this was fun. But no. I'm sorry."

"Sorry?"

"I agree that this was a great weekend. Let's leave it at that."

"It's more than that. You know it." He wound a lock of her hair around his finger. "We have a connection."

"It doesn't matter. It can't happen again." She wouldn't let it. Already she was fracturing, barely able to hold her fragile emotions together.

"Having a connection sure as fuck means something. At least to me it does." His voice was tight, irritation punctuating his words.

"I didn't mean to insult you."

"Yeah. You did. You were trying to put distance between us. I won't let you."

"Pierce." She lifted her hand to touch his wrist but dropped it back to her side. "I've been nothing but honest. I'm looking for a relationship. I need someone who will be around, who will sleep with me, stay the night, create a future. You understood that. We both did," she added the last part to remind herself.

"How about one who lights up your ass? How about one who leaves stripes across your thighs? Or crops your pussy and inflicts the right kind of pain to make you scream out an orgasm? Who fucks you in the backseat? Who gives you memories? That's not worth something?"

Because she couldn't resist the allure, she pleaded, "Don't."

"So that's it? Your fear of being hurt is worse than your fear of taking a chance?"

She squared her shoulders. "Take a chance? With someone who's leaving in a couple of hours? Who goes on missions so top secret no one knows what he does or where he lives? People think you do some kind of administrative work, that your biggest concern is a paper cut."

He loosened her hair with slow revolutions of his finger.

"I'm not ready to move to an army base."

"I don't live on post."

"That's not the point." She exhaled. "An army town where I don't know anyone, where I don't have a job, or support network. There's a lot of women who do that, and I admire them. But I think they're stronger than I am."

"You may be underestimating yourself."

"No." She shook her head. "I can't live in a new town where I'd be alone half the time. I can't. More, I don't want to. So where would that leave us? I'd stay here in Colorado and you'd visit every few years? I guess we'd have text messaging, or phone conversations, maybe video calls. But that's not a substitute for you being with me in person." When she was even more attached to him? When she had even more experiences to forget?

"What would it take?"

This was why she shouldn't have come to the party. He was so much easier to resist if she wasn't looking at him, seeing how handsome he was, remembering the feel of the cane punishing her skin while she was mesmerized by his stunning blue eyes. "It's impossible," she said, wishing it were anything but. "A relationship takes a lot of work and commitment from two people. You are not in a place to be involved with someone like me. I'm ready to settle down. I want the whole thing. A commitment. Marriage. Stability…a mortgage. I want someone I can share goals with and a companion who will go out with me on Saturday mornings for coffee and maybe a walk." All of the things he wasn't offering.

If she waited for him, she wouldn't be meeting new people, a solid man who was also looking for companionship and a future.

But what about the sex? Or the way she had connected with Pierce? That, she knew, didn't happen often in a relationship.

"Say you'll at least talk to me, answer my texts?"

"I can't. You'd be relentless." She knew her limitations. He'd wear her down.

He grinned. "Yeah. It's a text. What harm could come from that?"

She gave a half-smile, recognizing his tease from earlier when he'd asked.

Maybe she could, after some time had passed, after she'd sorted her life out again. "Not immediately."

"You've got a lot of resolve, Ella. You're tough."

"I never said otherwise." She brought up her chin a notch and reminded him, "I've been nothing but honest."

"It wasn't a criticism."

"No?"

"Tough is good. I admire your resolve. I might not like it, but I respect it."

Tears stung her eyes, and she fought them back.

"And I like the way you take the beating you ask for."

"Now you're not playing fair." She recalled his tactic to get rid of Morgan.

"Never do. Especially when I want something."

The success of Operation Fuck Ella Senseless at the Party was proof of that. "Am I the first person to tell you no?"

"And the last."

"If you'll excuse me?" She straightened her spine and retreated behind her business façade. "Safe travels."

"I can't change your mind?"

"Please don't try."

He stepped back and she dashed past him. Though, with his superfast reflexes, she knew he'd allowed her to.

She pushed the start button and the engine kicked into life.

He took three steps away, and she glanced in her mirrors, even though she knew there was no traffic. She eased onto the dirt road.

Pierce didn't budge. He was still there when she rounded the corner. Within seconds, the house faded from sight.

At the next stop sign, she dropped her forehead to the steering wheel and gave in to the tears.

He might believe she had untapped strength. She didn't. The truth was, she was a coward. But he had been one hundred percent correct when he'd guessed that her fear of being hurt was worse than her fear of taking a chance.

The trouble was, even though they'd only been together a short amount of time, she hadn't escaped unscathed.

Chapter Seven

Pierce remained in place, watching until Ella's tail lights faded from sight. Then, instead of moving, he stared into the night and listened to the distant rumble of the car.

How in the hell had their evening gone so wrong?

The backseat car sex had been smoking. Afterward, they'd been intimate, laughing, enjoying each other's company. Operation Fuck Ella Senseless at the Party had been a success. He was confident she'd enjoyed it as much as he had. Then all of a sudden, when he'd let her know how much she mattered to him, it was as if she'd embraced her inner ice princess to push him away.

He knew one thing for sure. Ella had run because she wanted him. That wasn't ego. It was an observation of the emotion expressed in her eyes, the ferocity with which she'd held on to him when they'd been making love.

He'd spent his entire life secure, confident, never questioning a decision. He decided what he wanted and pursued it.

And now? He didn't know what the hell to do.

He refused to tell her that he was considering taking a job with Logan. There were still too many uncertainties, and he didn't want her to expect something until he was certain it would happen. He wasn't sure he could live with her disappointment.

He wished he had words that would to encourage her to stay, let him pursue her, give them a chance.

Fuck. Even if he did take the job with Logan, Pierce wasn't convinced she'd want him, anyway. She thought she wanted someone solid and stable—an accountant, maybe? Or a salesman with regular hours? Not an EMT or firefighter or even an IT guy, though. They worked hours that might not mesh with her imagined, perfect schedule.

If she got what she wanted, he suspected she'd be restless.

Ella Gibson was an intriguing mixture of innocence and defiance. All of her emotions danced in her eyes. He could read her secrets. She had a wild side, loved having her ass spanked and her limits pushed. Even though she might not admit it, she was willing to take risks.

No doubt she'd been burned by her ex. But that didn't mean all military guys—or any man who worked more than nine-to-five with two weeks of vacation a year—were unreliable, a cheater or worse.

So how the hell was he going to convince her to take a chance on him? On them? Because he could never be the man she thought she wanted.

He massaged the back of his neck.

When it was obvious she wasn't returning, despite the ridiculous hope he harbored, he walked to his car.

Mindful of appearances and not wanting to behave in a way that would risk Ella's reputation, he tucked in his shirt, shrugged into his suit jacket then replaced his tie. His belt reminded him of her. He held it, allowing himself to remember the way he'd used it on her flawless skin and the way she'd responded.

Pierce fantasized now about laying it across her flawless skin while she writhed and begged for more even as he secured a promise from her that she'd never walk away from him again.

With that satisfying image in mind, he fed the leather through the loops then fastened the buckle that had warmed from his touch.

He returned to the party as the band was packing up. The bartender was loading bottles into a container. A few people were seated at the remaining tables, talking, in no hurry to leave. His mother and father were huddled with another couple near the patio. Farrah, Bon Bon and Walter snoozed on a patch of grass near the empty tent.

Fifi trotted over and followed him to the waterfall. The bottle he'd left there earlier was still perched on a rock, and he picked it up.

He heard the click of heels on stone as someone approached, and he glanced up a second before Morgan waltzed into view. She was heading his way.

"Is there something you want to tell me?"

"About?"

"Ella."

"Ella who?"

"You're not as smart as you think you are."

"Oh?"

"Earlier this afternoon, I knew Mom didn't want me. So that was a ploy for you to be alone with Ella. I want to know what happened last night after I left the bar."

"Why would you assume anything did?"

"Oh, for crying out loud." She rolled her eyes. "I saw you looking at her."

"I was looking at plenty of women."

"Not like that. And you stayed at the Neon Moon even after I left. I don't need to be a mathematician to know that two plus two equals four. Start talking."

"Morgan, don't you have someone else to bother? Aren't you supposed to be a hostess or something?"

"My duties are all but over. So I have time for you."

"Let me be a little more precise. There's nothing to know, nothing to discuss. We can change the subject or you can scram."

"Oh, my God." She grabbed for her necklace.

"What?"

"You…you've got a thing for Ella."

He remained silent.

Her mouth formed a perfect, stunned O. "My best friend. And my brother? This is not happening. This is *so* not happening. Tell, me, Pierce. Tell me this isn't really happening."

"Okay. This is not happening."

With a scowl, she said, "You can't even look me in the eye."

He finished his water then twisted the cap back on before giving her his full attention.

"Aha."

"Aha, what?"

"You're lying."

"And?" He took aim with the bottle, lobbed it at a recycle can and scored on a bank shot. "What do you want me to say?"

"How serious is it?"

"Darling, annoying, persistent sister, I wish you still had pigtails for me to pull. You're getting nothing out of me. My private life is private."

"Oh, Pierce. You do know she's looking for something serious. A relationship with someone who isn't in the military."

"So I've learned."

"Oh, my God. You're in love with her." She placed her fingers on his sleeve. "What are you going to do?" she asked.

"Have you always been so nosy?"

"Isn't that what little sisters are good for?"

"Go bother someone else. I think Mom—"

"I'm not falling for it twice. Nice try." Nevertheless, she dropped her hand. "Are you heading back home?"

"Yeah."

"To drink hemlock?"

Or formulate a new action plan. "You can come visit me in North Carolina."

"Have you washed that pile of dishes yet?"

That had been a unique experience. He'd been deployed without warning, so fast that he hadn't cleaned the kitchen, made the bed, emptied the refrigerator. The trash, thank God, he'd remembered. But she'd shown up before he'd arrived home, and he'd spent the first twenty-four hours of her visit asleep in his clothes and shoes. "I'll hire a housekeeping service."

"Then I'll definitely consider it."

"Let me know when."

"Can I bring a guest?"

"Quit meddling."

She smiled wide, bright, as if she were an angel. "Call if you need anything. Do me a favor? Keep an eye on Dad. Let me know if you think anything is odd."

"Come on, Pierce. There's always something odd about Dad."

He lifted a shoulder in a half-shrug. "Maybe ask Mom." Though he doubted she'd say anything. Despite the fact she didn't like him half the time, she never said anything negative about him to other people.

"And let me know if I can do anything for you…with Ella."

"Who?"

"You really are an asshole."

But that didn't stop her from falling into his arms for a hug.

"I'm going to miss you."

"My welcome mat is always out for you."

She pulled away and he saw a telltale sheen of tears in her eyes, so like his own. "I'm warning you."

"No one cries over jerks, Pierce." She swiped the back of her hand across her eyes.

"Call or text." He knew she would. Before he made it home, if his guess was right. Now if Ella would do the same…

But she'd made it clear that any contact had to come from him. Even then, she might not respond.

He started to walk away then stopped, turned back, met his little sister's gaze. "Stay out of it."

"Stay out of what?" she returned, her voice full of sass.

The couple who had been talking to his parents said their goodnights and went into the house. Since he needed to get to the airport, Pierce shook his head and pulled back his shoulders.

He joined his parents and gave his mother an air kiss. Fifi trotted over for a pet so that she wouldn't be

Enticement

left out. Walter cracked one eyelid and remained where he was.

"Your bedroom is always ready for you," Laurel said. "Please come home again."

He shook his father's hand. Throughout the night, he'd glanced over at Gerard. While Laurel had smiled and laughed as the belle of the ball, Gerard had been reserved. Pierce realized he might be suspicious because he was an untrusting soul, but he'd also been puzzled by Harold's behavior. The VP of Accounting at his father's headquarters had sat with him and Ella for almost an hour, dominating the conversation. If Pierce hadn't cut a getaway, they might still be there. "If you need anything, you have my number."

"Oh, no!" Laurel headed for the bar and Walter jumped up to chase her. "I need a wine before you close up."

"Of course, Mrs. Holden. Red or white?"

"A chardonnay, please."

Once they were out of earshot, Pierce leveled a look at his father. "I mean it."

"There's nothing for you to concern yourself with."

Gerard gave a tight nod. But he had no intention of ignoring his father's secretive behavior. Pierce might have to be the one to initiate phone calls and establish some sort of relationship. "I have a plane to catch."

"Goodnight." Without any further response, Gerard strode away.

Pierce took out his keys as he left the house. Another successful visit home. It had gone about as well as he'd expected. The highlight had been Ella.

How was it possible she had gotten to him so fast? He would have insisted that no woman had enough power to make him consider changing the course of his life. But now, he was obsessed with thoughts…

about her, a potential future, how to get what he wanted.

Morgan was more right than she realized. He'd fallen in love with Ella.

Fuck.

His mind reeled, knocked sideways by a blow he'd never seen coming.

So now what?

Pierce opened the car door then slid behind the driver's seat.

He smelled sex and remembered being deep inside Ella, making to love to her, claiming her.

He refused to let her go.

She had been honest with him from the beginning, but part of him hadn't wanted to believe she wouldn't yield. To him, the course of action was obvious. She should move to North Carolina. Having her to come home to would be mind-blowing. It would give him focus, ground him, get him through.

Hell, he'd have even compromised and let her stay in Colorado while he worked out his future. He'd make damn sure they spent plenty of time together. Flights weren't cheap, but that wasn't insurmountable, since it was a short-term problem.

But she'd refused to yield to him.

Pierce was left with only with one mission and one outcome. Pursuit and capture. Good thing his training had left him competent at both. Operation Fuck Ella Senseless at the Party had morphed into Operation Woo Ella and Keep Her Forever.

* * * *

Enticement

Ella swirled a piece of pasta in cream sauce, twirling the fork around and around, staring at the pattern it left behind.

"Who is he?"

Jolted, she looked up and across the restaurant table at her mother. The question shouldn't have surprised her. Her mother knew everything about her, always had.

Despite the fact it was a Sunday, Ella had thrown back the covers and crawled out of bed at four-thirty, disoriented and shaking. She'd had horrible nightmares of her father and Pierce, of loss and grief. Images of the two of them had intertwined, their features blending until they had been indistinguishable.

Desperate to touch them, to hold on, she'd reached a hand toward their blurred images. They'd morphed into grotesque smiles. She'd screamed as they'd vanished.

She'd returned to reality with a start, shaking and drenched in a cold sweat.

Unable to breathe, she'd climbed from bed and brewed a pot of coffee. When the first strong cup hadn't cleared the cobweb-like remnants of the dream from her psyche, she'd gone for a brisk walk around the neighborhood. Even that hadn't helped.

No matter how great the sex had been or how much she'd enjoyed his kisses and being in his arms for a dance, she was glad she'd refused to continue seeing him. There was little doubt in her mind that brutal dreams would be commonplace whenever he was deployed.

Around six a.m., he'd sent her a text message.

Since they didn't have a relationship, she'd ignored it. But she'd exhaled in relief, and she hated that she was grateful he'd thought of her.

At home, she'd drunk more coffee and watched endless episodes of television on a home improvement channel. Her gaze had been drawn to the picture of her and her father. Today, more than any time in the last twenty years, his absence tormented her.

With a sigh, she'd turned off the TV and decided to grab the vacuum and clean. As she'd walked around the house, straightening the coffee table, pushing in the barstools, making the bed, memories of Pierce had become more vibrant…and painful.

At eight, she'd texted her mom to see if she was available for lunch. Driving to Colorado Springs would take forty-five minutes to an hour and keep her from reaching for the phone.

Rather than soothing her, though, the journey had given her too much time to think. Turning up the radio hadn't worked.

"Ella?"

"How do you know the problem is a man?"

"You order carbs with a side of carbs and a glass of white wine when you have career or man trouble."

"Do I?" She looked at the food in front of her. Fettuccini alfredo and a second loaf of bread. Her water was untouched, but she had finished half of her glass of chardonnay.

"Last time we were here, you had a salad and a mineral water. If it was something to do with your job, you would have spilled it right away. So that makes me think you're having man trouble."

"Pierce Holden."

"Morgan's older brother? Didn't he bring you home one night when you were in high school and had been drinking at a party?"

"To be fair, we didn't know someone had put rum in the punch. But, yes." Even back then, he'd been a hero of sorts. Knowing her mother wouldn't judge her, she gave a complete synopsis of the weekend, except for the juiciest details.

"So what are you going to do?" Shirley took a sip of wine and sat back.

"Mope. Sulk. What else is there to do?"

"Move to North Carolina. Find out for yourself. Perhaps it won't work." She lifted one shoulder. "But then again, maybe it will. There's one way to find out."

Ella dropped her fork. She stared at her mother in open-mouthed shock. "I'm beginning to think the whole world has gone mad."

"Oh?"

"I don't know him."

"You know what kind of person he is. If he thinks enough of you to invite you to move in, there's a connection there." Shirley took one more sip. "The fact you're sitting here tells me that you're in agony. If you didn't care about him, you wouldn't be talking to me."

"I have a job."

"There are jobs in North Carolina."

"Mom. I have a house."

"Sell it. Rent it out. Or keep making the payments and keep it as an escape route in case you're right."

She blew out a breath that made a stray lock of hair flutter. "It's not that easy."

"Then go for a visit. Gather some more information before you make a decision."

With her fingertip, Ella made tiny circles on the tablecloth.

"What else is bothering you?"

"He's in the military."

"And?"

"It's some sort of super-secret, doesn't-exist-on-paper kind of thing. He lets most people think he's an admin geek. But he's not."

"That's a lot to consider."

"I don't want to go through that." She pushed her plate back. "Being alone would drive me crazy. I have no friends out there, no support system. No mom."

"It would be a big change, scary. You don't know how to make friends or live on your own. You can't make phone calls or video chat with me or Morgan or your other friends. And you'll never get another job. You're right. Move on. Go on a date with someone else tomorrow. Forget him."

"Mom!"

"Ridiculous, right?" Shirley grinned. "Made my point."

Ella tore off a piece of bread and dipped it in olive oil. "It's more than all that. I'm scared to lose him."

"I know." Shirley gave a wan smile. And when she continued, her voice was soft with heartfelt emotion. "Life doesn't come with guarantees, you know that. Just because someone is a manager in some building downtown, it doesn't mean that a freak accident won't happen. Even if I had known how things would turn out with your dad, I would have married him anyway. But I would also have savored the good times more, laughed, skipped the housework, not spent as much time worrying, fought less."

"Even with the hurt, it was worthwhile?"

"Every moment. To feel that kind of love in my lifetime? To wear his ring? See him smiling at the altar as he waited for me? To fight the demons of life together? Hold my hand as our precious daughter entered the world? *Every* moment."

Her mother's words added to her confusion about her determination to stay away from him. Ella wasn't sure she appreciated it. So she ordered chocolate cake for dessert.

"Have you heard from him since he left?"

She nodded. "He let me know he was home safe."

On the table next to her, the phone vibrated, dancing around on the white tablecloth.

"Is it Pierce?"

"No idea." To avoid temptation, Ella turned the device upside down. Since part of the reason she had driven to Colorado Springs was to shake off the upheaval of the last couple of days, she smiled at her mom. "Update me on you."

Shirley launched into tales about an airline pilot she was dating. "He's a silver fox."

And she'd made a picture of him—shirtless—her screensaver.

"What about the other guys you're involved with?"

"I change the background when I'm with them. Flowers." She laughed. "That he gave me."

"This sounds serious."

"Not at all. I just like staring at him. And having sex."

"God. Tell me you're using..." She blushed. "Condoms."

"Cherry flavored. Extra-large."

"God. Mother."

"I'm kidding. They're magnum sized."

"I need bleach for my ears." But her mother's outrageousness was the balm she needed for her soul. For an hour, a blessed hour, she was able to forget about Pierce. Until she returned to her car and looked at the phone.

When you masturbate, think of me.

Damn him. Of course she would.

Ella told herself to block his number, remove it from her directory and forget about him. She swiped the key to open his contact information. Before her courage could fail her, she selected the correct box. *Contact will be blocked. Continue?*

Her resolve fled. The pain of not knowing whether or not he was trying to reach her, whether or not he was in the country, whether he was alive and okay, was greater than the agony of ignoring him.

She pushed the red cross then deleted the message. Then she removed his phone number from her contacts to avoid the temptation of responding later.

Proud of her accomplishment, Ella dropped her phone into her purse.

As Ella drove home, her mother's words replayed. The ones about the silver fox and his condom size, Ella put in a mental incinerator, never to be thought of again.

But Ella considered the ones about Pierce.

By the time she arrived in Parker, thoughts of him crawled through her mind and heart.

When she was at home, Pierce texted again.

Even though she'd deleted his information, his name and number showed up.

She sighed.

This time there was a winking emoji and nothing else.

The man made certain she couldn't ignore him or dislike him.

Later, mentally exhausted, she took a bath. And that night, when she couldn't get to sleep, she looked in the mirror at her ass. The tiny red mark he'd left had almost gone. But the sensation of it still seared.

She took out her vibrator and climbed into the bed.

Even though a million emotional and sixteen hundred physical miles separated them, she fantasized about Pierce and his belt—warm from his body—leaving his mark on her.

Chapter Eight

I've been thinking about having you in the Holden Holy Hell position.

Oh, God...

Ella dropped her phone. It bounced off her planner and thumped onto her desktop.

Pierce.

It had been mid-May when she'd seen him, which was more than two months ago. Three weeks ago, he'd texted to say he'd be in touch as soon as he could. He'd provided no details about when he'd be back, where he was going, what he was doing.

For agonizing days that had dragged into weeks, her phone had been silent, more noticeable since he'd left voice mails and sent texts at least every eight hours before that last message.

Since the last time he'd contacted her, she'd driven herself crazy, wondering whether he was deployed, when he might be back, not knowing whether he was safe or even in the country.

Relief that he was okay careened through her and she almost typed a response.

But the realization she'd go through this often in the future if she responded made her leave the phone where it was.

Her phone dinged again. She considered ignoring it.

No matter how many times she told herself to do just that, her fingers and curiosity overrode her brain's orders. Relief flooded her when she saw the message was from Morgan.

You're coming to a meeting of the Carpe Diem Divas. Happy hour. Tonight. No excuses or I will drag your ass out of your house. Fiesta Olé! I-25 and Arapahoe. Five o'clock. And this is happy hour. Happy hour. Which means you have to act happy. For an hour.

Ella grinned. There were times she wasn't sure whether to hug Morgan or to smother her with a pillow. There was no doubt she and Pierce were siblings.

Before Ella could come up with an excuse to decline, her phone lit up again.

p.s. I know where you live, and I have a key. I will come get your ass. So do NOT even think about going home after work like you did last time.

Ella knew that seeing her friends would be good for her. She'd spent too much time at home recently watching Netflix and eating ice cream.

After replying that she'd be there, she grabbed several packets of information about the facility and catering options then went up front to wait for a future bride and groom and mother-of-the-bride to show them the room they'd be using if they selected the country club for their wedding reception. Having the bride's mother along always made these visits interesting, but it would help her forget about Pierce and the Holden Holy Hell position.

The appointment took longer than she'd anticipated, even though she'd budgeted extra time because there would be three people in attendance rather than the usual two, she was behind schedule when she left the office to drive to Denver to meet her friends.

When she walked into the restaurant's bar section, she discovered Morgan, Ava, Jennifer and Eden already sipping margaritas. She took the only empty chair and grinned when she saw a frozen drink at her plate, too.

She took a long drink of the sweet-and-sour beverage then shook her head at the bite from the tequila. "Is this a double?"

"No," Ava said.

"You just don't get out much," Morgan replied.

"I'm here now," Ella said. "Where's Noelle?" Though Ella wasn't an official member of the Carpe Diem Divas, she was sometimes invited when they were meeting at the south end of Denver. The Divas had started as a few friends supporting each other through recent breakups. Even though Noelle was now happily married to one of the area's renowned Doms, the group was so committed to each other that they didn't want Noelle to leave.

"She and Joe are up at their mountain house getting ready for a play party that they're having this weekend," Jennifer said. "I think Logan and I are going. Would you like to attend?"

"Uh." The invitation stunned her, but not as much as her reaction. "No." If she ever attended another club, she wanted to go with Pierce. He'd ruined her for other men. But the mention of BDSM made her squirm, remember the marks he'd given her and the orgasms that had ripped through her from his attentions. "I mean, thanks."

"Aren't you into that BDSM stuff?" Ava asked.

Jennifer pointed her straw at Ava. "It's not *that* BDSM stuff, like it's something weird. You should give it a try."

"Oh, fuck no. Ain't no man spanking this fine ass." She wriggled in her seat.

"You might like it," Morgan said.

"I'll leave that to the rest of you kinky bitches. I'm just looking for a man who likes to eat at the Y like his life depends on it. Which it might."

"Oh, my God!" Ella roared.

People from other tables glanced in their direction.

"Speaking of… How was your date last week?" Eden asked.

Ava shook her head. "Could barely introduce him to the kitty. Never did get him to pet it."

Right then, Ella decided to meet up with the Divas every chance she had.

As she was finishing the last drop of her cocktail, she became aware of Morgan's gaze on her. "What?"

"How's my brother?"

"What?"

"Pierce?" Ava demanded.

"What's this about Pierce?" Eden asked.

Blinking innocently, Morgan twirled the ice in her glass.

"Are you fishing?" Ella asked. Or had she heard something from Pierce?

"I told Pierce after the anniversary party I didn't have to be a mathematician to figure this out. I saw the way he was looking at you. And no one takes that long to walk someone to the car when they leave. And since you told me you didn't go home with Randall that Friday night, I figured that you and my brother were—"

"Randall?" Ava interrupted to stare across at Ella. "You were going to go home with"—she plugged her nose so that her voice had an upper crust, hoity-toity air—"Randall W. Thurston, Jr.?"

"No." Ella shook her head.

"You might have if Pierce hadn't put a stop to it."

"He's banned from Joe and Noelle's parties," Jennifer added. "Did you know that?"

Morgan replied for both of them, "Pierce told us."

Ava's eyes widened. "What does Pierce know about that? Is he a kinkster?"

Everyone fell silent and looked at Ella. "How would I know?"

"Tell us something." Morgan wrinkled her nose. "Anything."

"There's nothing to say. If you want more than that, you'll need to ask Pierce."

"Checkmate. He said to ask you."

Eden leaned forward. "I'm dying to know."

"There's nothing to tell. You all know I don't date men unless they're marriage material. And he lives in North Carolina."

Jennifer scowled. "Isn't he moving to Colorado?"

The bottom dropped out of Ella's heart. "What?" Her ears rang and the tequila soured in her stomach.

"He's been talking to Logan about joining the detective agency. It won't happen right away, but I know they've been having conversations." Jennifer scowled. "Shit, shit, shit. That's not a secret, is it?"

"I didn't know," Morgan said, her hand frozen in place.

Ella was too stunned to say anything.

"I must have misunderstood something," Jennifer rushed to say. "At any rate, I apologize for opening my big mouth." Her hand shook. "I'm going to be in trouble for this one. Repeating privileged information. All of a sudden, I'm not quite as excited about going home tonight. Confession may be good for the soul, but it's hell on my butt."

"I don't think you need to say anything to Logan," Eden said, always the loyal one. "You didn't know it was a secret."

"He'll find out. No doubt. And hiding it will make it more difficult for me to sit down when he does."

"You couldn't have known," Morgan reassured Jennifer. "None of us will say anything."

Conversation went on around Ella, like insects droning in her ears, but she didn't respond to any of it.

If he cared about her, wouldn't he have mentioned something so important?

A more rational part of her brain couldn't blame him. She hadn't replied to his numerous texts. Of course he wouldn't share intimate details of his life.

The server arrived with the bill and Jennifer picked it up, saying, "It's the least I can do for ruining everyone's evening."

"You didn't ruin anything," Eden assured her.

"I'll pay next time," Ava promised.

"I'm going to kick his sorry soul into the next zip code when I see him," Morgan said. "He hasn't said a word to Mom or Dad, either."

The gathering broke up, and Morgan walked outside with Ella.

"Ella. I'm sorry. I had no idea what I was starting," Morgan apologized. "I wanted to get you out, have some fun, maybe learn some salacious details about my brother. But I had no intention of hurting you."

"He has sent me text messages and called me a few times since he went back to Fort Bragg, but I've never answered." The small disclosure was as much as she would reveal. "But Jennifer's announcement is news to me. He said nothing."

"He can be an ass at times." Morgan stopped near her car. "He must have wanted it to be a surprise."

"Well, it worked."

"He cares about you. I know it."

Ella gave a brave smile that she was afraid would shatter. "We're friends. Nothing more."

"I hate him a little right now."

"Don't." Ella shrugged. "At least not on my behalf." She knew what she'd been doing. At least she thought she had.

"There's nothing I can say to make this better, is there?"

"I'll be fine." Though the last thing she wanted was company or obligations, Ella wanted to make Morgan feel better. "Let's have happy hour again next week."

"Same place and time?"

"The margaritas are good." Ella nodded.

"Call me if you want to talk or go out or go shopping. Or anything."

"I will." That part was a lie.

When she was in the car, Ella looked at her phone. The screen was blank.

She wished she had been surprised.

* * * *

At work the next afternoon, Ella's desk phone buzzed. From the extension on the display, she knew it was from the receptionist at the podium.

"Hey, Ella. I've got a gentleman who'd like to talk to someone about membership. And Barb left about twenty minutes ago."

"I'll be right there."

Typically, potential members scheduled an appointment in advance. Barb would show them the facility and sometimes treat them to a meal or a beverage in the bar. Every once in a while, someone would show up without calling, and on those occasions, the club provided information and encouraged the visitor to return for an official tour.

She shrugged into her black blazer and took a vanity second to look in the mirror to ensure she didn't need to dab on some eye cream. She hadn't slept well last night, waiting for Pierce to text and say something. Anything. But he never had.

Deciding she wouldn't frighten the visitor, she grabbed a folder filled with informational material. Then she pasted a practiced smile on her lips as she walked through the public areas of the club toward the podium.

She missed a step when she saw Pierce in the lobby. He was so handsome in a polo shirt, navy slacks and a blazer that her breath lodged in her throat.

"Ella, this is Mr. Holden," the receptionist said.

Unable to speak, she nodded.

Since he extended his hand, she had no option but to accept it, even though every instinct warned her not to.

Instinct had been right.

His grip was reassuring, promising, strong, and most of all, welcomed by the most feminine part of her. The one that was unable to resist him.

She extracted her hand faster than was polite. "Staff Sergeant Holden, is it? Rather than Mr. Holden?"

The receptionist turned to greet a couple of ladies dressed for tea.

"It is."

Had Jennifer been wrong last night? And what was he doing here? Her knees knocked together, and she forced herself to stand up straight. "I'm sure you heard that Barb, who handles new memberships, isn't available? You're welcome to come back for a formal tour of the premises. In the meantime, I'm happy to answer any questions you might have."

In response, he dropped to one knee. Her mouth opened and heat flooded her body.

The receptionist, and the ladies who were there for afternoon tea, all turned to stare.

"Pierce?"

"I do have a question, Ella." His eyes were brighter, more intense than she'd ever seen, and a serious frown had settled between his brows.

He reached into his pocket and pulled out a ring box.

She lost her grip on the folder and it fell to the floor.

"Will you marry me?"

"*What?*"

Instead of responding, he opened the box.

The princess-cut diamond was ginormous, the overhead lighting bouncing off its brilliance and refracting all the colors of the rainbow.

"I don't understand."

"You made your position clear. I want you. I will do whatever it takes to deserve you. It will take some compromise from you, because it will be a while until I get my official discharge. I'm transferring to Fort Carson. That's the closest I can get to you. And I've made post-retirement plans to work with Logan Powell in his detective agency. So we have a lot of decisions to make. About where to live, how to manage your doubts. Things won't be perfect for a long time. I shouldn't have to deploy, but if I do, we'll get through it together." He took a breath, but not long enough for her to respond before he continued. "No doubt you'll have issues with me working with Logan, but we'll deal with that, too. Together. This is everything I have to offer you, Ella. Please tell me it's enough, that you're willing to try as hard as I am. Freaking yield a little. I'm begging you."

Words failed her and emotion flooded her.

"I love you, Ella. It took me some time to wake up to that fact. And I was frustrated that you wouldn't give in or compromise. Being away from you, knowing I couldn't talk to you and that you wouldn't respond to any of my texts, made me a madman."

One of the ladies fanned herself.

"Okay. Now say something. Anything."

"I..." She wished she could. But all of her dreams—of being with a fantastic person, a caring Dominant, someone who would support her and push her—were right there. It thrilled and overwhelmed her.

"Put me out of my misery, Ella, please. This is my new version of the Holden Holy Hell position."

Tears spilled from her eyes, and she laughed through them.

"Is that a yes?"

"Yes!"

He pulled the ring from the box, and the two ladies clapped.

Her future husband slid the ring on her finger.

It looked like hope and promise rolled into one.

"*You're mine.*" Then he stood and raised her hand and kissed it. "I'd planned to come to your house tonight, but I couldn't wait."

"I'm glad."

The ladies and the receptionist came over to shake hands, give hugs and share their best wishes.

Then he backed her into a portico. "We can't," she protested when the wall prevented her from moving any farther.

"The fuck we can't. I braved IEDs and the entire might of the US military to get to you, red tape, bureaucratic bullshit, then airplane reservations, rental cars. If you don't think I'm kissing my future bride—"

"You'll get me fired!"

"Good. That will give you the opportunity to practice being my sex slave. I'll teach you a few more of my favorite positions."

She giggled. "When you put it that way…" She tried to glance around, but he captured her chin and imprisoned her.

"Open your mouth."

"Yes, Sir," she whispered. Ella breathed him in, the scent of determination and sexual charisma. Her body vibrated with recognition that he was the man she'd been waiting for her whole life. He cared enough about her to make big changes to his career and future to accommodate her. It wasn't a perfect solution, but it was better than she'd dared hope for.

Thrilled, nervous at the idea of being caught, she leaned into him, wrapping her arms around his neck so that she could look at him and her engagement ring.

He claimed her mouth, took what was his, everything she had to offer.

His mouth was hot and he telegraphed sensual need.

"I've got to get you home."

Everything he wanted, she did, too. "I can leave in about an hour."

He glowered.

She might have laughed at his expression if she weren't afraid he'd toss her over his shoulder and carry her out of the front door. "I'll see if someone will cover for me."

"I'll meet you at your place?"

"Perfect."

Ella's boss allowed her to go home early to celebrate, and within half an hour, she was pulling into the driveway at her townhouse, heart pounding, anticipating what was ahead.

He was lazing against the hood of his rental car, somehow managing to look badass even though he was dressed for the country club.

He pushed away, strode over to her, opened her door then helped her out.

"You're more beautiful every time I see you."

He always took her breath away.

"Let's start this relationship the right way." His voice was edged with dominance, and corresponding pleasure rushed through her, making her clit throb.

"Sir?"

He held out his hand for her keys, and she tossed them to him.

Before she knew what he was about, he had her off the ground and over his shoulder. Breath whooshed out of her.

"Carrying you across the threshold."

"That's not how it works," she protested, kicking.

"It does in this relationship." With a flick of his hand, he closed the car door.

"Pierce! Put me down!"

Instead, he brushed her skirt up a little and gave her ass a hard spank.

She melted. He understood her so completely, perfectly.

He was worth the wait.

His steps were long and confident as he walked to the house, unlocked and opened the door. After he carried her inside, he kicked it closed behind them.

"It's time for you to learn the Holden-Gibson Forever pose," he said, lowering her to the floor. "Shall we get started?"

"Oh, Sir. I thought you'd never ask."

Chapter Nine

"Put down your purse and come here, Ella. You're not quite ready to leave."

At the implacable tone in Pierce's voice, her heart leaped then settled into a wild gallop. She turned to look at Pierce, her Dom, her fiancé, her world. He was holding a butt plug unlike any she'd ever seen. Her tummy plunged. The thing was gorgeous. A work of art. It was crafted from glass with a stunning spiral of deep blue sneaking up the interior. It was also gigantic. At its thickest, it had to be twice the size of the biggest one they'd ever used. And even the stem was much thicker than she was accustomed to. There was no way her sphincter would adjust to that monster, no matter how long she was forced to wear it.

Some part of her should have expected his order. Pierce often stunned her with the unexpected, keeping their relationship fresh.

The past two months had been difficult. She'd flown to North Carolina to spend some time with him and help him pack his belongings. He'd shipped most of his personal items to her townhome since he would be living temporarily in barracks at Fort Carson. Their time together while they waited for his discharge to be processed was limited. Every reunion, though, deepened her love for him. And she was becoming addicted to his dominance. Or had been. Until this moment. "Uhm…"

"Do I need to tell you twice?"

"No, Sir. But…" She trailed off. "The size of that thing. And, aren't we pressed for time? I mean, with traffic, we might be late. I hate to keep Morgan waiting."

"We'll be later with each second that you stall."

"Pierce…"

He didn't say anything. Instead, he remained where he was, watching her squirm. And damn him, he looked so handsome in an athletic-fitting T-shirt that showed his lean runner's physique. She had a rush of sexual hunger every time she saw him.

"Ella? You're stalling. That won't go well for you."

"Maybe we should put it in after we get home." And she had a chance to distract him and make him forget the enormous thing existed.

"We could do that."

She smiled. Then she exhaled a breath she hadn't known she was holding.

"But we're not going to."

Ella glanced back toward the door, making certain he understood her preference to leave. But the frustrating man didn't budge or acknowledge her wishes. "That thing is bigger than your cock." It wasn't. But it intimidated her nevertheless.

"I could stretch you out with my dick first, if that puts your mind at ease?"

"No!" They hadn't done that yet, and she was in no hurry to do so. Small plugs were enough for her.

He grinned. "Then get your ass over here, sub."

After releasing her grip on her purse, she walked to him.

Pierce placed the plug on the coffee table next to a bottle of lube before removing the bottom cushion from the couch so that the fabric-covered frame was exposed. "Squat on the edge here."

"Have you lost your mind? What if I go through that material?"

"Your weight will be on the edge, on the steel frame. You won't be anywhere near the middle. The couch and your hot little body will both be safe."

In true Dom style, he said no more. He'd responded to her objections, but he didn't argue or cajole or invite questions. Instead, he waited for her compliance.

She stood there, contemplating. But she knew he wouldn't relent.

With a sigh, she kicked off her shoes then wriggled out of her panties. "Shall I take off my dress?"

"No."

Out of reasons to stall, she climbed onto the couch then lowered herself into the awkward position he'd said.

"Come my direction a bit more."

"I will fall off."

"You won't. Spread your knees to shoulder-width, then put your weight on the balls of your feet on the edge to help. You can hold onto the back for balance."

"Is this another version of the Holden Reverse Half Squat?" She realized there was nothing *half* about it.

"There are a number of modifications I've been thinking of. Keeps me awake at night. But I will tell you this, I like having your pussy and ass available for my use like this. You're vulnerable."

"Because my life is at risk."

"I've heard enough." He snatched her panties from the floor, wadded them. "Open."

"But…"

Pierce seized the opportunity to shove the lacy material deep into her mouth. Then he took hold of her chin and turned her to face him.

God, how she had missed him when he'd been gone. His gaze bored into hers, his deep blue eyes compelling her not to look away.

"This is going up your ass and you're going to be a good girl and take the whole thing without complaint. And at dinner, I'm going to find the hardest chair in the restaurant and force you to sit flat so that it's driven high inside you. Every time you move or breathe, you will remember I'm your Dom."

Even though the plug was nowhere near her, her ass cheeks clenched.

"I will enjoy watching you suffer. And if you're lucky, I'll let you go into the ladies' room and masturbate."

"*Let me?*" Since her mouth was stuffed full of lace, the words were garbled.

"If you're lucky."

He lifted her dress and rolled it up to tuck the hem inside her fitted waistband. She wasn't sure how he accomplished it, but the material stayed in place.

A soft pop told her he'd opened the lid on the lube bottle. She imagined him smearing the smooth surface with the viscous liquid, and before she was ready, Pierce cupped a hand on her left shoulder to hold her in place while pressing the rounded tip against the entrance of her rear.

"*Oww.*"

"I haven't started yet. I will put it in the freezer for a few seconds if you continue to misbehave."

She shook her head frantically.

"In that case, shall we?"

Even though she hated to, she nodded.

"Bear down."

Ella sucked in a breath, and when she exhaled, he started forward with inexorable force. "*It...*" The word, even to her, was incomprehensible.

The pressure became too much, and she rocked forward, frantic to escape.

"Get back in place, if you please."

Now she just wanted to get it over with. The less time she was in agony, the better. Resolved, she deepened her squat, offering him greater access to her body.

"Such an amazing sub, princess." He began the slow, relentless torment again.

She prayed the thing was at its widest because she was certain her ass couldn't be stretched any farther.

"Almost there. Damn, I love watching it go in you. I'm not sure I'll ever use anything other than glass on you." Without warning, he let go of her shoulder to grab her hair and tug her head back. He kissed her forehead, distracting her enough that she didn't move when he pressed the plug all the way in.

She gasped. And the thing seemed to settle in. Ella sighed with relief as her muscles clamped around the post.

"Perfect. Stay there for a second." He kissed her again, and she knew she'd endure anything as long as he rewarded her with that smile and expression of pride in his eyes.

He grabbed a damp cloth that she hadn't noticed before and wiped the excess lube from her skin. "Knowing that's inside you will torture me all evening."

He helped her to stand before turning her to face him. After smoothing her dress into place, he plucked the panties from her mouth.

"Torture *you*, Sir?" She placed her hands on her hips.

"Yeah. I'm going to have a hard-on all night."

"So sorry for your anguish, Sir." She bent to slip into her panties.

Pierce grinned and offered his arm. "Shall we?"

Outside, he helped her into the car before sliding behind the wheel.

He watched her squirm as she tried to get comfortable. She tightened her ass cheeks. When that didn't help, she relaxed them. That was every bit as unsuccessful. "The plug is too big."

"Uh-huh." After checking the surroundings, he pulled from the parking spot.

"Can I have any sympathy? A single drop of kindness?"

"Nope. That will only lead to more and a request for me to allow you to take it out."

Relaxing wasn't easy.

He talked about his day and asked about hers. When his phone rang, Logan Powell's name appeared on the screen in front of them.

"Sorry. I've got to take this call."

"Go ahead."

"Holden. You're on speaker phone."

"Want me to call back later?" Logan asked.

She pulled out her phone to play with while he spoke.

"No."

"There's something here. Want us to move forward? Or should we drop it?"

Ella glanced up from her screen.

A tiny muscle ticked in Pierce's jaw. "I want to see it first."

"Tonight? Tomorrow?"

"0800."

"My office." Logan ended the call.

Pierce gripped the steering wheel so hard that muscles in his forearms jumped. He drove with complete competence even though he was silent.

"Do you want to talk about it?" She slipped her phone back into her bag and focused on Pierce.

"When I was home for my parents' anniversary, my dad was acting a little..." He shook his head. "I can't describe it. I had a hunch he wanted to talk about something, but he didn't. And the way his CFO behaved at the party..."

"Maybe he was trying to tell you something?" Among the stupid jokes about pushing paper and needing an army to help them.

"So I asked Logan for his opinion. I don't know what it means. Not going to guess. But I'm going to deal with it."

"We don't have to go out tonight. I can call Morgan and cancel."

He relaxed his grip. "In the army, I learned to eat when I can. Sleep at every opportunity. From you, I'm learning to enjoy life. As you said, it's important to spend time with friends as well as family. And think about fucking you and the way your ass even now is wide open because I want it to be."

She leaned to one side. "This thing with your dad is important."

"And I'll know more details tomorrow. Then I'll consult with others and decide on a course of action if necessary. Everything in due time. Nothing hurried. This could take days. Weeks. Months."

Calculated, like everything else he did.

"Please, not a word about Dad in front of Morgan. I don't want her worried. If she needs to know something, I'll inform her."

Ella nodded.

They arrived at the restaurant before Morgan.

Once they were seated at a table near the window with margaritas in front of them, he looked across at her.

"Take off your panties."

Startled, Ella glanced around the restaurant to see if anyone had overheard Pierce's outrageous order. "What?"

"You heard me."

"I did, Sir." His command caught her off guard, stunning her and shooting an illicit thrill through her body, straight to her pussy, making her tighten her grip on the plug.

"Then?"

"In the bathroom?"

"Right here. Right now."

His blue eyes blazed with uncompromising demand. She had no doubt he meant it.

Thanking the stars for the white linen tablecloth, she reached her hands beneath her dress and worked her thong over her hips and down her thighs. When she reached her knees, she hazarded a glance to be certain no one could see her then pretended to look on the floor for something as she pulled her feet from her sandals and worked the panties the rest of the way off.

When she sat up, he was smiling.

"Hand them over."

With a sigh, she wadded the material into a ball and offered them to him.

"You may be excused to the ladies' room to masturbate. I don't care whether you orgasm or not." She knew his words were more than a suggestion.

"Yes, Sir."

With his free hand, he snagged her wrist as she walked past him, forcing her to stop. "I love you, Ella."

"I love you, Sir."

He kissed her hand before releasing her.

The stalls in the ladies' room were luxurious, with floor-to-ceiling wooden louvered doors, giving her plenty of privacy. She hadn't thought she could come, but the moment she touched her clit, she groaned.

Everything he'd done—from his tone, to the gentleness of his touch, to his commands, to the oversized plug that split her apart—turned her on.

She parted her labia with her left hand and stroked her clit even harder, pretending Pierce was stimulating her. The thought of him made her close her eyes and she surrendered to the fantasy. She pressed her lips together so she didn't moan again, and she rubbed harder, faster.

So damn good.

His power over her was complete. And she loved it.

She pushed the balls of her feet down, and the angle change made the plug move. The friction on the thousands of nerve endings in her anus pushed her over the edge. She came hard. Even though she tried not to, she moaned as she dropped her head forward onto her knees.

It took her a few seconds to recover before she pulled herself together and headed for the sink to wash her hands and finger-comb her hair into some semblance of normalcy.

When she returned to the table, Morgan was there. She'd stolen Ella's margarita and stood to give her a big hug.

"I can't believe I get to see the two of you together."

Pierce stood to pull out her chair. Against her ear he said, "Sit flat on your ass, princess."

She did, shifted, then stayed still.

He never stopped watching her.

The waiter returned with another round of drinks and a basket of chips to go with a fresh bowl of salsa.

They gave Morgan all the news on the move and job situation. Ella noticed he never mentioned their parents.

Morgan looked from one to the other. "Have you set a wedding date?"

"She's stalling."

"I'm not." She scowled at him over her chip. "I want us to be settled and spend some time together before we make it permanent."

"Settled?" Morgan sat back. "When does that ever happen? I think you should set a date and figure it out."

"Same thing I keep telling her." Pierce looked at her. "You're the one who told me you wouldn't get in a relationship unless it led to marriage."

"You can't use my words against me."

Morgan grinned. "He did that."

They were probably right. Life might not get much easier when he was working for Logan. "I'll set one." She crunched her chip.

Morgan licked salt from the rim of her glass. "I'll nag you until you do."

"*That*, I believe."

They all laughed. Under the table, he touched Ella's leg above the knee.

And within an hour, they were back at home.

He closed and locked the door while she placed her purse on a nearby table.

"You masturbated at the restaurant?"

"I always do what my Dom tells me."

His pupils flared. "And did you come?"

"Right away."

He shook his head. "I have to have you."

"I would have been happy to stay at home with you all night, Sir."

He tossed his keys into a metal bowl on the table, one she'd put there for him. Maybe Morgan was right. Maybe it was time Ella set a date. In many small ways, she and Pierce were already settled into a relationship.

"Next summer."

"For the wedding?"

"That will give us time to plan, reserve a venue —"

"Spoken like a person who handles events. How about we actualize our own vows in the mountains and then have a party later? No one has to know. I want you as mine, now."

"Spring."

"This winter."

She exhaled. "How about you fuck me?"

"Are you trying to distract me?"

"Is it working?"

"I have incredible focus. If it works, it would be temporary." He grinned. "Take off your dress. And crawl to the bedroom. I want to see your ass move. I want to see the plug."

As always, he gave her plenty of opportunity to shake off her self-doubts.

Ella pulled off the dress then removed her bra before lowering herself to floor.

Pierce sucked in a sharp breath, and that made her confidence soar.

Even though she blushed, she crawled to the bedroom. He followed behind, telling her how gorgeous she was.

"On the bed. On your back."

She exaggerated her motions, pretending to be a sex kitten.

After undressing in record time, he rolled on a condom and climbing onto the bed on top of her. "It's going to be tight with the plug."

"I know." But her pussy was already wet. "Fuck me, Sir."

Instead, he tormented her clit a dozen times with his tongue then said, "I want your knees on my shoulders. I want to be as deep inside you as possible."

She lifted her legs and he moved toward her, pressing his shoulders against the backs of her knees. "*This.* Yes, Sir… Exactly like this."

"God*damn.*"

His strength and power seemed to split her apart. But she took him, all of him, everything he wanted her to have, everything she needed.

He called out her name as he came, the sound broken into two distinct, guttural sounds.

Once he was replete, he didn't collapse on her. Instead, he lifted his body and looked at her. "Still need a little more?"

"The plug and the angle is…I don't know."

He toyed with her, stroking her clit, paying close attention to her.

"Pierce!"

"You're almost there."

She closed her eyes and gave herself over to the sensations. She squeezed her butt cheeks, clamping down on the plug.

Then he maneuvered his body so he could tease one of her nipples with his tongue.

"Damn." So, so close.

He bit.

She arched. He stopped biting and instead sucked hard. Then he plunged a couple of fingers into her heated pussy and flicked her clit with his thumb until she shattered from the sensual overload.

Pierce stayed there until she rode it out. She wasn't sure she'd ever be able to move again. More, she wasn't sure she wanted to.

For thirty seconds, maybe more, she floated, somewhere quiet and peaceful as her heart rate returned to normal.

When she opened her eyes, he was looking at her. He grinned. "Put your hands over your head."

It took some effort since her limbs felt wooden, but once she managed it, he clamped her wrists.

"This is my favorite version of the Holden-Gibson Forever pose. You're mine, Ella. *Mine.* To love. Nurture. Protect."

"And spank my ass?"

His blue eyes seared hers. "I wouldn't have it any other way."

"I wouldn't, either, Sir."

"Good. Then set a date." He paused. "For the wedding."

"You're relentless, Pierce. Do you ever stop?"

"You're vulnerable. I plan to take advantage of it. Next week."

"No. No. No. *No.* Next summer. June."

He continued to stare at her. "January."

"April." Before facilities got booked for proms and weddings.

"Done."

She glared at him. "Was that the date you wanted?"

He grinned.

"Did you just win? You won. That's not winning, that's cheating."

"And?"

Instead of waiting for an answer, he swooped in for a kiss so deep and thrilling and emotional that words weren't needed.

When he finally ended it, with her mouth swollen from the way he devoured her, he said, "Tell me you're not upset."

"Pierce, in all the ways that it counts, I'm already your wife. I love you."

He grinned and gave a slow, sexy, searing look that reflected his devotion.

Her insides melted. No matter what the future held, she had the confidence they would deal with it together.

"In that case, Mrs. Holden, let's get started on the honeymoon."

About the Author

Sierra Cartwright was born in Manchester, England and raised in Colorado. Moving to the United States was nothing like her young imagination had concocted. She expected to see cowboys everywhere, and a covered wagon or two would have been really nice!

Now she writes novels as untamed as the Rockies, while spending a fair amount of time in Texas…where, it turns out, the Texas Rangers law officers don't ride horses to roundup the bad guys, or have six-shooters strapped to their sexy thighs as she expected. And she's yet to see a poster that says Wanted: Dead or Alive. (Can you tell she has a vivid imagination?)

Sierra wrote her first book at age nine, a fanfic episode of Star Trek when she was fifteen, and she completed her first romance novel at nineteen. She actually kissed William Shatner (Captain Kirk) on the cheek once, and she says that's her biggest claim to fame.

Her adventure through the turmoil of trust has taught her that love is the greatest gift. Like her image of the Old West, her writing is untamed, and nothing is off-limits.

She invites you to take a walk on the wild side…but only if you dare.

Sierral loves to hear from readers. You can find her contact information, website details and author profile page at http://www.totallybound.com.

Totally Bound Publishing

Made in the USA
San Bernardino, CA
08 August 2017